Before the Earthquake

Before the Earthquake

Maria Allen

**Tindal
Street
Press**

First published in February 2010
by Tindal Street Press Ltd
217 The Custard Factory, Gibb Street,
Birmingham, B9 4AA
www.tindalstreet.co.uk

A CIP catalogue reference for this book is available
from the British Library

ISBN: 978 1 906994 04 4

Typeset by Alma Books Ltd
Printed and bound in Great Britain by
CPI Cox & Wyman, Reading

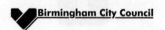
Birmingham City Council

For My Parents

PART ONE

I

It was gone midday and Concetta was asleep, sunk into the central dip of the bed she shared with her sisters. Immacolata, on one side, waged her sleeping war of attrition, restless hands constantly pressing for more space. Nunzia, on the other, lay immobile and immovable, arms locked across her chest like a stone effigy.

They had been out in the fields since before dawn, raking for potatoes while there was still the thread of a chill in the air. The night would bring the dark moon, a phantom moon they called it, invisible and unwholesome, and nothing could be planted while it lasted.

Concetta woke for no reason that she could fathom. Perhaps it was the point of an elbow in her back or the sudden surfacing from a dream. She slipped a dress over her head and shuffled into sandals. She pushed the slats of the blinds apart and, through the glare, she saw how still the birds were, perched on trees like tiny black figurines. She walked through the other room where her mother and father and brother were sleeping and then out of the stone dampness of the house into a block of dense sunlight.

In the deserted street, she fancied she heard the strain of something uprooting. A metal pot clattered onto a hard floor somewhere and rolled around on its rim. Beyond the houses, a breeze moved through distant branches and, opening her hand to feel the wind's direction, she wondered where the push was.

A jolt, and she staggered. The stalled start of something bigger. She glanced up to see glass shooting out of windows. Shifting glitter against the sun.

A door opened and an old woman in black stumbled out. 'Earthquake,' she said. 'It's the earthquake.' Her voice, strangely flat, was like a bell tolling.

Concetta looked away and up at the sun.

It was the dust that made her cough. Everything on top of her shifted. More rising dust and she wanted to put a hand to her mouth but, wherever it was, it was heavy and she couldn't locate it. There was no feeling anywhere except for a burning pain in her left foot as though a flame were being held against it. An age seemed to pass before she understood that her foot was the only part of her body above ground and that it was skewered by a shard of glass. She could feel a lick of warmth on it from the sun.

Time passed. Slowly? Quickly? She couldn't decide. She felt herself slipping into blackness and then rising out of it, forgetting where she was, and then opening her eyes into the same blackness. She felt this happen again and again and she thought that this must be limbo. Later, though, she knew she was still alive because she could feel something, life she supposed, leaking out of her. Even the burning in her foot was lessening, an echo of the pain from before.

She thought more and more of her foot, the only part of her above ground; the glint of the glass flagging her whereabouts. She willed her foot to move and was rewarded with a sharp bite of pain. The debris on top of her creaked and readjusted and dust came trickling down over her eyelids, her cheeks, her mouth. It seemed as if she were facing downwards even more now, falling head first into her grave. She could feel herself sinking again, the familiar lethargy creeping back. She could hardly breathe; the dust was in her throat now. She didn't know if it was the same day or a new day, but she thought she could still feel the warmth from the sun and she imagined the glass in her foot catching its dying rays.

A hundred shouting hands. Concetta was heaved up and passed along. It felt like levitation, not dead and rising, but almost dead and side-winding. She was finally placed on the ground. A disembodied shout. 'Who is it?' The rubbing of roughened fingers against her face. Nails to scrape away the grime. The smell of charred wood on them. The fingers stilled and she felt the eyes all over her face. Another voice, stopping, dog-tired but insistent: 'Who is it?'

She wanted to laugh out loud and shout, 'It's me, Concetta!' But she couldn't move a muscle, not even in her foot. She was mute. The fingers rubbed again, but gentler this time. They brushed the dust off the face of a girl far too young to be showing the first lines of wear. Thick, dark hair with no curl to soften it. A heavy stamp of eyebrows, a finer dusting in between. A sturdy peasant girl reared for survival.

He knew her. 'One of the Salierno girls,' he shouted over. 'The youngest.'

'Alive?'

She tried to open her mouth to speak.

There was a finger at her wrist. A pause. The voice was doubtful. 'Only just.'

*

9

Concetta could feel herself stretched out on dry grass on a blowy hillside, a crocheted blanket pushed under her head for a pillow. Her mother, Anna, had sat for a long time cradling her head and was now running her fingers over the nicks and grazes that patterned her body. She was astounded to find no broken bones and told Nunzia so when she arrived with a bucket of silty water from a nearby stream. They washed Concetta down together, removing the last of the earth and dust. The water was powerful with the smell of rotting reeds.

Nunzia unwound the bandage from around her foot. It already needed changing, the blood still running freely from the wound. When she finished, she sat stroking it, as if that simple action would stem the flow. Every so often, her mother leaned over and passed a hand over her mouth to feel for the soft passage of air. To prove she was still alive, Concetta exhaled the essence of a creature trapped in an airless room.

Nunzia began to cry. 'She must have known it was coming. She knew and tried to run.'

There was an edge to her mother's voice. 'She couldn't sleep and got up. Let her have some peace. She's in God's hands.'

Concetta was glad to feel Nunzia's hands on her foot. Before, the pain had been the only way that she had known she was alive; now her foot felt numb. She could feel the blood ebbing from it and the same weary feeling moving over her. It felt as if she were receding back into the ground again; there was no wind on her face any more.

She wasn't going down, though, but up. She felt herself lift off from the ground and circle above the bent heads of her mother and sister. Then, suddenly, she could feel the wind in all its briskness. She could feel the draughts of air from shifting bodies, blades of grass flattening underfoot. Higher still, she could see the masses of people grouped on the hillside. Families banded tightly together, whole streets recomposed and neighbours reunited again. Relief in some stunted routine. Old enmities suspended only for the time that it took for the ground to stop rumbling. She could see the village to her right, broken on the crown of its hill. She saw the aftershocks as they shivered across from great distances and then, below her, the responding murmuring and stirring and moaning.

Concetta hung for a time above it all and then she felt herself drifting back down. Her father, Rocco, was there now, Immacolata and her brother, Tino, too. Ringed around her was a small crowd of people. They were drawing close and running their fingers over her. They were pushing back her hair, stroking her cheek, wrapping hot palms around her ankles. It was as though they might transfer the heat of them, the life that pulsed within them, and enliven the part of her that was dying.

Towards nightfall, the crowd shrank back to the distance of respect. Nunzia had her head in her arms. Tino and her father looked forlorn and her mother's sharp features seemed blunted. She had a pinched look, the one she wore when there was nothing more to be done. Everyone was on their feet.

Concetta was torn. A part of her was down there at the centre of the scene – after all, she could see herself lying on the floor – but another part was pulling away. She gathered her strength and willed herself to shout, but only Immacolata looked up towards the sky, her face with its usual vexed expression. Immacolata glanced down and back up again, frowning even more, and then fell forward onto her knees as though her legs had buckled from beneath her. In a great hurry, she picked up the empty bucket beside her and, before anyone could put a hand out to stop her, she brought it down with all her force on Concetta's bandaged foot.

*

The shock travelled up from her foot and her heart made as if to jump out of her body. It was pumping fast now; she felt the blood whirring in her ears, knocking against her skull. When it settled, she was back in the place where everything was cramped and dark again. Just her heart beating through her foot. A dull boom. She couldn't see the hillside or the village or her family, but she was most definitely down here again, and not up there.

As she felt more and more present in her body on the ground, she began to remember more. There had been an earthquake. She was lying here marooned like this because she'd been struck by something heavy falling on her. An earthquake, one that devastated, struck the village every fifty years or so. Once a lifetime, people said, sometimes twice. If the air was too still, they called it 'earthquake weather'. If the moon was bloated, red as fever, someone would pronounce it 'earthquake red'. The birth of a malformed goat, a coop of hens that wouldn't lay, end-of-summer rains that packed the skies but didn't fall. Earthquake. Earthquake. Earthquake. They'd been expecting it for as long as she could remember, and long before that.

As always, though, it had struck without warning. Even the women who slept with their eyes open, like the cows in the fields, had missed the deftness of its step. They were part of a long line of people, constantly being felled, always fooled. How could they not be humble? They lived their lives in this jittery way then, between one earthquake and another.

2

When Concetta woke, she was lying alone in the bed she shared with her sisters. It was daylight, though not yet hot enough to be midday. She tried to sit up, but her bones felt as though they'd been fused together and the mattress, impregnated with the familiar musk of bodies, chafed her in places already sore. She sank back down again and fixed on the wooden crucifix lashed against the wall opposite. It was the thing she always saw on waking in the grey first light. A long spidery trail radiated out from its tip across the ceiling and there was another one, fainter, which she traced all the way across the room to the door.

The door opened and Immacolata stepped in. She moved across the room without glancing towards the bed. Concetta closed her eyes again and tried to breathe softly but, after a moment, when she heard a rustling on the other side of the bed she couldn't help but flicker her eyes open. Her sister was busy rummaging through a chest of clothes. She could have been invisible, Concetta thought, or dead for all the notice her sister took of her.

Immacolata was the middle sister, the pretty one, taller than Concetta and Nunzia by a head and more solidly built. She had black hair, thick and wiry, which she always wore in a single plait as wide as a man's fist. This she grasped now and threw behind her where it quivered like a live thing. She bent deeper into the chest and sorted through the mainly old work dresses and frayed underthings, pieces which were too threadbare to hand down, and the knitted shawls and stockings stored for the colder months.

A voice came from the other room, her mother's, calling Immacolata.

'In a minute,' her sister shouted, half turning towards the door. 'I'm washing her.' She turned back to the chest and bent in, elbow deep. After a moment, she stopped. She turned her head fractionally towards the bed and then back to the chest and began drawing something out.

It was Concetta's best dress, a gift from her *comare*, her godmother, given on her Confirmation day. It was the dress she wore on feast days, weddings and baptisms, on days to celebrate and be happy. It was modestly cut with a neat white collar that hugged the neck and a skirt that brushed the ankles. It was the pretty blue floral pattern, she knew, that Immacolata liked best.

Her sister held it out for a moment to take the full measure of it and then she pressed it against her to see where it fell. She kicked out against the skirt and then an idea seemed to come to her. Still holding the dress, she walked briskly towards the door and pushed it shut. She walked back again and slipped off her work dress and slid the blue one over her head. She had to tug to fit it over her hips and shoulders. It rode up slightly above her ankles and pulled a little too taut across her back. She patted the material down and, without even a glance at Concetta, walked over to Nunzia's side of the bed and thrust an arm underneath to find a piece of cracked mirror. This she held out in front of her. She put a hand up to smooth down the finer hairs along her hairline, which had a tendency to spring up and frame her face in a dark halo and then stepped back to admire herself. The blue of the flowers, a dark cobalt blue, complemented her black hair and sun-darkened skin.

Concetta could see, despite its fit, that the dress suited her sister far better than her. She closed her eyes again and felt relief at blocking out the light. The room was warm and stuffy. She made to shift her left foot because it felt oddly numb, but an unknown dread came over her and she didn't dare. She wondered what she was doing here at this time. It must be mid-morning, not the hour to be lying in bed. She'd never been ill before, but her foot must be injured, she reasoned, and she was here resting up.

She opened her eyes again. The crucifix before her wavered and the lines leading off from it seemed to multiply. On the far side of the room, she saw a blue blur. She fixed on it until it clarified and she saw the smile first, a genteel one for an imagined audience. Immacolata was turning this way and that, admiring herself in a cracked piece of mirror. Concetta shifted her foot, which had deadened, and heard herself sigh loudly at the unexpected pulse of pain.

Immacolata dropped the mirror and screamed. The smile, both real and reflected, vanished.

Concetta couldn't speak. The pain had winded her and her mind was a fog. She wondered if she were seeing things. Her sister was standing in front of her wearing her best blue floral dress.

Immacolata opened and then closed her mouth, her hand fluttering at the collar. After a moment, she glanced down and seemed so taken aback at finding herself wearing the dress that she began to sob.

The door opened and Nunzia hurried in. She looked towards Immacolata first, frowning at the dress, and then, as if afraid, she followed her sister's gaze and turned towards the bed.

Villagers, scrubbed up after a day out working in the fields, spilled through the door. They came to see Concetta for themselves, respectful cap in hand, an armload of figs or plums, some still draped in the black of mourning. It was rare for someone to come back from the dead, so it was no wonder they talked of miracles.

Concetta heard how on the hillside her mother, who was never mistaken about these things, had pronounced her dead. Tino had been sent to fetch *don* Peppino, the village priest, hours earlier when her mother knew she was slipping away. He had arrived too late to administer final rites and it was while he was giving words of comfort to the crowd of mourners that Immacolata had suddenly taken it upon herself to act as she did. Concetta was told how she had jerked with the force of the impact, and then sighed once and loudly.

Concetta's father had tried to grab at Immacolata and hadn't known whether to hit or embrace her and, in the midst of the commotion, *don* Peppino declared it a miracle. Concetta, he said, had returned from the dead. It was a gift from God at a time of profound despair. For the week or so that remained before the people returned to the village, they gathered around Concetta, their symbol of hope, holding vigils and praying for her to wake.

Nunzia had taken it upon herself to attend to *don* Peppino at the vigils and, later, during his visits to the house. She said that as the days and then weeks had dragged on, the priest had admitted disappointment. He'd wondered if he'd been too quick to declare a miracle. After all, there was only Anna Salierno's word that her daughter had died, and it was not uncommon for a mother to assume the worst.

After the move back to the village, Concetta had lain unconscious in her bed for three weeks. The well-wishers dropped away, the vigils ceased. Concetta's mother had quietly taken the precaution of calling in *don* Peppino to administer final rites. A coffin was put together and lined and Nunzia had even managed to find a bride's white gown to bury her in. The villagers, and even the family, were losing faith.

Concetta woke to more joy and fêting than she could ever have imagined. The miracle was intact, as reaffirmed by *don* Peppino. She'd survived an earthquake, burial and death itself. A mass of thanksgiving was celebrated a few days after her awakening to which she was taken, hoisted on the shoulders of her father and Tino. The villagers stood at their doorways clapping, lining the streets, and then thronged behind her in a singing procession towards the church.

Her mother had insisted she wore the bride's dress and draped a pale lilac scarf over her hair and across her shoulders. Immacolata was wearing the blue floral dress. It was her reward, she told Concetta, for acting so promptly with the bucket.

The church of San Rocco in the main square was roofless, and the whole of the left wall was dangerously unstable, but the villagers had cleared away the rubble inside and wiped down the pews as best they could. Concetta was placed on a chair at the front of the church and the first mass in the village since the earthquake was celebrated within its walls.

Concetta sometimes wondered whether she were still lying unconscious below ground. Her life on waking seemed far more likely to be part of an elaborate dream. The enormous relief, the fêting, the joy; it all seemed unreal. Yet, she didn't feel relieved in herself; she didn't feel joyous. She didn't feel anything at all.

She tried to take an interest in what had happened in her absence. There was a steady stream of well-wishers, who continued to troop through the house bringing her vegetables straight from the fields; flowers, nuts and berries. She caught fragments of how things had been. Some things she knew. They'd been preparing for the earthquake all their lives. They were from a long line of people who had always got on with life. She heard how there'd been no time to mourn because of the numbers of dead, how the incessant heat meant they'd had to bury in a hurry. She heard how every family had to tend to their injured and then had braced themselves for the suicides (a handful from shock and despair). They'd slept out in the open for a few weeks and, once the aftershocks had subsided, they'd drifted back to the village to begin the work of rebuilding.

It didn't last long, though. The first excitement of tearing down and starting anew was replaced by the bickering of families in overcrowded lodgings. Those that came to see her began to reminisce about how things had been in more settled times. Concetta's interest in the earthquake waned, too. She was beginning to feel stronger now, able to sit up propped on cushions. She smiled and nodded when she needed to because she saw that her mother still watched out for this, but more than anything now she wanted to forget. She wanted to put the earthquake behind her. She thought of that last memory, traced the trajectory of it. She'd roused herself from sleep. She'd walked out of the house into the street and had had to push her way through the heat, which came at her in waves. Then the ground had moved and glass was shattering above her and the old woman in black began to speak, the same words over again.

*

The end of summer brought the distant boom of thunder. Storms that never arrived. The expectation of them hung in the air. It made people scratchy, fussy about details, about how it was then and how it was now. One night after Concetta's godparents, her *compare* and *comare*, had gone home, they continued the dispute in the kitchen.

'Hand on my heart, I've never known heat like this year,' said Nunzia. 'We should have known it would bring no good. Earthquake weather.'

Half the village were talking like this. Looking back for omens.

'Ah,' said Immacolata, waving a hand at her dismissively, 'you see signs where you want to see them.'

'There was something different about the sun,' said Nunzia. 'That's what people were saying.'

'Listen,' said Immacolata, 'the sun looks the same today as it did then.'

'We said it was getting closer,' said Nunzia, turning to Concetta. 'Didn't we?'

'Everybody was saying that,' said Immacolata. 'Just copycat talk.'

'I don't remember,' said Concetta, laughing and shaking her head at Nunzia. 'I don't remember the heat being any different. Every summer seems hotter than the one before.'

Nunzia looked over at Concetta. 'You had your hands in bandages for a week.'

Concetta frowned. She struggled to recall an incident.

Nunzia leaned in. 'Your hands swelled up. They looked as though they'd been stung by bees.'

'But it wasn't bees, it was the sun,' said Immacolata. She stood up and yawned. It was nearly time for her to leave with Tino. They would head towards the fields to take their father's supper. Tino would remain there. He and his father often slept overnight at the *pagliaro*, the stone hut, so as to be able to start work with first light. Everyone had lost valuable time because of the earthquake. 'And the dog,' Immacolata said. 'Don't forget old Paolo's dog.'

'Chained to a gate for a whole day with no shade and no water,' said Nunzia. 'Poor thing.'

Concetta looked down at her hands folded on her lap and spread out the fingers. She tried to recall them red and swollen, encased in white crêpe.

She thought of old Paolo's dog; a grey, scrawny thing with a long tail that curved underneath its body. It would often bound out from behind a small haystack by old Paolo's house on their way to the fields in the mornings. It would always bare its teeth at the girls and then trot along behind them for half a mile or so wagging its tail. It was said to be half-dog, half-wolf and Concetta always fancied that it was there to protect them against evil spirits.

'He's not there any more?' asked Concetta.

Nunzia looked at her oddly. 'Not unless it's his ghost come back from the dead.'

'Smelly, bad-tempered thing,' said Immacolata. 'Thank God we don't have to put up with him scaring us any more.'

Their mother returned. She'd walked some visitors back to their house a few streets away and now started busying herself wrapping some food in a piece of cloth, enough for a late supper and breakfast. Concetta smiled and nodded, following the thread of winding talk in the kitchen while desperately trying to think back to the weeks before the earthquake. The chatter about heat felt familiar to her, just the tired talk of summer that was bandied about at the hottest part of a long July day. The kind of day, though, that Concetta couldn't separate from those that had gone before and those that came after. Nunzia had expressed it well enough. Easily spent words. Throwaway talk.

But what about her swollen fingers? And the poor wolf-dog? She tried to imagine these events from the little her sisters had said. She tried to fix them in a time and place, hoping to spark a memory. But all she could see, when she tried to think back, was the giant orb of the sun just as it was when the earthquake struck.

Concetta was sitting in the kitchen shelling broad beans. Her mother still insisted that she keep only to light housework. Outside, she could hear the rebuilding work now in full swing. The banter of the men, the clanging of metal on metal, the whoops that went up when a wall was about to fall, the hiss of rising dust.

Immacolata came in, slamming the door. She brought half a loaf of bread and a couple of brown speckled eggs. She brought resentment, too. She and Nunzia had had to shoulder Concetta's share of the field work. The plums, apples, walnuts and figs were dropping off the trees, she said, and the sweetcorn were hardening inside their husks. Their mother and Nunzia had gone to see an old widow, *signora* Clara, who lived by the cemetery on the other side of the village.

'How is she?' asked Concetta.

'Bad,' said Nunzia. 'Crying all the time.' One of *signora* Clara's sons had died during the earthquake. They'd made a grave for him in the end, but they'd never found a body. 'She still says she won't believe he's dead until she sees for herself. She's been on her hands and knees digging. That's when they sent for our mother.'

Immacolata went to the fireplace, raked the ashes away and lit a fire. She put two eggs in a pan of water to heat through. She stepped back and opened her palms to stare at them in disgust. Her hands were sore and newly calloused.

They sat in silence for a few minutes and then Concetta walked over to the fire and fished the eggs out. She cracked one into the heel of the loaf and handed it to her sister. She tore off a smaller strip of bread for herself; after all, she wasn't doing manual work now and needed less, and emptied the other egg in.

Immacolata finished quickly. She'd always liked her food. She watched Concetta eating for a moment and then eyed the remaining bread. She looked away and back at the fire. The rest of the bread would be for her father and Tino who'd spent yet another night at the fields. 'Signora Clara still finds time to gossip,' she said, turning to Concetta with a sudden smile. 'She remembers you being at the cemetery gates. She told you it was too late for a girl on her own.'

Concetta laughed. 'Not recently.'

'No,' said Immacolata, 'before the earthquake.'

'It could have been anyone.'

'She says it was you.'

'Oh, it probably was me then.' Concetta turned back to the fire. She didn't have the energy to argue.

'At night? Waiting, like some loose woman?' Even Immacolata isn't prepared to believe this.

'The woman has just lost one son, and her other son is far away with never a word or message sent back.' Concetta tapped the side of her head. 'She's lost her mind, and it's no wonder.'

'I'm only telling you what she said.'

'She's an old woman with a broken heart.' Concetta got up to brush the crumbs from her apron into the hearth. She felt bad about losing her temper at *signora* Clara. 'Her eyes are failing, that's all.'

'Her eyes,' said Immacolata, 'are the one thing she doesn't complain about.'

Concetta's time to recover was coming to an end. There were no more visitors and, this evening, her family were mostly absent. Only Immacolata was at home, kneading dough to make *fusilli* for the week. Her father had taken the night off to play cards at the *Vecchia Osteria*, the wayfarers' inn, outside the village on the old Roman road, and her mother and Nunzia were with *signora* Clara again and had sent word that they would be late.

There had been no word from Tino, and Concetta imagined that he would be working through the night again, as he so often did at this time of year, catching a few hours' sleep in the *pagliaro* with the sheep and goats. Instead, he turned up very late, entering the kitchen quietly. He hadn't eaten anything since breakfast and he had a wary look about him that spoke of real hunger. Concetta cleared a place for him at the end of the table and gave him a piece of dry bread and half a raw onion. She drained the last of the wine into a glass, dregs and all. He ate in silence. Tino was always frugal with his words.

Concetta had felt a surge of gladness at seeing him come through the door so unexpectedly. She was feeling low from spending her days alone in the house and she missed Tino in particular. She'd hardly spoken to him since her waking. He hadn't slept on the small wooden bench in the kitchen that served as his bed for a week or more and the times he did appear, like this evening, it was because he craved the comfort of the kitchen and the hearth. She didn't dare tax him with her silly cares. She was on the mend, as her mother said with a satisfied nod, and that was all that mattered.

Concetta took his plate away to clean outside and Tino waited for her to come back in before speaking. 'They found sant'Emidio.'

Immacolata stopped kneading and clapped a floury hand to her mouth. Concetta, still by the door with the plate in her hand, looked first at one and then the other. Sant'Emidio was the village protector against earthquakes, a waist-high statue that stood on a plinth in the main church.

'Where?' asked Immacolata.

'Behind the altar in Santo Stefano, under the floor-boards.'

'What was he doing there?' asked Concetta. Santo Stefano was a dilapidated church in the south of the village, deconsecrated after it had been damaged in the last earthquake, over fifty years ago.

'Hiding probably,' said Immacolata with a laugh. 'He knew what was coming!'

'Is he in one piece?' asked Concetta.

'Except for his nose and that was from last time.'

Concetta came over to the table by Tino and sat down. 'It's more than a miracle. Found, and in one piece.' Her voice was full of awe. The girls in the village had a lot of affection for sant'Emidio. At mass, they jostled to be on a pew close to him. They admired his dark blue bishop's cape with its jewelled clasp and the boyish frizz of light curls under his mitre. His hands were raised, palms slightly turned out in restrained welcome. His feet were usually hidden by the disintegrating mulch of flowers pulled hurriedly from the roadside: bunches of daisies, all stalks and wilting heads, and sunflowers sweating petals that curled and died at his toes. 'How could they lose him before the earthquake? How could they have let that happen?'

She looked up to find Tino's eyes on her. 'What's wrong, *sorellina*, little sister?'

It wasn't until Concetta heard herself speak that she acknowledged the truth. She hung her head. 'I've lost time,' she said. 'I can't remember things, a lot of things.' It was as if she'd fallen down a well into a black hole. A yawning place without light or sound. She'd been bumping up against its edges for some time.

'You remember the earthquake,' said Immacolata, her voice sharp.

'I remember that day. I don't remember before . . . days, weeks, maybe months . . . I don't know how much time before.'

'How do you know that you can't remember?' asked Immacolata, her voice probing. 'How can you tell?'

'Things people tell me. I say I remember, but I don't.' She looked to Tino, but his expression was difficult to read in the dimness of the room.

'Sometimes people forget on purpose,' he said finally. 'They don't want to remember.'

'Like what? What do I want to forget?'

Tino shrugged. 'I don't live your life for you.'

Immacolata suddenly clapped her hands and hooted with laughter as though she'd just thought of the funniest thing. 'At the cemetery gates,' she said. 'It *was* you.'

3

The Feast of the Immaculate Conception came and went and then it was time to cut up the pigs. Every family needed a houseful of people to do it. Not to kill it, a man and his son could do that, but family, in-laws, neighbours, and others besides came to work on the pig after the slaughtering. They'd slit the pig's throat in the morning and then leave it to bleed. The next day, in the evening, when the heat of the day had gone and the helpers were back in from the fields, they'd carve the pig up. They'd bash the flesh from the bones, section the stomach and cut off the haunches. They'd scrape the fat away and collect it in dishes. They'd lop off the extremities: the trotters, the flaccid snout, the papery gristle of the ears, the soft, hairy testicles, the hard twist of the tail.

Then came the hard work. The mashing and bagging of meat scraps, gristle and fat into slithers of lining to make the various *salumi* and sausages, and the stuffing of the pigs' trotters, *cotechini*, which they'd save to eat at midnight on the last day of the passing year. Nothing was wasted, not a whisker or an eyeball or a tooth.

These slaughter days always had a festive feel to them. They meant going out to toil in the fields and then coming home to work through the night. They meant the faces of everyone you knew crushed into the tableau of a warm, poky kitchen. They meant thinking about the succulence of the meat, its potbellied bountifulness right there in front of you. Even though the pig had to last the year out, it was being stripped down, organ by sticky muscle by bone, and you could imagine its preparation, the smell of the fat sizzling, the piny, clean scent of the rosemary, the blood-thickened juices of the steak meat.

What people loved most about those slaughter days, though, was the *sangonaccio*. This dish was prepared late in the evening when the pig had been stripped. It needed some of the stretchy tubes of intestine and nearly all of the blood. It had other ingredients, too, like aniseed and orange peel, but mostly it was made of solidified blood and was eaten in thick slices with bread. The children would pester all evening, hands grabbing, trying to cajole their mothers into making the *sangonaccio*. The mothers would slap them away, but talk about the starting of it, and the children would stampede in groups from one end of the room to the other, drunk on the smell of blood and the lateness of the hour.

On the day their family's pig was to be killed, Concetta and her sisters got up early. They felt around for their clothes and nudged through sleeves and collars with the blindness of newborn creatures. It was November, and winter had brought a soupiness to first light. Water sluiced outside. Their father was scraping a blade across his neck. Through the shard of glass on the wall, he pinched his chin out of the way and then tracked the blade carefully up his neck.

Concetta and her sisters passed the trough on their way to the fields and stopped to look in on the pig for the last time. The pig lifted its snout off the ground and flared it at them.

'Her time has come,' said Nunzia. She leaned over the fence and tapped the pig's head.

'Lucky for us,' said Immacolata.

They watched it for a few moments rooting around in the rindy mush. There was the crunch of eggshells as it foraged.

'They can tell it's the end,' said Concetta, 'just by the way you walk towards them.' She couldn't remember who'd told her this but, watching the pig, she felt sad that it might be true.

'She seems happy enough to me,' said Immacolata. She stepped away from the pen and tossed her plait over her shoulder. 'Come on. Let's go.' She waved at the pig. 'Bye-bye, pig.'

'Shush,' said Nunzia and pointed over at the house. Their father and Tino, booted and dressed, stepped out of the door. Their father held a knife. A toothless one with a thick tongue of a blade. The girls turned away and headed for the fields.

That evening, on their way back home to the village, Concetta noticed the blood. A brown speckling over faded cotton-print roses. Immacolata was walking just ahead of her. 'There's dirt on your skirt,' said Concetta.

Nunzia took hold of Immacolata's skirt and lifted it. 'That's not dirt,' she said, letting it fall. 'Change your dress when you get back.'

'Cover me,' said Immacolata. 'One of you walk behind me.'

'When we get to the village,' said Concetta.

'What if someone sees?'

'It's blood,' said Nunzia. 'What are they going to say?'

Concetta stopped short. The other two turned round, cupping their eyes against the slanting rays of a low sun.

'What about tonight?' she asked. 'The pig.' Menstruating women were forbidden to touch freshly killed animals. It soured the meat.

'I can't believe it,' said Immacolata. She grabbed at her skirt, trying to twist it round to see better.

'It's blood,' said Nunzia, walking on again.

'What will they do?' asked Immacolata, running up behind her. 'I can come for the *sangonaccio* at least.'

'They'll send you away. Just in case.'

Immacolata stopped walking and stamped her feet in frustration. The others walked on and, after a minute when it was clear they wouldn't stop, she ran up behind them and grabbed at Nunzia's arm. 'Why do we have to tell them? No one need know.'

'No!' Nunzia was firm. 'No more bad luck this year.'

'Why should I be the one to suffer? Why me?'

'What makes you different?' said Nunzia.

'How do I know it's not your time,' said Immacolata, 'or hers?' She jabbed a finger at Concetta.

'Because of the way we live.'

Concetta felt the truth of that. They lived in such close proximity that they couldn't help but be aware of each other's bodily functions.

'I'm not because I'm not,' said Nunzia. She nodded over at Concetta. 'She's not because she hasn't been right since the earthquake.'

The trauma, the recovery, the continuing amnesia had all affected Concetta's cycles. She used to grumble about the messiness of her monthly flow, but now its absence left her feeling strangely unhitched. The blood, the long, seeping flow of it that passed through the torn sheets of cloth that she packed herself with and into the ground, that blood was the fragile thread that made her a part of everything else. It felt like a loss.

'You should count yourself lucky,' she told Immacolata.

They got to the village's far-flung outer reaches.

'One of you go behind,' said Immacolata, searching around for invisible eyes. 'Cover me,' she said again and walked on ahead.

It was Concetta's turn to make the weekly bread and Pina, the woman who ran the village oven, had already given her cursory rap on the girls' bedroom window a few hours before dawn. Concetta gathered her strength and pushed the heaviness of sleep away by reaching across Immacolata for her shawl on a chair. She climbed over her sister and padded out to the kitchen. Her mother and father were asleep in their bed shoved against the far wall, but Tino was already awake, having slept just a few hours on his bench. He was going to the river but had waited for her to get up. He wanted to tell her about a time he'd been eel fishing.

On moonless nights, men from the village would fish for eels. Eels prefer the dark. They hunt at night. They lie in wait, suspended in the dim sparkle of rising silt. But catching an eel, catching enough to make an all-night visit worthwhile, was not easy. Many of the men knew that squatting by a bend in the river on a cold winter's night was often time squandered.

Tino had the right temperament for eel fishing. He went willingly and, at bottom, he explained to Concetta, this was the only secret you needed to know. He recognized the ritual in trapping eels, that some stiff inner part of him was being tested. He liked to feel the pinch in the air, the blackness of the night, the lonely winding walk down the hill through the even blacker mass of trees and then out along the gurgling rush of the river. He liked to study the careful conjunction of earth and water and sky that revealed the best spot.

They fished for eels all year round although early December was when Tino liked it best. Cold, but not too cold. Eels become inactive when temperatures drop too low. Tino always wondered how inactive. Sleeping, he supposed, not feeding, just being, dorsal fin ruffled by the river's onward sweep.

Since the earthquake and Concetta's prolonged absence from the fields, the winter had hit them hard that year. Tino knew what this meant better than their father. He felt the responsibility of it more keenly. His father dealt with a crisis when it was already upon him. Tino knew to recognize it from a distance. Already, at nineteen, he was different from his father, a better man, although this knowledge brought him no particular pleasure.

Tino came over to the kitchen table where Concetta was working and pulled out a chair. They mouthed their words, careful not to wake anyone.

'Which time?' asked Concetta.

'It was the summer,' Tino said. 'Before the earthquake.' He remembered stepping out of the dark plume of the trees and heading down to the river. Along its banks, he saw other men from the village, crouched in muddied niches, probing the unseen depths for sinuous movement. 'Old Carmine Caputo was there,' he said, 'sitting on a stool.' Tino had a distinctive fluting whistle, which he used as a greeting. Concetta could picture him, tongue between his front teeth, no hands, old Carmine turning to wave.

'The Di Rienzo brothers, too. Peppe and Francesco were round the bend further on. They said it was a slow night.' Peppe and Francesco were *signora* Clara's sons. Peppe was the one whose body had never been recovered after the earthquake and Francesco had left soon after that night at the river for the other side of the world to make his fortune. He'd never sent word back to his mother and she continued to lament this, and the fact that her son had heard neither of the earthquake nor of his brother's death.

31

As Tino talked, Concetta began to wipe the table down. She emptied the flour onto it, made a well in the centre and, pouring water from a jug, began to knead.

'Peppe told me Pasquale had just passed by, that he'd been looking for me.' Pasquale was a cousin of theirs, as different from Tino as it was possible to be. 'He said that Pasquale had gone looking for me in the direction I'd come from.'

Tino hadn't seen his cousin for some months and he wondered whether he, too, had suffered in the heat and gone to ground somewhere. Tino knew that he should have sought him out sooner. He hesitated and then finally doubled back on himself and followed the curve of the river. He walked on, but never caught sight of his cousin and decided in the end he was just too far ahead. Carmine hadn't seen him and when he came to the place where the Di Rienzo brothers had been sitting he found them already gone. They'd probably found the night too slow to be worth the wait. Further ahead, he passed another man. 'A face from the village,' he said to Concetta. 'I don't know the name.' Their father sometimes boasted that he could name every man in the village, but Tino knew only those he wanted to know and those he did not. This was a man that Tino would only nod at. Concetta knew the man he meant. A mournful-looking wife, a clutch of scruffy children. Poorer than they needed to be.

Tino continued to follow the river until it came round to a small outcrop of trees. It was the point where the woods met the river, where trees had fallen in previous earthquakes and lay half submerged, where wild animals sometimes came to drink. It was here that Tino said he heard Concetta's voice. He turned towards the trees and was transfixed as he saw her running and dodging in and out from among them. 'I thought I was dreaming,' he said. 'I'd left you just a few hours before. You'd been in the *pagliaro* fast asleep with your sisters.'

Tino had recovered himself and sounded his breezy whistle. 'You stopped and turned. You were startled,' he said. 'You didn't know whether to run or face me down. Then you called my name.' Tino waited a few moments before moving towards her. He covered the ground in long strides and took hold of her arm.

He'd known there was someone with her. 'Who's here?' he called out. A twig snapped from somewhere close by and he looked round. 'You had your eyes on my face so I knew there was someone with you, someone out there, breathing as quietly as the trees.'

Concetta's hands were still. She had stopped kneading a long time ago. She had no doubt that the story was true. Tino never lied. It felt like he was talking about someone else, though. She couldn't believe it of herself. How could she have done such a thing? She glanced at the bed where her father slept. She knew what he would have done. He would have taken a handful of her hair and dragged her towards the man who thought to save himself by being invisible. He would have put a fist to her face because he would have known that this was the way to draw the man out. Her father would have thought more of getting his hands on the man than of saving a wayward daughter.

Concetta looked down. Her hands were embedded in the dough. She began to work it again, slowly.

'I don't remember anything,' she said after a moment. 'Who was he?'

Tino shook his head. 'I didn't see him.'

'What did you do?'

'I took you back to the *pagliaro*,' he said. 'I pushed you through the door and went back to the river. No one knew you'd gone. But I should have done more. I should have stayed to force this man out.'

Concetta realized that Tino had wanted to tell her this for some time, that he'd been waiting for the right moment. She thought he was ready to leave now, but he didn't move. He hadn't quite finished.

He had returned to the river that night to retrace his steps. 'I wondered about every one of them,' he said. 'No one was there any more. The riverbank, the woods were empty.'

Concetta let her eyes drop to her hands. The dough was beginning to dry.

'You must remember something.'

Concetta shook her head, her eyes closed now. She had the briefest flash of a memory. Jumping across stepping-stones on the river, running through trees. Then a yawning black hole.

Tino had been deep in thought when he rejoined the river and began to walk back along its bank. As he rounded the bend where he'd last seen Peppe and Francesco, a hand had loomed out of the darkness and clamped his shoulder. Tino had had to quell the shout that rose in his throat.

'Cousin,' a voice had laughed in his ear, 'are you following me?'

After Tino left, Concetta made her way back to bed for a few hours, the time it took for the dough to rise. Well before dawn, she got up again to divide it into loaves. She placed them on a plank and lifted it up onto her head and, bracing herself for the cold, walked through the as-yet quiet streets to the communal oven in the main square. She didn't have the heart that morning to exchange the usual greetings with the other women and lingered only for a moment to hold her palms out to the heat of the furnace before turning back on herself and hurrying home.

She was hungry when she got in and ate a helping of *minestrone*, washing it down with some wine. She drank straight from the lip of the bottle and then returned to her bed for the hour or so before it was time to start the day.

Concetta woke feeling groggy. She had felt the acid of the wine in her throat while she slept. Her sisters were rousing, too, and she heard them sighing as limbs unfolded and unshod feet padded across the floor. Material was being eased over the contours of a yawning body. Concetta opened the door and walked through into the other room. Her father was sitting up in bed, scratching his head, his face stubble-dark. There was a nip in the room. Her mother had just gone out and the winter air had stolen in.

Concetta walked out the house and watched her mother rubbing herself down with a torn strip of material. Moisture hung in the air. She could detect the mustiness of mould, rinds and peelings rotting in a pile near by. Her mother pared the damp strip away and, for a brief moment, before she stepped into her drawers, she stood naked, slack breasts puckering in the chill.

'You next?' she asked.

Concetta looked around for the other bucket of water.

'Your brother took it. For the eels.'

'Ah.' She'd forgotten.

The slip her mother was smoothing over her hips was so old it had become a fragile wisp. The grain of cotton weave had unravelled in places with use and starch. Her mother shoved the bucket towards Concetta with her bare foot. 'Before the others get here. Save yourself the arguments.'

Concetta fidgeted with the sleeves of her nightdress and felt suddenly shy. She didn't want her mother's scrutiny today. She felt how her mother saw her youngest as an extension of herself: a body to be picked at, spit-cleaned, wiped down. Concetta wanted to move out of her keen-eyed orbit, but since the earthquake she'd lost the will to do even this.

Fragments of a whistle came from the direction of the trees, snagging in the damp air. Her mother turned. It came again, a cheery trill, a fluttering ribbon of sound that stirred an uneasiness in Concetta as she recalled the talk of the night before.

'A good night,' her mother divined.

'It's too cold for eels.'

'Your brother knows what he's doing.' Their mother's trust in Tino was absolute. She moved off towards the door and Concetta took the opportunity to slip her nightdress off and, gritting her teeth against the cold, she poured the water over her and moved a nub of soap over her body. Her breasts and belly felt taut. It occurred to her that she perhaps hadn't finished her growing yet. She seemed to be growing more solid in shape, more like Immacolata, and less like Nunzia with her softer roundness and looser skin.

She slipped on her work dress and, despite the cold, waited for Tino. He appeared on the path that led from the woods and moved towards the house with that unhurried pace of his. Immacolata stumbled out of the door, bleary-eyed.

'Good catch?'

'Sounds like it,' said Concetta.

'Maybe snow on the way,' she said, squinting up at the sky. Shivering, she turned back inside.

Concetta stayed to greet Tino.

'Not a bad night's work,' he said.

Concetta looked into the pail: three eels lay coiled in a puddle of water. She had an overwhelming desire to taste the greasy flesh. She put a hand in and drew the length of one out of the bucket. She walked inside and over to the kitchen table and smacked it, head first, on the edge. She felt a kick, a last kick, undulating through and then something unexpected, a jab, a response from inside her. It was as though, somehow, the very life from it had slipped up her arm and into her belly.

*

Concetta dreamed of the eel every night for a week. She wondered if the spirit of an eel, perhaps knowing its moment of death was near, could leap out of its skin and slip inside a person. At night she was breathless with anxiety as she pictured it growing, blind and skinless, nudging its pink, scaleless length through dark interior passageways.

She was at her grandmother's one day when she felt it again. She'd brought a pair of winter boots, resoled, from the cobbler's. Her grandmother was taking her time to inspect them, rubbing a finger across the ancient leather, bending the tongue back and forth, sniffing inside.

Concetta put a hand to her stomach and felt a fluttering. She closed her eyes and imagined the fluid sweep of an extended dorsal fin. Hundreds of flexing spines brushing along the roof of some inner canal. She swayed forward onto a chair and waited for the sensation to pass.

When she opened her eyes, her grandmother was holding the boots out to her, the soles upwards. 'They're used,' she said. 'Look at this.' She tugged at the new piece of leather that had been nailed over the old.

Concetta sighed. Her grandmother, Maria, her father's mother, was starting to forget things. They had first noticed it the winter before. She had always had an iron grip on the order of everyone in the village, who was related to whom, who was family and who was not. She took these matters very seriously. Then she'd started to get things back-to-front, linking people up the wrong way, confusing neighbours with cousins, accusing people of trying to trick her when they put her right. She'd have days, even weeks, of perfect clarity when she remembered the way things stood and then she'd get up one day and the world was mixed up again.

Concetta's father, Rocco, couldn't believe his luck at first. All his life, she'd been right. God, he said, had finally, in her old age, made her wrong. Once a large woman with a round, moon face, she became slighter, her skin sunken and etched with worry. It was as if something had been slowly sucked out of her.

'You asked me to take them to be mended.' Concetta kept her voice even.

'They're not mine.' Her grandmother let them clatter onto the floor. 'They're too big. Man-size. What do I want with a man's old boots?'

Concetta sighed. 'New ones cost money. We don't have any money for new boots.' She felt a wave of irritation and suppressed it, imagining how her mother would be. Calm but firm. Always respectful. Instead, Concetta had sounded like she was chiding a wayward child.

'Where did you get them from?' Her grandmother was suspicious. 'Who died?'

Then she felt it again. A swish, something twirling deep in the pit of her stomach. She remained crouched at the floor, afraid to move lest it should come back. The time had come to tell her mother. She would play the youngest child for a little longer. She would tell her mother that an eel from the river, in the split second it took to bash the life out of it on the kitchen table, had jumped out of its own skin and into her own.

She turned to get up and her grandmother was suddenly bending towards her. 'I told you before,' she said. 'Nunzia does what her mother tells her to do. But what are we going to do with you, eh?'

Concetta was taken aback at finding her grandmother's face up close. She'd lost that faraway look and seemed lucid.

Concetta struggled to her feet. She felt tired and sore from crouching on the ground. 'What did I do?' she said.

'I told Rocco that you'd need watching. Too soft for your own good,' she said, nodding. 'Easily led astray.'

'*Nonna*,' said Concetta, sighing. 'You're thinking of someone else.' She'd had enough of this nonsense. She needed to talk to her mother now. She moved towards the door and was already on the threshold.

'Wait!'

Concetta took a deep breath and turned round.

Her grandmother walked over and handed her the boots. 'Take these out of my house,' she said. 'A dead man's boots are no good to me.'

It wouldn't be the first time that Concetta's mother had had to deal with troubled spirits. Anna knew for a fact that the dead fretted, that they sometimes felt compelled to replay over and over a scene from their lives already lived. She knew that they could get trapped, lost in the new texture in which they found themselves, and would tap at a window or flit across a darkened room or breathe against a sleeper's cheek. They had no peace.

She told Concetta about the time when she herself was a small child. She was with her mother, Filomena, droving the animals home from the fields and she had been tied to one of the goats by a piece of string so she didn't go wandering off by herself into the woods. It had been late, past midnight, so they had taken a different path, a shortcut which meant passing a tree where a murder had been committed a few years earlier.

The murder was forgotten now, Anna said, but then, people still talked about it. 'Because it was so brutal, and so unexpected,' she said. 'He was a courteous man. The kind who would run next door to beg for a flask of wine to offer you if you passed by. We couldn't understand what would trigger a man like that to murder.' She could remember his wife as a frail thing, indisposed for many months after childbirth.

39

Concetta and her sisters sometimes passed the tree on their way to the fields and she sometimes imagined seeing a woman's stunned face trapped within the confusing crisscross of branches.

Anna couldn't remember much about that night. She was very young and it was very late. They'd approached the spot and as they drew nearer to the tree, the animals began to paw at the ground and wouldn't move forward. The string that was attached to Anna became slack and her mother took a stick to the donkey at the front of the pack, but the animals all began to rear up and fall backwards. Anna's mother shouted at them and tried to pull them forward.

Her mother wouldn't look up towards the branches, but Anna did. She remembered seeing something, but the form it took was so unlike anything else she'd ever seen, so indistinct, a wraith or a cloud perhaps, that she could never afterwards, even as an adult, describe it to anyone. She tried to recall the image many times, but it was too amorphous and she had been too young. She had the shell of it fixed in her mind: the place, the murderous circumstances, the late night, her mother shouting, the braying animals, but the vision itself was lost to her.

The next day, Anna recalled, her mother, Filomena, had told a crowd of people in the square about the sighting. She told them how her little daughter, Anna, hadn't flinched when the goat staggered backwards and nearly crushed her. She told them that, in the end, she had had to make the sign of the cross to calm the animals and only then had she been able to lead them all safely past the tree.

'She just made the sign of the cross and the animals stopped?' asked Concetta.

'Yes,' said her mother, 'but she didn't tell them what happened before that.'

Anna, who had barely yet uttered a word in her short life and had been small enough to need tying to a goat, had begun to shout at the tree. Terrible things, fully formed words, and with such a fury.

This time, though, Concetta's mother did not suspect the dead. This, she said, was mischief that hailed from the living. Concetta had escaped death and her memory was not yet fully restored. Many, though, had lost daughters or wives in the earthquake and her mother knew the strangling power of envy.

'It's not possession?' Concetta asked.

Her mother laughed. She sometimes found her youngest daughter's confused ideas endearing. 'By an animal? An eel?'

'I felt it kick.'

'This is worse,' she said. 'A human snake.'

'Worse?'

'Evil,' her mother said. '*Lu maluocchi*. The evil eye.'

When someone was watching you, when someone was hoping that harm might befall you, when someone was wishing it so much that it did in fact happen to you, that was when they said you had 'the evil eye'.

Her mother knew how to check for this. She took a bowl of water, freshly drawn from the well, and threw a few gobs of olive oil into it. She studied the gentle lap of its surface. If the oil sat on the surface, intact, there was no curse. If instead the oil dissolved, there was the proof of affliction.

They both stood and watched the water until it finally stilled. Most of the oil had filtered through. A few spots, almost invisible, pockmarked the surface.

Her mother frowned. 'Some envy,' she said eventually, 'it looks like.' She pored over the bowl again. 'I can't see, though, that this is the main thing.'

'I definitely feel something.' Concetta's hand drifted to her stomach.

Her mother looked round sharply. 'Are you keeping something from me?'

'I'm telling you that I can feel it moving inside.'

Her mother was about to say something, but stopped herself. She got up and crossed into the backyard and poured the oily water into the chicken coop. She came back in and went to stand over by the window and stared out. After a while, she turned to Concetta, who still had her hand resting on her stomach, but looked away again. She seemed to collect herself then and cursed. 'That envious water,' she said, rushing outside, 'it's in with the chickens.'

4

Nunzia wouldn't stop crying. She held onto Concetta as though her sister was dying all over again.

Concetta was expecting a child.

'But how?' asked Concetta.

'How? How?' Her mother threw her hands up in the air.

'And I was saying how you were doing so well,' said Nunzia between sobs. 'I thought you were just putting the weight back on that you'd lost.'

They looked at Concetta and they could see that she was bigger now, broader, her belly protruding.

'How could I have missed it?' The three of them were standing in the girls' bedroom and their mother swung round, aiming her question at the crucifix on the wall.

'Since the earthquake,' said Nunzia. 'She's not been right. We put it down to other things.' She drew her sister to her and patted her hair down with damp hands. She started crying again. 'She's fifteen. She's still a child.'

'No,' their mother said, still staring at the crucifix, 'she's not.' Concetta had never heard her mother sound so bitter before.

43

Concetta lay quietly back against her sister. She couldn't think what she'd done wrong. She couldn't remember. But she had. Her belly, and the strange restless creature moving around inside, was the proof of it. It didn't seem fair. She felt she might cry now, because of the unfairness of it all.

'The earthquake,' she said. 'I remember afterwards but not before.'

'You remember who it was at least?' her mother said carefully. She had swung away from the cross to face Concetta.

Concetta shook her head. There was a pair of long needles lying at the bottom of a drawer in the other room. She put her hands to her face as she thought of them. Her mother knew how to deal with unwanted children. Women often called on her for help.

'It's too late for that,' her mother said. 'You're too far gone.' There were times when her mother could read her thoughts.

Nunzia started up again, weeping. She sat Concetta down on the bed and rocked her from side to side like a child. '*Papà*,' she said, 'we'll have to tell him.'

'Of course,' their mother snapped. 'What do you think? He'll have to make sure this man does the right thing.'

'I can't remember him,' Concetta said. 'I don't know who he is.'

'You must know,' said Nunzia. She cupped her chin. 'You have to. Think.'

Concetta closed her eyes and was again back running in the woods. Breathless, zigzagging between the trees. It was dark, no moon. Someone ahead of her, or was he behind her? She knew him. He wasn't a stranger. She was running, trying not to make any noise. Just her heart bumping and the pad of her feet against the undergrowth. No name. No face.

Nunzia still had her hands on her face. 'Don't worry,' she said, forcing a smile. 'We'll find him.'

Their mother walked towards the door. 'The time for laughing,' she said as she went out, 'is over.'

Concetta's grandfather, her mother's father, killed a man once. He did it not for himself, but for a friend whose wife had been faithless. Concetta had heard her grandfather tell the story only once before. Now, with an ear at the crack in the door, she heard it again. His account, reduced to a few sentences, had not changed.

It was very dark and her grandfather was glad that the man, the woman's lover, was made faceless by the long shadows thrown by the trees across the clearing. He had never killed a man before and had imagined it would be like butchering a calf, so he had brought a hefty knife with a smooth blade and some strong twine. In the end, though, he hadn't needed the twine. The man, he recalled, smelled powerfully of earth and dewy grass and the scent of fear, animal fear.

Her grandfather had been brought by Tino to tell his story again. He sat steaming on a stool by the fire. It was raining hard outside, the water driven by the wind to slap against the windowpane. At times, the noise obscured his voice. Concetta's father and Tino sat sombrely facing the logs, which crackled and spat in the damp air. There was a feeling of shock. A gathering of strength before action.

Concetta had escaped lightly. Her father, Rocco, was a short man with large, gnarled hands that seemed too big for the rest of his body and he had a loud clap of a voice. He was not a man to shy away from violence. When her mother told him of Concetta's condition, his initial burst of anger had fizzled almost immediately. Her mother had made sure that Tino was on hand, but her father had seen a way out and it pleased him that he had understood how the matter might be resolved.

He had sent Concetta out of sight and made Anna leave with Nunzia. Then he had sent Tino to fetch his father-in-law. Concetta, closed up in her bedroom, had pressed her face against the doorframe and listened.

'You didn't do it for nothing,' her father said after a while.

Another long silence. 'We were like brothers.' Her grandfather sighed. 'It's difficult to talk about it now. They were different times.'

'It was a lot to ask,' said Tino. His voice was neutral.

'He would have done the same for me.'

'So, what happened that you're not close now?' asked Tino. Her grandfather had little to do with his friend now.

'Ah, Pietro wants to forget. We hardly pass the time of day any more.' Another pause. 'We all want to forget.'

'Old friends like you should make peace before they die,' Tino said.

'He does well for himself. He's put that trouble behind him.'

Her father's reply was quick. 'Thanks to you. Thanks to you.'

Concetta adjusted her position to see better. When she looked again, she could see all three of them staring into the fire. The rain outside was easing off.

Her father turned to Tino, as though by way of explanation. 'Pietro has a good piece of land out there by the flour mill. It must take some tending. Not so bad, though, when you have five sons to help you, eh?'

Her grandfather nodded. He knew where this was heading. He had waited a long time for it. The time had come to call in past debts. Tino seemed to understand, too. He put an arm on his grandfather's shoulder.

'A lot of sons,' continued Rocco, 'and even more grandsons, eh, Tino? Your generation.'

Tino nodded. 'The oldest grandsons are married, Gino and Giuse' Totila. A few of the others, too, but most of the younger ones not yet.'

'Pietro had all *maschi*, boys,' said her grandfather.

'*Complimenti*,' her father said.

'It's the girls you need to worry about,' continued her grandfather. 'Pietro always used to say that.'

Concetta could hear the scrape of the chair as her father got up. '*Papà*,' he said, and walked over to where her grandfather sat. '*Papà*, he wasn't wrong there.'

Immacolata was the last to find out the news. She'd been sent out of the way to attend to *signora* Clara and was back late. At this hour, they would all usually be fast asleep, but tonight Concetta was awake and sensed that Nunzia beside her was, too. Immacolata crept into the bedroom and undressed in the darkness. She clambered into bed and kicked Concetta's leg away for more space.

'Leave her alone,' said Nunzia.

'You awake?' Immacolata said, sitting up. She reached under the bed for a candle and lit it. 'Why didn't you say?'

The light flickered uncertainly. Concetta sighed and sat up, too.

'What's wrong with everyone today? *Signora* Clara is still crying. She wants her son back.'

'Still grieving?' Concetta asked. Her own shock felt like grief.

'She won't accept he's dead without the body. They've told her that he must have been swept into the river and drowned or fallen down the side of a cliff when it struck.'

'Poor *signora* Clara,' said Concetta, shaking her head.

'And the other one, Francesco. She's still had no word from him since he left. I'm tired of hearing about him, too.

I told her she ought to prepare for the worst. He might be dead for all she knows. Anyway, why is it always me these days who has to listen to her crying?'

Nunzia sat up. 'Stop thinking about yourself for once.'

Immacolata stopped. It was not like Nunzia to be so testy.

Before Nunzia had a chance to say anything, Concetta spoke. 'I'm having a baby. Five months gone. It happened before the earthquake. I can't remember . . . I don't know who he was.'

Immacolata's face seemed almost grotesque in the jumping candlelight. 'And they believe you?' she asked. 'That you don't remember anything?'

'She's not been right since the earthquake,' said Nunzia.

'Even if you don't remember him,' said Immacolata, 'he must remember you.'

Immacolata was right. Concetta turned it over in her mind.

'What kind of man is he?' asked Immacolata. 'You lay here dying and he didn't come to see you even once.'

'He couldn't come to see her openly,' said Nunzia. 'What would *Papà* say?'

'Either he's a coward,' said Immacolata turning to Concetta, 'or he never loved you, and this is the man you took such a stupid risk for?'

The words stung. Concetta couldn't believe her sister was right. 'He can't have known what's happened since,' she said.

Immacolata sunk her face into her hands. 'This is terrible. What's going to happen to us?'

Concetta frowned. She had seen this as only her own downfall. She realized now that her sisters would be ruined, too. A child born out of wedlock. No father to its name. The whole family would be tainted.

'*Papà* is dealing with it,' said Nunzia. She reached for Concetta's hand and squeezed it. 'She'll have a husband and the baby will have a father.'

Concetta had been so shocked by the news and so caught up in trying to replay scenes from the past that it only dawned on her now that this is what everyone had been preparing for all day. Her family was practical. Her father couldn't stay angry when there was work to be done. As her mother had said, the time for laughing was over. The time for remembering, too.

'But what about us?' said Immacolata. 'She can't marry before us.' There was a strictly observed custom in the village. Daughters were married off in order of age.

'Well, I'm the eldest,' said Nunzia, 'and I don't want to marry ever.'

'It's not right that she goes first,' said Immacolata. 'People will know something is wrong because we've overturned the proper order of things. It's not right.'

The candle guttered and went out. It left a long plume of smoke hanging in the air and a powerful smell of burnt tallow. Immacolata slid off the bed and crouched down. There was a tearing sound as she scraped a match. As she brought the candle up to the level of the bed, Concetta could see that she was crying. Their mother always said that Immacolata was only capable of crying for herself and she did so now, softly. Her face was blurry in the stuttering light.

Concetta placed a hand on her belly and realized that she had seen countless women in the village make this gesture. Protective towards something they knew nothing of yet. She extended her hand towards Immacolata and touched her arm. 'I don't want to marry either,' she said. She tried to smile to show that she was being brave.

Immacolata wiped her eyes with the back of her hand. 'Who cares what you want?' she said. 'Do you think you

49

have a choice now? You've made your mistake and now you'll have to pay. We all will.' The candle bobbed and went out again. She didn't relight it this time, but settled down into the darkness and yanked the blanket towards her.

Concetta woke early while everyone was still sleeping. Even though the windows were tightly shuttered, she knew it was still dark outside. She lay in bed for a while listening to her sisters' light breathing and that of her parents and brother in the other room. Beyond, she could hear some soft sounds from the only remaining room in the house, where the animals were penned in together out of the frost. She could hear the cows shifting their weight. They sensed the coming of the morning, too.

Today, Tino, her father and grandfather, and her cousin Pasquale would go to pay their respects to Pietro Totila, her grandfather's friend, and his son, Giovanni, after morning mass. The meeting had been arranged formally through a third party, and some of Giovanni's sons might also be there. The women of the family would serve some food and wine, perhaps some dark brown *nocino*, strong walnut liqueur, because of the gravity of the occasion.

Concetta knew that there was much at the meeting that her father would not say. He would not insist his family was owed a debt even though his father-in-law was beside him. Nor would he talk about the terrible thing hanging over the two families, a stain which continued to tie them through three generations. Even if there had been no one to see what had happened in the woods that night, no one to say who was lover and who killer, who marked man and who hunter, the time had come to put the past to rest. But her father would never say it.

Instead, he would thank Giovanni Totila, and his father, for seeing them. He would say that he had a daughter, a good girl, not afraid of hard work, no beauty but of cheerful temperament, his youngest. He had come, he would say, because Pietro had hard-working sons. He'd heard that they had done well for themselves, were kind people, and in their turn had produced healthy, hard-working sons of their own. He wouldn't say any more than this. It would be Giovanni's place to speak of marriage.

Concetta knew the family only slightly. She tried to picture the faces of some of Giovanni Totila's sons. They were mostly fair, quiet men, some of them stockier than others. The oldest few were married with wives and children, but she didn't know any of the wives well and nor did her sisters. They lived next to each other on the other side of the village in a series of houses down a winding street that led to the flour mill. Some of the men worked at the mill, but the family owned a large piece of land just beyond where they kept sheep and goats. They were people who kept themselves to themselves, although they attracted the landless in leaner times, giving food as payment for a day's work. They were hard-working and honest and that was why her father believed they would agree to this plan. They were people who understood a grievance.

A cockerel some distance away began to crow and it sparked off a brief, answering chorus. Concetta climbed off the bed and shrugged into a dress and shawl. Breath streamed out in front of her, and her feet, stockingless on the stone floor, felt numb from the cold. These were the bleakest days of winter. Everything was hard, bound up tight. Even those fortunate enough to own an ox couldn't break the earth.

She moved quietly through the next room, past her sleeping parents and brother, and slipped outside. There was no light yet and heavy black clouds made the sky darker still. She pushed her feet into work boots and opened the door to the room where the animals slept. Inside, she groped around for a shovel and basket and began collecting the muck. One of the goats greeted her with a solitary bleat, but otherwise the animals were mute. Even the cockerels were silent now.

It was early still. The animals knew it and refused to shift out of the way. Not even they, she thought, would do her bidding. Concetta slumped forward and rested her forehead against the handle of the shovel. The night felt like it had seeped inside her. She waited for tears to spring, she willed them as she thought they might bring some relief, but none came and she could only think that they might be needed for later.

She found a dry place on the straw and sat down to face the small opening that acted as a window in the stall. In the dark, the rank smell was overpowering but the animals were made quiet by the cold and the long night and soon she felt herself calmed, too.

Some time passed and she came to. She had dozed off for a moment. She put her hand to her hair to brush out the straw and it came away sticky with oil. It was too cold in winter to wash long hair and she had to put cooking oil through it to stop it from tangling. She'd have to go back in to run a comb through it soon because today was Sunday, the day of rest, and in an hour or so she would have to be presentable for first mass.

Light was inching through the window. She picked up the shovel and began raking up the muck.

Her father had been confident that the matter could be resolved quickly and, awkward in their best clothes, the men returned from the meeting with the air of those who might have pulled off a difficult feat. Giovanni Totila had said himself that his father and the girl's grandfather were tied by more than friendship, but he had not spoken of either murder or marriage. 'Things,' Concetta's father said to her mother, 'will take their course.'

Concetta was still in disgrace and, when not out working, confined to her room. She waited until her father and
grandfather left to play cards at the *Osteria*, the old inn,
before emerging. Tino was shrugging out of his best shirt
when she came into the main room and Immacolata was
there too, eager to know what had happened.

Immacolata handed a glass of wine to Pasquale who,
still in church clothes, was leaning against the wall. He
had spent much of his childhood at their house when his
mother, their aunt Ada, got ill with scarlet fever, and he
had been like a brother to them. They saw little of him
these days, as he worked the fields on the other side of
the village. Their father had wanted Pasquale to come to
Giovanni's. 'The debt is to the whole family,' he had said.
'It's only right he comes.'

'So Giovanni Totila said yes?' asked Immacolata.

Concetta stoked up the fire in the hearth and then
took Tino's shirt from him and laid it out on his bench
to fold it.

'He didn't say anything,' said Tino. He turned to
Concetta. 'I think he's a good man, though, and he'll help
if he can. I believe that of him.'

'They owe us,' said Pasquale, draining his glass. 'Debts
are there to be repaid.'

Immacolata turned to look at Concetta. 'You're saved,'
she said. 'Do you know how lucky you are? Do you?' She
said it with awe, as though not quite believing the way
things had gone.

'Let's not rush,' said Tino. 'We don't know anything
for sure yet.' He stood shirtless and Concetta pulled a
vest and his thickest woollen jumper from a pile and
handed it to him. She watched him as he dressed. He was
tall and bony, his ribs visible. Concetta wished he would
eat more, rest more. But he didn't seem to need to. She
had never heard her brother complain.

'Were any of Giovanni's sons there?' she asked after a moment. She felt shy asking it.

Tino shook his head.

'Not even the married ones?' asked Immacolata.

'No,' said Tino. 'Perhaps Giovanni decides these things alone. Some families work that way.'

'What do we do now?' asked Immacolata.

'Sit and wait,' said Tino.

'They can't leave it for too long, Tino. She's already showing.' Immacolata's voice was rising.

Pasquale put an arm around Immacolata and drew Concetta to his other side. 'Don't worry. We'll take care of it. They know what they have to do. They're just making a show of taking their time over it.'

'A man has a right to think,' said Tino. 'Any father would do the same.'

Despite the warmth from the fire, Concetta felt a shiver pass through her whole body. She shrugged Pasquale's arm away and walked over to her brother. 'He won't say no, though, will he?'

Tino sat back down on the bench. 'No,' he said. 'He won't say no.'

The next few days passed slowly. No one mentioned Giovanni Totila, not even Immacolata, but as the week wore on without news Concetta tried to imagine how life, with a child, might be without a husband, and couldn't. She heard her mother say to Nunzia that they would give it a week. And then what? thought Concetta.

The following Sunday morning, the family walked to church in silence. They went together, which was unusual as they usually made their way individually, calling on family, godparents, friends on the way, only regrouping once inside. Today they walked in a single block. It was as if they had formed a wall, one strong enough to resist shock. The tears that wouldn't flow for Concetta the week before threatened now. The church, San Rocco, was in the main square, on higher ground and, as they passed through the crumbling ramparts of the old village boundary, Concetta gripped herself. She mustn't cry.

She had to hold herself in throughout the service. There wasn't a moment when she could relax. Outside the church, pinned between her mother and Nunzia, she nodded to people and leaned over to kiss, all the time her eyes wide open and bright. Her jaw ached with all the smiling she had to do. Her godmother, *zia* Carmela and her mother's sister, *zia* Filomena, and their families walked with them most of the way home as they too lived in that *contrade*, that part of the village. Concetta stood by Nunzia and Immacolata to wave their relatives goodbye from the doorstep and, as soon as they had turned the corner of the street, she darted inside and went straight to the bedroom.

Again, she had to check herself from crying. Immacolata had come into the room. Concetta turned away from her sister and walked over to the window and opened it. She felt a desperate need to be alone. Immacolata began to strip off her good dress. 'Shut the window, for God's sake,' she grumbled. 'Can't you feel how cold it is?'

Concetta had discarded her best shawl in the other room. She glanced around the room, picked up Immacolata's shawl, which had been flung across the bed, and heaved herself up onto the window ledge. Her sister, the dress over her head now so she couldn't see anything, grumbled again about the cold. Concetta jumped through to land on the scrub below. It was a little too high from the ground to land comfortably and she fell onto her side. She picked herself up, rubbed the bruise that would surely form, and reached up on tiptoe to shut the window from the outside. Immacolata, in her vanity, would only wear her light shawl to church on Sundays and Concetta had to wrap it around herself twice. The day had started off bright but clouds were forming now, dulling the light. The wind was brisk enough to bring snow. On this side of the house there was a patch of wasteland where the chickens roamed and, further on, the sty where the pig used to be. Concetta found the path on the periphery of their land that led down to the fields and, as she did every day of her life, she headed down the hill.

For some minutes, she wasn't aware of anything. She only knew she'd been crying when she tasted the salt and then she felt all at once the cold whip of the wind against her damp cheeks. The rhythm of her feet against the dusty track was a solace. After a moment, she stopped. A voice reached her from far away. It was the sound of her name, snagging in the wind. Nunzia. She loved her sister, but she felt for the first time ever a rumble of resentment. Why couldn't Nunzia leave her to cry in peace? Why couldn't she ever have time to herself? Why was there always a sister or a parent or an aunt calling for her or looking for her or telling her to do this task or that?

The voice came again. Not angry, but urgent. Concetta took the end of the shawl and wiped her face. It came away grimy. She had walked into a dip in the land so she could see Nunzia, but her sister couldn't see her. Nunzia was turning this way and that, running forward and then stopping and putting her hands up to lift her voice above the wind. Concetta walked back on herself for a few paces and waved a hand overhead. She began to trudge towards her sister. Nunzia, one hand on her head now to keep her headscarf in place, ran to meet her.

'Quick,' she said when she reached Concetta. She took hold of her arm and turned back towards the house, pulling Concetta along with her. 'Felice,' Nunzia said, so out of breath she was hardly able to speak. 'His name is Felice. He's finally come.'

Concetta wanted to go back through the window to clean her face and tidy her hair, but Nunzia wouldn't hear of it.

'He can't think you come in and out through windows. Here.' Nunzia stopped by the pail of water outside the door. She took an old rag hanging off a hook and dipped it into the water, wiping Concetta's face hard. 'He mustn't know you've been crying,' she said. She untied Concetta's headscarf, flapped it in the breeze and retied it under her chin. 'I can't do anything now with your hair. Go, don't keep him waiting.'

'Does he look kind?'

Nunzia smiled and kissed Concetta on the cheek. 'He looks like a good husband.'

Concetta put her hand on the door and pushed it open. She entered, with Nunzia following, and had to wait a few moments for her eyes to adjust to the light in the room. Seated next to her father on the bench was a fair-haired young man clasping a hat between his hands. He stood up when the two women entered and Nunzia nudged her forward. Concetta took a step and bobbed her head. She didn't dare look closely. It felt improper. As soon as her father resumed what he was saying, she backed away, keeping her eyes to the floor. Her mother was pouring some wine and searching on a shelf for the *taralli*, savoury biscuits, that she kept for special occasions. Concetta walked over to her and, only from here, a dim corner of the room, did she allow herself to look at him properly.

He was younger than she had imagined. Tino was standing at his shoulder and her brother seemed to be of a different order from Felice, almost a different generation. It was as though one had lived a whole lifetime already and the other had yet to begin. Felice had a pale, delicately moulded face and hair that was tan-coloured with the soft, springy texture of a newborn's. The dimness of the

57

room gave him a sallow, melancholy look and Concetta wondered if he was ill. It was not unheard of for families to keep disease hidden.

Once her mother had handed the men a glass of wine each, she retreated again to the hearth and busied herself tidying and clearing things away. Nunzia, exchanging a look with her mother, came over to help. Concetta hung back at her mother's side, but she saw that Immacolata had drawn up a chair and was sitting with the men. She had managed to change into her favourite dress, the blue floral one that used to belong to Concetta.

Felice didn't seem to be saying a lot. Her father was doing the talking, asking about family, the flour mill, some of the men they knew in common. Concetta could tell that her father's chatter was partly relief at bringing to a close a disastrous situation, but he was also more outgoing than usual. Like most men of the village, he treated strangers with scepticism, but he had put his arm on this man's shoulder. Felice was already family.

As the talk wound on, her mother would occasionally break in to ask about an aunt or a neighbour or a cousin. She knew most women in the village. Felice seemed brighter when answering her mother's inquiries, but Concetta noticed how tense he seemed sitting here among them with her father's arm on him. Occasionally he glanced at Immacolata, who was seated directly in front of him. Concetta chided herself for seeing how every time Immacolata moved an arm to adjust her headscarf or rose from the seat slightly to straighten her skirts, Felice noticed too. Once, only once, he averted his gaze from Immacolata and caught Concetta's eyes with his own. Concetta quickly looked away again, but then she feared he might be ashamed to look at her directly. Perhaps he was afraid she might already be showing.

She squeezed her eyes shut and felt the room recede.

Shameful, she thought, she had done a shameful thing. And he had come to save her. Yet she felt nothing for this man, who was turning his hat in his hand on the bench, shrinking from her father, eyeing her sister. He was nothing to her and yet he must be everything to her. She would have to learn how.

Finally, when her father's talk dried up and there was a lull, Felice cleared his throat. 'I'm at the age when I need to take a wife.' He looked down at his hat and stopped turning it. 'And I've talked to my father, Giovanni Totila, about my intentions.'

Concetta's father nodded and put his arm again on Felice's shoulder. 'I know you have, son. I know you have.'

While he was speaking, Immacolata rose to collect the empty glasses and went to the hearth to wash them in a bucket of water. Felice looked at her back for a moment and then down at his hat. He spoke in less of a rush now. 'I've come about one of your daughters. I've seen her before, and admired her, and I'd like to make her my wife.'

Her father stood up to squeeze Felice to him even before he had finished speaking. 'And we're very happy to have you in the family. Welcome. Welcome.' The rest of the family stood up, too. Immacolata came away from the hearth to join them.

Concetta felt her mother at her side and she turned to kiss her. There was more relief than joy in the embrace and Concetta felt all over again what a terrible thing she had done. She couldn't help crying now, her tears flowing freely, and Nunzia came over and started crying too. Concetta couldn't bring herself to look at Felice and she hung back. Her father and Tino offered to walk him home. They would go in to pay their respects. Giovanni Totila had made good on his debt.

5

The nights were getting longer and the last days of the year were a time of waiting, of gathering forces. As the year had brought only bad luck, the wedding was fixed for the first day of the new one. What was done on the first day of the year, they believed, would stay with you for the rest of it. They would make the day a success and so it would be, reasoned Concetta's mother, for the year itself and beyond.

One Sunday, a few days before Christmas, Concetta's mother sent Immacolata and Nunzia ahead on their visits to friends and family in other parts of the village. She'd barely spoken to Concetta since the day Felice had come to the house. It seemed so long ago that Concetta had yearned to move out from under her mother's skirts. It had seemed too difficult at the time and her mother too unwilling to let her go. Then, overnight, it had happened. She was no longer a child but an adult, and she felt like a stranger to her mother.

Her mother wanted to speak about the *corredo*, the dowry that Concetta would take with her. A *corredo* was part of the contract. A husband would expect it and so would his family. A woman who was to marry would spend a year, longer even, embroidering sheets and pillowcases, weaving cloth for nightdresses and good underwear, and knitting bedspreads for future winters. It would all be taken in a procession by the women to the bride's new house.

Concetta had never given her *corredo* a thought until now. 'How can I take what I don't have?' she asked.

Her mother pursed her lips. 'To not have one is as good as saying to the world that there's no hope for you.' She went over to the bed where she and Concetta's father slept and from beneath it she dragged out a large wooden box. She searched the waistband of her dress and fished out a small, rusting key. It was not often her mother was on her own in their small and sparsely furnished house and yet she had managed to fill this box and keep it a secret. Concetta had never seen it before. She wondered if even her father knew of it.

She signalled to Concetta to help her lift the box onto the bed. It was much heavier than Concetta expected. Her mother took the key and hesitated slightly before levering up the lid. The hinges creaked as though they hadn't been used for a long time. Her mother wiped her hands down against her apron and then counted out six carefully pressed sky blue sheets, six pillowcases to match, six towels of the same blue cotton, three crocheted summer bedspreads, three woollen winter ones, three pairs of summer drawers, three heavier worsted pairs, three delicate shifts, three light nightdresses. There were some coins, too, which seemed to have been tossed inside the box at random, and a silver pendant with an obscure figure holding a staff crafted on it.

Concetta found her voice. 'I've never seen these things before. Where have they come from?'

'People give me things, for payment or as thanks. I've never asked for anything, but I see now that I did need the help of others.'

Concetta nodded. Her mother was always helping the villagers, especially the women, the old and infirm, and the sick of spirit. She reached over and ran a fingertip along the delicate ridges of a beautifully embroidered petal.

'They're yours,' her mother said. 'The other two have time enough to make their own dowries, and it's better that they do.' She started putting the pieces back into the box, but Concetta put a hand out to stop her.

'I'm sorry,' she said. 'I'm sorry that I never said sorry before. I just didn't know what I'd done wrong. I couldn't remember.'

'And now you do?'

Concetta shook her head. 'I wish I'd never caused all these problems for you, for *Papà*, for everyone. I wish I could remember what happened before the earthquake and why I did what I did.' She stopped to catch her voice.

Her mother sighed. 'What's the use in this kind of thinking? Think of your husband. Make it up to him. I just hope he's a good man, that he won't hold it against you.'

'I'll make it up to you all, I promise.' She would have to make things right. It was all that was left to her.

Concetta's mother nodded briefly, then turned away and began returning the items in neat piles to the box. Concetta watched her turn the key and wipe the box down with a cloth. Her mother was a practical woman. The world was different now. Concetta had made it so. As with all strangers, her word meant nothing.

Christmas Day was one of the few days of the year when no work could be done. Most people went to early morning mass, then lingered in groups outside the church, chatting and paying respects, and waiting for their turn to go back in to confess. This would take most of the morning and then, once the family units were intact again, they struck out in every direction to visit others to wish them a good Christmas and a fruitful coming year. Concetta had borrowed a capacious coat of her grandfather's to cover her broadening figure. It was a cold, crisp morning and anyone who hadn't yet guessed her condition, she hoped, would think nothing of her wearing it.

After they had dropped in to see aunts and uncles, cousins and neighbours, and a polite *don* Peppino, Concetta's mother decided that she ought to go to see poor *signora* Clara as well, being as she had no family left in the village. She elected to take Concetta with her.

Concetta hadn't seen *signora* Clara since the earthquake. Her mother and her sisters had been to tend to her since she'd lost her mind with grief. She'd become attached to Concetta's mother as though she were the daughter she had always craved and who would now look after her in her troubles. It was thanks to her mother that *signora* Clara had finally accepted that her son, Peppe, was dead, even without a body to grieve over. Now *signora* Clara had turned her attention to her other son, Francesco, the one who had gone overseas to America and who she was convinced she would never see again either.

Signora Clara lived east of the village, close to the cemetery. To get there they had to cross the village and take a dirt track, which fell away sharply from the crest. A lot of people worked the land out this way, past *signora* Clara's house, further down the hillside, as water was plentiful. There was a well connected to a natural spring here and a small river, which only dried up on the hottest days of the year.

Concetta and her mother walked in silence. Her mother was never one to talk when she had nothing to say and she was even less inclined these days. Out here, the cottages became sparser and there were fewer dogs straining at the leash to bark at them as they passed. Between dwellings, straggles of goats and sheep chewed at grass and shrubs and the lower branches of fruit trees. At night they would be taken indoors as sometimes the cold drove wolves up to these parts. They'd come in packs, eyeing the village from just beyond its edges.

Concetta wondered whether she ought to mention what Immacolata had told her, that *signora* Clara had seen her standing at the cemetery gates and had gone out to reprimand her for being out so late. As they walked that way now, it struck her that it was a long way to walk at night.

She was beginning to feel the extra weight she was carrying from the pull in her back. At other times she simply forgot that she was carrying a child. Of late, it had quietened down. It didn't move around inside her as much as before and Concetta imagined that it, too, like the plants and animals around her, was lying dormant, collecting its energies.

When they got to the cottage, a low, simple construct with two small rooms and a tiny stall for the donkey, Concetta's mother stepped up to the door and rapped against it. When she didn't get an immediate answer, she banged the tiny windowpane. Concetta hung back in the front yard. She felt afraid all of a sudden that this woman might have some vital clue about her past movements, which the sight of her standing there might trigger. She felt a wave of shame wash over her. She couldn't even visit people in the normal way any more for fear that someone might point a finger and reveal her for the sinner she was.

The lock scraped as the door, a solid, old-fashioned one, was heaved open. *Signora* Clara appeared, wrapped in a thick black woollen shawl, which she had put over her hair. 'Anna,' she said, and pulled the door open wide. 'Come in out of the cold.'

Concetta's mother put a firming hand against the old woman and raised her voice slightly so she could hear better. 'I've got my other daughter with me.' She turned to Concetta and beckoned her forward. 'You remember Concetta?'

Signora Clara stepped away from the door and peered out into the yard. 'Ah,' she said, 'she's come too?'

'Yes, she's with me.'

The old lady seemed resigned. 'Come in then. Come in.'

Concetta followed her mother into the house and had to push her back against the door to close it properly. The room was dark. The day was bright, but there was only a small, narrow opening high up to let the light in. A candle burned on the table in its holder and the surface of the table was mottled with old wax. This was a house where candles were needed every day. Concetta glanced around. The cottage, she could see, was very old. Originally, it must have been built as a place for animals. An old stopping-off post perhaps, for shepherds as they drove their flocks down from the hills to graze in warmer pastures.

Her mother had brought *signora* Clara some *zeppole*, some pieces of fried batter, sprinkled with sugar. She had also brought an orange and a handful of walnuts. Her sister, she told *signora* Clara, had bought the oranges and walnuts from the market in San Michele, a bigger village, a day's walk away.

'Thank you, thank you,' said the old lady. 'You didn't keep them for your own family?' She picked up the orange and offered it to Concetta.

'No, no,' said her mother. 'It's for you. It's Christmas.'

'Ah.' She sat down and lapsed into silence.

Her mother began to tell her about morning mass and the people they'd seen outside church and those who had wanted her to pass on their regards to her, and *signora* Clara nodded at everything sorrowfully, as though hearing a tragic tale rather than the details of a festive day.

Concetta felt relieved not to be included in the conversation. She sat back on the hard chair and squeezed her greatcoat around her. Her eyes wandered around the room and she got to thinking about the sons that *signora*

Clara had lost, one straight after the other, and she looked for signs of them in here. A worn man's felt hat hung off a nail by the door and a couple of benches pushed against the back wall were all that indicated their presence. A large chopping axe lay on its head by the hearth, which Concetta thought would have been too heavy for *signora* Clara to wield herself, but there was a pile of splintered wood beside it and the embers of a dying fire. There would be neighbours, of course, who would help with the heavy work. It must have been hard to lose a husband, not so many years ago, her mother had said, and then both sons so quickly. It was no wonder she could make no sense of the world any more.

One of them was not dead, though, only gone. It was not uncommon for men to leave the village, never to return, and sometimes never even to be heard of again. The journey was far, too far, and sending letters was laborious. You had to pay for paper and writing materials and then go round to the priest and ask him to write it for you. Even then, you had to entrust the letter to someone, a passing pedlar, to take it to the provincial town, a walk of three days there and three days back. All this, if you had a place to send it to, and *signora* Clara did not.

Concetta realized that the old lady and her mother were looking at her expectantly, waiting for an answer. She shook her head slightly and sat up.

'*Tanti auguri*,' said *signora* Clara. 'Best wishes for your marriage.'

'You must come to the service,' said her mother, 'and to raise a glass afterwards and have a bite to eat. It won't be a feast. You know what kind of year it's been.'

'Yes, please come,' said Concetta. She felt awkward and childish again, parroting her mother.

'She's young, isn't she,' asked *signora* Clara, 'to be getting married? What about the others?'

'He is a nice man,' said her mother vaguely. 'It's the right thing to do.'

'I don't understand people any more,' said *signora* Clara, sighing. 'They do things for themselves, never for the family. It never used to be like this. Look at me. An old woman sitting all day in these four walls waiting for my son to come back.' She bent her head and took out a rag from under her shawl and began dabbing at her eyes. 'I never meant for it to be like this. Be careful, Anna, it doesn't happen to you too. You can't trust these young people any more. My son promised he'd come back and look what's happened.'

'Don't cry now,' her mother said, leaning over to touch her shoulder. Her mother didn't like tears. 'You won't go without.'

'He might come back,' said Concetta uncertainly. She felt like she ought to say something. She wanted to be a comfort to this woman, too. 'If he said he would, then maybe you just need to wait a bit longer.'

'He said he would write, but I've received nothing, and the days pass.' She sighed. 'And the days pass.'

'But he left before the earthquake, didn't he? If he sent a letter then, it would never have got through. He won't know about the earthquake.'

Signora Clara blew her nose and put the rag away. 'He promised me he would write. He said he wouldn't abandon us. He wasn't going to make his fortune there. He was just going to make enough to buy a house, a piece of land for us, and then come back. I told him, "Don't be tempted. Don't forget about us," and he said, "Never".' She spoke in a monotone as though she'd said the words a hundred times in her head. 'He doesn't know about Peppe. He doesn't know it's just me to look after now. He needn't work so hard. But I can't tell him that, can I?'

'He'll be back,' said Concetta. 'He wouldn't have promised to return if he didn't mean it.'

Signora Clara looked up at her. 'You remember how he was. Always a good son.'

Concetta frowned. She didn't know Francesco at all. She'd seen him once, a long time ago, when Tino had stopped to talk to him after mass, but then Tino was well liked and would often stop to talk to acquaintances. She couldn't even picture his face now. When she'd asked after him, Tino had only shrugged to say there was nothing much to say.

'What is, is,' said her mother, turning to Concetta. 'We can't know the future. Lots of things can happen so far away.'

'I just meant that there's still hope.'

'We're all praying,' her mother said. 'That's all we can do.' With this, her mother brought talk of the son who'd left to an end. Concetta could see that she didn't want *signora* Clara to think of him too much. She believed he had gone for good. Nunzia, too. 'Better she believes him dead,' Nunzia had said. 'Better to accept the worst. That way she won't be disappointed.' Immacolata had agreed. 'Why would you go all that way only to come back?'

Concetta's mother wanted to do a few odd jobs while she was here and she made Concetta clear the hearth while she went outside to check on the hens and rabbits. While Concetta was bending over, raking the ash, she felt a light touch at her elbow.

Signora Clara had sunk down beside her. In the dark room, with her black shawl like a cowl over her head and her hands outstretched, there was something grasping about her. Concetta tried not to shrink away.

'One day before the earthquake. It was long past sundown, it was late, too late. You were out by the cemetery gates. It was no place for a girl to be, no place.'

Concetta tried to stand up, but the grip on her elbow

68

had stiffened. 'I don't know what you mean, *signora*. It wasn't me.'

'It was you. It was. Francesco was with me. We heard noises outside. We thought it was wolves so Francesco took the gun.'

Concetta wanted to shake her off, but the old woman's hand was like iron clamping her down.

'You were startled to see us. You jumped and looked around you. I wanted to know who was there with you. I told you to go home, that I knew your mother, that she's a good woman. And I meant to tell her, even though Francesco told me not to, but then there was the earthquake and everything, and I didn't.' Her hand slackened and fell away. 'I didn't say anything to her in the end.'

Concetta got to her feet. Her knees ached from crouching. She helped *signora* Clara back to a chair and sat her down on it. She walked over to the door and put her head outside. Her mother was putting feed out for the hens and indicated to her that she was nearly done. Concetta went back inside and sat beside *signora* Clara. She waited for the heat in her face to pass before speaking. 'You never saw him?'

'A scoundrel,' she said with distaste. 'But, no, I didn't see him.'

Concetta felt an odd relief and let out a sigh. It struck her that now, after all that had happened and all that was about to, it would do her no good to know who this man was.

'But Francesco did.'

Concetta felt a shot of nerves through her stomach. The baby shifted. She put a hand over her belly to soothe it, but she could feel her hand shaking.

'Francesco knew him. But he wouldn't say any more. "A good-for-nothing," he said. "Just a good-for-nothing."'

Concetta closed her eyes. Francesco had been right to dismiss him as worthless. He had slunk away into the undergrowth, into obscurity, leaving no tracks. He was a coward and he had got away.

The heavy door scraped open against stone floor. Her mother stamped her shoes to get rid of the muck and came back in to say goodbye. Concetta rose to her feet. She was ready to leave.

Out of Concetta's way, there had been discussions about her future home between her father, Felice and Giovanni Totila. Her father had brooded for a while about whether to move his mother out of her house, which was not far from his own, and have her come stay with them, but the old woman had reacted with fury and threatened to bolt herself in. Concetta's mother said there was to be no trouble on the first day of the year and so to let it be. 'She can't be on her own for much longer anyway,' she said. 'She's losing her memory. Leave the house for Nunzia or Immacolata.'

Giovanni Totila was understanding. He said he would offer the couple what he had: a ramshackle cottage, just a single room, which sat squat by a lonely roadside beyond the flour mill. It would need cleaning out as it had been uninhabited for years. Rats, bats and other field creatures had invaded it a long time ago, and the place was rank with them.

Concetta's father and Tino had gone to see what other work needed to be done and found there was no glass in the windows and the top of the roof had caved in. Together with Felice and some of his brothers, they took care of the repairs and cleared out the vermin. They beat down the thorny bushes and wild undergrowth which, if not kept in check, would creep towards the houses and into the village. They even built a rudimentary sty to keep a pig or to hitch goats in, as there was no covered stall to pen animals. In winter, though, animals would have to stay in the house, tied up in a corner on a bed of straw.

Afterwards, the women, Concetta's mother and sisters and some of Felice's family, came to dust the place down. They brought a few sticks of furniture, enough to eat and sleep on, and then prettied it up for the arrival of the couple: a couple of bronze candleholders, some roadside flowers threaded through the neck of a bottle, a simple iron crucifix to bolt above the door.

The day before the wedding, they prepared the *corredo* to be taken to the bride's new house.

Concetta and her mother and sisters were joined by her *comare*, a neighbour, an aunt and three younger giggling cousins, and Concetta's mother handed each of them a basket with a few of the items from the *corredo* to place on their heads for the walk over to the other side of the village and out to Concetta's new house.

Concetta had woken that morning feeling anxious, but it was such a bright day, the sun out so early that it seemed like a blessing, and her cousins' good humour readily infected her and the other women, so that when Concetta tried but failed to mount the donkey to accompany the *corredo* through the streets they all shouted with laughter. Concetta felt the gaiety flush her face and even though she knew the reason she couldn't get up was because of her protruding belly, for that moment, it didn't matter. She was just a giddy bride-to-be, excited that her household goods were being moved from her parental home to her future marital one.

After the women had pushed her up so she was able to swing side-on to the animal's back, they picked up their baskets, balanced them easily onto their heads and began their march through the centre of the winding streets, along the *corso* and through *Porta Vecchia* into the main square. Concetta felt the heat gradually ebb away from her cheeks. There was a sharpness to the light of the overhead sun, but no real warmth, and the women were settling down now, picking their skirts up here and there to avoid animal dung and other debris strewn along the roadway. The donkey's hooves clopped against the cobblestones and then the women started up singing songs, popular *serenate*, one about a lover who had gone far away and never written, and a humorous one which started off, 'My fiancé is the ugliest man in the village.' Concetta wondered why it was that while the men sang of ideal beauty and happiness, the women's *serenate* were all laments.

'Hey, Concetta,' someone shouted from a ground-floor window. '*Auguri!*'

Concetta angled her head towards the voice and raised an arm to wave at her *compare*'s brother, Nino the carpenter. He bowed and raised his hat. Most people would be out in the fields at this time of day, but some were left behind in the village and they emerged, crowding onto doorsteps to watch the women walk by and sliding windows open to lean out and wave. Some women, who could never resist taking part in these events, hurried into coats or shawls and joined them. Someone even got hold of a tambourine to keep the beat.

It took them over an hour to wend their way across the village and down towards the Totilas' land. There was a fair group of people now; some old men, too, had tagged along, walking with their hands in their pockets, glad of the company and the women's cheery bustle. The procession stopped briefly at Giovanni Totila's house, where his wife Franchina and her daughters-in-law were standing ready outside. They had pulled fresh water from the well and brought it round in tin cups. They handed out some chestnuts, too, that had been charred on the hearth.

Concetta remained behind while the procession completed the last stretch past the flour mill to the house. She wasn't allowed to cross the threshold of her new home until she was married. Some would raise their eyebrows that she had even come this far, as it was possible to make out the tiny cottage from the Totilas' backyard. Concetta left the donkey tied to a post outside and went in for a drink of *orzo*, hot barley water, to warm herself up. Franchina predicted snow on the way, and her daughters-in-law, Lucia and Mafalda, nodded and stared. Concetta couldn't think of what to say. She brought her coat around her tighter despite the roaring fire on the go. They know about the baby, she thought. They know, but they can't say.

'Big day for you tomorrow,' said Franchina. 'And for Felice, too. He won't mind me saying, but he's nervous, and who can blame him?'

Concetta smiled and nodded at this. She was going to say that she felt sick with nerves, but checked herself. It didn't seem right to say that to her future mother-in-law and there was a note in Franchina's voice that she hadn't reckoned on. 'It's come round so quickly. I can't believe it,' Concetta said after a long pause.

Franchina came to sit down at the table across from her. She was an energetic-looking woman with big hands like a man's and hair that was straight and grey with a widow's peak that came down low on her forehead. 'Your mother will miss you, being the youngest,' she said. 'Your sisters, too. You were close, weren't you?'

'I'll still see them,' said Concetta. Her voice had become small like a child's.

'Of course,' she said. 'But you must start to think of your husband first from now on. And we're here, too. We're your new family.'

'Oh yes,' she began. 'Thank you.'

'No need,' said Franchina, turning round to face the others. 'My son is the one you should thank.'

6

Concetta woke while it was still dark. She continued to lie in bed, not wanting to rouse herself to the day, thinking that this would be the last time she would wake to the snuffling sounds of her sisters sleeping beside her. Everything she had known would end today. She shivered and closed her eyes. She wished the blackness she had just come from could take her back again. She would go willingly.

'Concetta?' Nunzia had woken. She stretched her arms overhead and then settled back down under the blanket. 'God, it's cold.' She lapsed into silence and Concetta knew that she was also thinking that this was the last time the three of them would be together like this. She propped herself up on an elbow and laid the back of her hand against Concetta's cheek. 'In summer, you know, when Felice sleeps out at night, you can come here and be with us again.'

'But it won't just be me. There'll be the baby.'

'There's room for the baby too,' laughed Nunzia.

Concetta nodded and tried not to cry.

'It will be all right,' said Nunzia. 'I promise.'

'I will see you, won't I, just like before?'

'Silly! Course you will. Maybe not quite like before, you'll have your husband and baby to take care of, but almost.'

Concetta considered. 'I'll be the older sister really, won't I? I'll be able to tell you and Immacolata what it's like being married. How funny!'

Nunzia sighed. 'I don't want to get married.'

'Of course you do.'

'I mean it. It's not for me. I've thought about it a lot.'

'Nunzia, all women get married. That's what they do.'

'Not all. I could join the church. I've spoken to *Mamma* about it, but she doesn't agree.'

'Not get married and join the church?' Concetta felt a kind of awe. The idea seemed amazing to her. Surely it was something you'd only do if you were forced to. 'But, Nunzia, you're pretty; there are plenty of men who look at you along the *corso* and in the main square. You only need to give one look back and they would come to ask for you. There's no need to join the church.'

Nunzia shook her head. 'It's not that. I just don't want to go through all that. I've been with *Mamma*. I've seen the things women suffer. Look, it's not the time to talk about it now. It's your wedding day.'

Concetta frowned. She only had a dim understanding of what Nunzia meant. Her mother had never taken her along when she went to help those women. She said she was still too young to know about such things. Nunzia was always her obedient helper and she would often come back, dog-tired, and wouldn't want to talk. She'd only say that it was a difficult childbirth, or that a woman had had a child too many, or that it was the hysteria women got when they couldn't cope. 'They have a right to it,' Nunzia would say. 'A woman's life is too hard. They need to let it out. Better that way.'

Immacolata grunted and threw an arm across the bed. 'Go and talk somewhere else.'

The door opened and her mother came in, blinking sleep away. Her heavy grey shawl was wrapped around her shoulders and she had her thick stockings on. She slept in them when it was cold. She signalled to the girls that it was time to get up, lingering a moment before closing the door again.

As a child, Concetta had always begrudged the first day of the year. Everything you did would stay with you for the remainder of the year, which for a child was for ever. So it meant you had to do things right. She and her sisters would have to be nice to each other and they would have to work faster at prising cabbage heads from the ground, boot-hard from the frost, huge piles of them, and then they would have to rush back to clean the house down, top to bottom, almost as thoroughly as if they were doing the spring clean. It wasn't just that everything had to be done, but that it had to be done well and so it would be for the rest of the year. Hard labour begetting more hard labour. Concetta couldn't see how this was reward.

This year would be different. There would be no house-cleaning or walking out to the fields to harvest winter spinach or *cicoria* or cabbage. Today was her wedding day. The most important day of her life. A fresh beginning. A chance to put things right.

Mid-afternoon, her mother and sisters and Tino, after much fussing by Immacolata, who wanted to wear her spring shawl despite the cold, left ahead of Concetta and her father. As soon as they had gone, Concetta felt her nerves return. She felt jittery like the time she'd had coffee at the market in San Michele. Then as now, she couldn't decide whether her palpitating heart was excited or ill.

Wedding dresses were always recycled; all the daughters in a family would often wear the same one, and so they were made to accommodate all sizes. Even so, when Concetta had climbed into her mother's dress, leaning forward onto her mother's shoulders to balance, it was a squeeze and her mother had to tug at the buttons that ran up the back to close it. The cotton was a stiff, durable one, made to last, and came up high, to the chin, as was considered proper before a holy sacrament.

Concetta felt encased in the dress, trapped in its panels and folds. She could only walk with difficulty and would have to make an effort not to hobble. Her feet were in a pair of boots at least, she did not possess shoes, and these were hidden from view by the length of the skirt. She wrapped her shawl, a bulky, white, cable-knitted one borrowed from her *comare*, around her shoulders and draped the lace veil over her face. She picked up the piece of mirror that Immacolata had tossed onto the bed and tried to hold it at such an angle that she could see her whole body. She touched the bulge of her stomach and drew her breath in as far as it would go, and then let it out again with a heavy sigh. The bump was noticeable, but it was just possible that people might put it down to simple weight gain. She dropped the mirror on the bed and then stepped through into the other room. Her father rose wordlessly to his feet.

The day was icy and getting colder and there was a strange blank quality to the light, a woolliness that enveloped everything: the sun, clouds, the fading moon. The local church, dedicated to sant'Antonio, was stark against it, as were the people huddled outside on the steps. When Concetta rounded the corner into the square, they moved as one inside the church to be in their pews ahead of her.

Concetta stumbled slightly as she made her way up the steps. Her father's hands steadied her, but when she looked round, she read the warning on his face. It wouldn't do to fall today.

Inside the church there was a powerful smell of incense; it hung suspended in niches and where the light poured in through the rose windows. It was even colder in here than outside. The stone floors and columns and marble statues retained no heat. Concetta felt herself glide the short distance to the altar steps and then her father's arm was no longer there. She felt its absence along with the shawl that was taken from her shoulders and then Felice was at her side, but looking straight ahead at *don* Peppino. He was mouthing words and she realized the mass had started.

She struggled to catch up for the rest of the service. Her shins on the stone steps were like planks. The Latin words she mouthed by heart, without fully understanding their meanings, and she could only listen mutely to the supplicating voices and the heartfelt alleluias. She lowered her eyes when *don* Peppino read the Wedding at Cana and then spoke of miracles, of water becoming wine, of surviving earthquakes. The prayers and the responses slipped by, and she was only dimly aware of them being intoned. She screwed up her forehead and told herself to concentrate to make sure she said the right things in the right places, and she was thankful for the veil that hid her face. It was only because of the man at her side, his pressure on her arm, light but not unreassuring, that she knew when to kneel and when to stand.

When the time came to exchange vows, the priest turned her to face Felice and she could look at him squarely for the first time. He was wearing a dark, ill-fitting suit that must belong to some taller, broader brother, and hobnailed boots, shined for the occasion. There was something different about him: he was less melancholy but grimmer, as though he'd sloughed off his old skin and still hadn't got used to the fit of this new one. There'd been something uncertain and yielding about Felice when he'd come round to her father's house, but she couldn't see that it was there any more.

She managed to follow the words of the priest; her voice, almost a whisper, repeating his, and she listened as Felice did the same. Then *don* Peppino pronounced them man and wife and she thought to herself that it was done. It seemed only a few minutes ago that she'd come into the church on her father's arm and now she was being shepherded to the side of the altar to a wooden chair as the priest prepared for Communion. For a few moments the church lapsed into silence and in that lull Concetta became aware of the congregation massed to the side of her. There was a rustle of low-pitched voices; whispering from the back. A boot banged heavily against a pew.

The priest raised the host and the chalice and after she and Felice got to their feet to receive it, the priest prompting her to lift her veil, he turned away to minister to the people streaming up in a long line that ran all the way back to the entrance and round the sides. The church was small and the congregation had spilled out onto the square; she could see that there were faces peering in over shoulders from outside. It would take time for everyone to receive their host.

Concetta glanced at Felice. His head was bowed, his hands pushed together in prayer, the shoulders of his suit sagged. Concetta turned back to watch the people receiving Communion for a few minutes and then, despite the veil, she started to feel self-conscious as people nudged forward, running their eyes over her, some trying to spark a smile. She turned instead to the priest. High above him, beyond the rose window, she saw that the sky was brilliantly white and falling down in pieces. They had hoped the snow would hold off for today.

Above her, on a side wall, Concetta noticed a small, delicate painting. She recognized it because it had been removed from the ruins of a nearby sanctuary destroyed by the earthquake. The portrait was of Our Lady of Consolation, although the villagers called her the Madonna of the Pomegranates because of the bulbous fruit that festooned the painting's upper corners. It had spent a week on a table in the central aisle of the *chiesa madre*, the main church San Rocco, decked in ivy and glossy holly leaves, but now someone had thought to bring it here to this out-of-the-way corner of Sant'Antonio. Since it had been recovered, Concetta had filed past it many times with her sisters after Sunday mass. A Madonna and child, she'd thought, just like any other. Now, though, she saw it differently. It was as though the painting had been subtly altered. Mary seemed sullen. She had the child, a sickly baby, pinned between fingers which tapered to points like blades. Concetta quickly looked away. The picture stirred a feeling of bad omen and she wished she were not sitting in its presence. She wished now for the service to be over, but there were people still in the queue shuffling forward, heads down, to receive the sacrament.

At last, the priest brought Communion to an end and everyone stood for the final blessing of the married couple. Felice and Concetta moved to the centre of the aisle again and knelt, Concetta girding herself for the wince of pain from the hard stone, and their hands were joined by the priest. Felice's hands were smoother than she'd expected and warmer than her own. Nothing about the day, though, was as she'd imagined.

She and Felice followed the congregation out of the church into the square and the snow, soft and hairy through the window, had turned into hard pellets, which zigzagged down, buffeted by wind. People laughed, slapping at it as though trying to shoo away a swarm of bees. A muffled cheer went up and dry rice and *confetti*, hard, white, sugar-coated sweets, were hurled and in the swirl Felice relaxed his grip and Concetta felt herself borne away.

There was the fleshy suction of cold lips at her cheeks, a tangle of arms and grasping hands, brief clinches against chests, palms pounding her back. She fought for breath and for a familiar face, but managed neither. Snowflakes penetrated the lace veil and she felt them seeping onto her eyelashes and into the corners of her eyes. She blinked and the world became blurry. She felt a sharp pain at her cheek and she lurched forward to find a shoulder, Tino's, and leaned heavily against it. They were carried along by the sheer will of the crowd, which had started to make its way down the steps. As soon as she was able to breathe again properly, she put a finger to her cheek and found a small wound. The chipped edge of a well-aimed *confetto*. Tino produced a handkerchief and she dabbed at her face before the blood had a chance to stain her veil.

The procession snaked out of the square and along the *corso*, through *Porta Vecchia*; the same route Concetta's *corredo* had taken. As then, people who hadn't made the service came out of their houses and hung out of windows to shout greetings. The young girls in particular were keen to see Concetta. 'Where's the bride?' they shouted. 'Where's the bride?' Concetta had to step forward, turn round on her heels to show off her dress and raise her hands to wave. Applause went up. The first time she blushed, but they made her do it again and again until by the end she couldn't help but do it with a little flourish.

She caught sight of Felice ahead. He was among a group of men, his brothers most likely, and they had their arms flung around his shoulders. She could see that he no longer carried the solemnity that he'd had in church:

he was being jostled and was trying to duck out of the way. Concetta was glad. The good spirits around her had enlivened her, too. She wanted more than anything for the day to go off well.

She searched around for her sisters. The light had faded and what seemed like the beginning of dusk was already settling over the street. She located them together, making up the rear of the line; Nunzia had taken their grandmother's arm and Immacolata was helping *signora* Clara and looking unhappy about it. They were proceeding slowly. Concetta felt a moment's hesitation at facing *signora* Clara, but quashed it. No more secrets, she thought, and made her over way to embrace them all.

'How hot you are!' said Nunzia. 'Do you have a fever?'

Concetta shook her head, grinning. 'I'm just happy it's all gone well.'

'I told you it would, silly girl!' Nunzia chided.

'Hey, *bambina*,' shouted a voice. Concetta turned round. It was her cousin Pasquale with Tino. She hadn't kissed him yet and stumbled slightly as she moved forward to embrace him. 'Careful!' he said.

Concetta froze for a moment, thinking that he would mention the child.

'You're a married woman. No falling.'

Concetta tried not to blush. Pasquale pinched her cheek. 'Come on now,' he said, 'no more modesty. I thought this one would be the first to get hitched.' He nudged Immacolata, who pushed him back, trying not to smile.

Then he cupped his mouth and shouted to the front of the line where Felice was among his brothers. '*Figli masculi!* Here's to a good crop of male offspring!'

They rounded the dirt track that led down towards the Totila house. The snow had lifted, but had left the ground damp and slippery. Concetta raised her long skirts and picked her way along. When they reached the house,

Giovanni Totila, who had been at the head of the line, herded everyone into the principal room. They'd opened up the bedrooms, too, and cleaned out the stables so as to accommodate everyone. They'd laid planks of wood out on chairs to make up a large table, and there was already food laid out: braised rabbit, boiled potato, winter salad, pizza bread flecked with mint. Enormous straw flasks of wine were brought in by Franchina and put at either end of the table. People swarmed in, leaning against the walls, crouching down on their heels, already overflowing into the other rooms. Franchina and one of her daughters-in-law came in with bowls of *maltagliati*, the first course. Concetta's mother, too, relieved herself of her shawl and pushed her sleeves up. She disappeared outside where a huge cauldron was hung above a fire, and then came in with more plates of pasta. Concetta was summoned by a ringing voice, Giovanni Totila's, and pushed down into a seat next to Felice. His hair had been mussed up and one of his brothers took his half-drunk glass of wine from him and refilled it, standing all the while with his hand on the neck of the flask, until Felice had finished and then proceeded to refill it again. 'Drink up,' he said.

Franchina came in and pushed the older son away. 'Paolo, *basta*,' she said and directed generous plates of pasta towards the newlyweds. 'There's plenty of time for that later. Everyone eat first. Now, who hasn't got a plate?'

Concetta tried to eat, but people kept shouting *auguri* to her above the clamour so she had to stop chewing and respond by lifting her glass with them. The red wine was sharper and stronger than she was accustomed to at home. Her head was beginning to feel fuzzy and, even though she knew she ought to eat to soak up the wine, she had no appetite and left her pasta half eaten by her chair on the floor. More food was brought in: baked eel, cabbage stew, bulbous heads of *caciocavallo* cheese, boiled chickpeas and

83

roasted chestnuts, already split open and steaming. Guests were arriving all the time, and Concetta felt her head spinning as she rose again and again to greet people.

Later, when the food was gone, the men spilled out into the backyard. Now they'd drunk, the house couldn't contain them. A few neighbours departed noisily to get some more wine and Franchina, satisfied that everyone had had something to eat, gave the signal for the women to start clearing up. Felice, his face flushed, could barely hold himself upright and was led outside by his brothers.

Concetta went to the doorway and leaned against the doorframe to watch the men. The effects of the wine had begun to wear off now, leaving behind a faint throb at her temples. A fire had been lit in the hearth in the kitchen and it had gathered strength despite the door being left ajar so the women could pass in and out while completing their tasks. Concetta felt the lick of the fire at her back. The night air had a bite to it and she wondered that the men didn't feel it; some had stripped down to their shirtsleeves and nearly all were hatless.

A group of men emerged from the stable and one of them, a raucous Pasquale, was holding a cockerel by its legs. Its plumage, black with red tail feathers, was fluffed up and untidy. Pasquale headed towards a chestnut tree in the yard, unsteady on his feet. With one hand holding the cockerel, he attempted to climb the tree, but fell back again to great shouts and bellows from the other men. He put his free hand up in resignation. 'All right, all right, I give up,' he said.

'Can't hold your wine, my friend,' Paolo shouted.

'You come and try then,' Pasquale yelled back. Then he caught sight of Tino, leaning against the stable in half-shadow under an awning. 'Tino, you do it. Here.' He thrust the cockerel towards him. 'You're the only man sober enough.'

'Come on, Tino,' one of Felice's brothers shouted. 'Before the groom falls asleep.' Felice was swaying against the brother, unable to keep his eyes open.

Tino pushed off from the stable wall and strolled over. He grasped the cockerel from Pasquale – the bird had begun to squawk in protest and he quietened it, in the way that Tino could – and then, indicating to Pasquale to form a step with hands, he pushed up from it and swung onto a branch. From there, he made his way smoothly to the top.

Concetta forgot the cold and stepped out of the doorway into the yard. She found Pasquale by her side and he threw an arm around her shoulder. The women, who had been bustling backwards and forwards, stopped what they were doing and they, too, moved closer to watch. There was a wan moon, which seemed to bob just above the top branches where Tino lashed the cockerel. The moon gave off an uncertain, wavering light and Concetta could just make out the bird's beak stabbing at it.

Tradition held that the groom's aim when shooting at the wedding cockerel would reflect the fortunes of the marriage. An accurate shot, where the bird died instantly, would bring good fortune for the couple. If, instead, the groom missed or didn't kill the bird cleanly so that it suffered a lingering death, then the bride should brace herself for hard times and much sacrifice in the months and years to come. Some in the village held it to be a true forewarning, but Concetta's mother was doubtful. She'd seen plenty of birds shot straight through the heart and yet the bride had had misery all the way. Even so, Concetta felt a flutter of apprehension as Felice was pulled up by his braces and positioned a good shooting distance from the tree. Paolo handed him an old-fashioned hunting rifle with a long thin muzzle and fancy silverwork on the barrel.

'Steady now,' Paolo said. He put his fist around the muzzle and pointed it at the top of the tree.

Felice immediately collapsed forward under the weight of the barrel and several men had to pull him back upright again.

'He'll shoot his own foot if he's not careful,' Concetta's mother said.

It had started to snow again, just a light dusting, and Concetta looked up to see that the moon was now hidden behind clouds. She squinted at the top of the tree, but she could no longer distinguish the cockerel's beak. There was no movement either, no flashes of red against the branches. Without the moon, it looked very obscure up there, indistinguishable from the sky.

Paolo had his hands on Felice. 'All right?'

Felice nodded and Paolo backed away slowly. Felice trained the rifle towards the top of the tree and a hush fell. The gun cracked, followed by a faint echo. Felice staggered forward again and was caught just in time. Paolo tried to stand him up, but he flopped down.

'He's out,' said Paolo. He took Felice's face between his hands and tried to talk him round, but then shook his head. 'Let's take him in,' he said to some men close by. They each took an arm or leg and huffed under his dead weight as Franchina directed them towards the new house, beyond the mill.

Concetta stared after the men as they made their way across the yard. She wondered if she ought to follow.

'I don't think your husband will be of any use to you tonight,' said Pasquale in her ear. Her arm was threaded through his and she could feel the length of him swaying against her, using her as a support. She was beginning to feel cold again and stepped away so as to wrap her shawl tighter. She looked around for her mother.

It was true that people were still milling about talking and laughing. Felice's departure didn't seem to be the signal for festivities to end. Usually, people would start to make their way home when the bride and groom left for their quarters.

'Was it a hit or a miss?' shouted Pasquale to the men standing closest to the tree. In the commotion, everyone seemed to have forgotten the poor cockerel. 'What's the verdict, eh, Tino? Can you see from there?'

Tino was close to the tree trunk, but didn't seem to be in any hurry to find out.

'It's too dark to see.' Her mother had appeared at Concetta's side. She glanced over at the men struggling with Felice and then back towards the tree.

'But it doesn't mean anything, does it?' asked Concetta.

Her mother shrugged.

'Tino, what's got into you?' shouted Pasquale. 'Is it dead or alive, man?'

Tino circled the tree and peered up. After a moment, he levered himself up onto a branch and proceeded to make his way to the top again, scattering snow as he went.

After a moment, they heard Tino call out, his voice muffled.

'Hit or miss?' bellowed Pasquale.

'No,' they heard.

'No *what*?'

Tino began to climb down. He straddled the last branch and jumped cleanly to the ground. 'No bird,' he said and lifted up the string.

Concetta stared at it.

Even her mother was speechless. 'Well,' she said, lifting her shoulders. 'I don't know what that means.'

'*Zia*, Aunt,' said Pasquale, 'either that bird is lucky or cunning or both. That's what it means.'

Everyone fell to laughing at the cockerel that got away, even Concetta's mother and, because it felt strange not to, Concetta joined in too.

7

It was late, but there was still nearly a houseful of people warming their hands and faces in front of Giovanni Totila's hearth. Concetta's mother said that Concetta ought to leave now and make her way over to the other house. She called for Immacolata and Nunzia to accompany her, as it was bad luck for a married man or woman to enter a newlyweds' house on the day of their marriage.

Their job is done, thought Concetta as she embraced her parents. She turned to Tino, who was walking *signora* Clara home, and she saluted the remaining guests. Franchina came over to the door and handed Nunzia a candle in its blown-glass holder and the sisters stepped out of the kitchen, its pool of light, and into the cold darkness beyond.

Both Nunzia and Immacolata had been to the Totila place regularly over the last few weeks but, with just this feeble, bobbing light, the way to Concetta's new home was unfamiliar to them. 'We should have let Mafalda come,' grumbled Immacolata. 'She would have known the way like the back of her hand.'

'No,' Concetta said. 'I don't want Mafalda. I don't want any of them here.'

'Why? What have they done?' asked Nunzia in astonishment. She linked her arm into Concetta's and drew her in.

'I just wish I were going back with you, going home. I know I can't. I know that.'

'Don't be so childish,' said Immacolata. 'Of course you can't.' Her voice rose. 'You're lucky. Very lucky how things have turned out. It could have been different. It makes me angry that you still can't see that. Even now.'

Immacolata walked slightly faster ahead of them so that Concetta couldn't see her face any more. She had moved out of the dancing circle of light. They walked on in silence, stumbling occasionally on the overgrown footpath that led from the yard and skirted a small field.

'It's done now. You're a married woman,' said Nunzia after a while. She said it in a cheering way as though it were a great thing to be married and then Concetta remembered their talk earlier, before the rest of the household had roused, when her sister had spoken about joining the church. It seemed so long ago now, yet it was the same day.

Concetta felt her eyes growing used to the dark. She recognized the whitewashed structure of the flour mill, with its crooked chimney, up ahead and it seemed like a beacon penetrating the darkness. Immacolata glanced up at it as she passed and then put her head down again. She was trying to go quicker, so she could take her leave, go home. Immacolata liked her sleep and it had been a long day. Concetta felt contrite then. It was true that she was lucky. This was the most she could have hoped for. 'I'm still full of the day. I can't settle, that's all,' she said by way of apology.

'That's normal,' said Nunzia with a short laugh. 'I feel the same.'

They walked on past the mill and then the fields were very deep and black beside them and Concetta felt as though it would be easy to lose your footing here, where the weeds grew in abundance and snagged at your boots. She would have to be careful walking home alone in the dark.

The footpath veered off to the left, a raised, grassy platform, and the fields continued to fall away either side. Here they walked in single file. Ahead, a dark plume of trees was visible and then, as the path swerved round, the tiny house, low and white, revealed itself. The candle that Nunzia was holding extinguished itself and she cried out in dismay. They had to be even more careful now and grasped the back of each other's shawls to keep close. Concetta, in the middle, leaned over to her right, to see past Nunzia. The cottage stood in perfect darkness. There was no candleglow at a window to show the way.

They walked around the cottage to the door and Concetta glanced at her sisters before softly rapping her knuckles against it. There was no reply, so she did it again. She put her hands against the door and pushed it open. There was a faint scent of soap and paint, but the overwhelming smell was sharp and musty, of animals and undergrowth and soil. It was just one simple room. She walked through using her hands to feel her way around. There was a small fireplace and, beside it, wood piled into a bucket, a couple of rickety chairs and a small table with some holly inside a glass jar. On the other side of the room, away from the door, was a bed: two benches pushed together with a thin mattress laid over the top where Felice, still in his best clothes, lay face down. He hardly made a sound.

Concetta shivered. Her sisters had come in, too, and were looking around the room curiously, as though seeing it for the first time. They hung back near the door and Concetta felt their awkwardness at being in her house and again she had the feeling of being a stranger to the people she knew best. She gestured at them to come in further, as she didn't want them to leave immediately, but Nunzia shook her head. Immacolata took a moment to study Felice's prone form and then turned round and walked back outside. Nunzia followed her.

'It's time for us to go now,' Nunzia said in a whisper.

Concetta wanted to ask them to remain a few minutes longer, just enough for her to absorb the shock of being in a strange house with a man she hardly knew, but she thought again that all was as it should be and that she was lucky to be standing outside her new house with a sleeping husband within.

'Think of the baby,' said Nunzia as she embraced Concetta, holding her tight.

Concetta nodded and turned to Immacolata. 'It's all gone well, hasn't it? You'll be all right now.'

Immacolata allowed herself a short smile. They embraced and Concetta followed them round the cottage and stood watching as they made their way along the path and towards the flour mill until they disappeared into the night.

She came back into the house, pushing the door open gently and then closing it. She had searched around earlier in the dark for some matches, but she couldn't find any to give her sisters for the lamp. It seemed odd that her mother, or whoever had prepared the room, had forgotten to leave matches. Glancing around now, she couldn't even see any candles. The men must have simply offloaded Felice onto the bed and left, taking the light they were carrying with them.

She walked across the room. Felice was still on his front, his arms and legs sprawled over the whole bed. She would have to move him if she went to lie down there and she didn't want to wake him. She had an urge for him to sleep for ever. She didn't feel tired, though. She felt out of sorts and buzzing and it was true what she'd said earlier. She couldn't settle. The house seemed so empty. The bits of furniture seemed insignificant; if anything, accentuating the bareness of the room. Everything else that was familiar: her family, her friends, even the village itself, was far away, a good, long walk away.

She drew one of the chairs over to the table, making sure not to scrape its legs against the floor, and sat in it for a while, just staring into the darkness and thinking about the day, the crowds of people, the laughter, the snow. She didn't feel the cold now, that was how unsettled she felt. She could feel a pulse in her throat, her heart pumping. She made an effort to calm herself and laid her head on one side against the tabletop so that she could feel the uneven grain of wood against her cheek. She stayed that way for a long time until her heart, the beat of it in her ears, had quietened.

A wind had blown up. The windowpane was rattling in its frame. Concetta woke with a start, her neck ricked and aching. It took a few moments for the place to make sense to her. It was still pitch black. She walked towards the bed and saw that Felice had moved onto his side. He'd tugged his shirt out of his trousers and pushed his hands together under his cheek to form a pillow. He was moaning lightly in his sleep.

Concetta wondered whether, now there was the space, she should undress and lie down next to him. She felt tired now. The short sleep had seeped into her bones and the baby felt heavy as she unwrapped her shawl. She heard the window rattling again, this time more insistently, and it came to her that there had been no wind earlier. She walked back towards the window but there was something about the quality of the noise that stopped her in her tracks. She was in an unfamiliar place, as good as alone, and it occurred to her that she didn't know what spirits or mischievous entities lurked in this isolated place. She was suddenly very frightened. Her scalp prickled. There was another noise at the window, not a rattle, a kind of creaking movement as though someone were trying to push against it and then – she felt herself nearly fall in fear – there was a flitting movement outside, beyond the window. She backed off towards the bed. There was a figure at the window and then she saw the silhouette of a face press against it. She fell onto the bed in terror and cried out. She put her hand to Felice to wake him. He moaned and turned away from her. At the pane, a hand was rubbing the glass and then an eye appeared, trying to peer in.

Then she heard a low, fierce whisper. 'Concetta,' it said. 'Are you awake?'

The terror lifted, and she looked at the window in amazement. Tino!

She ran to the door and, steadying her hands, which were shaking still, she lifted the latch. She'd forgotten her shawl in her excitement and the cold air cut through her dress like a knife. 'Tino!' she said. 'I was so frightened. I didn't know who it was. Come in, come in.'

'No, I'll stay here,' he said, his voice low. 'I'm sorry to come like this. I shouldn't be here.'

Concetta took a moment to understand what he meant. 'No, no,' she said. 'He's still out. He's sleeping.'

'That's what I thought.'

It struck Concetta that something terrible must have happened for Tino to come to find her tonight at this late hour. 'Tino, what has happened?'

'Nothing, nothing. Don't worry.' He hesitated. 'Are you all right?'

Concetta nodded, but she felt anxious. He had come to tell her something. 'Wait,' she said, 'let me get my shawl.' Her neck felt raw from the cold. She went back inside and drew her shawl around her throat. Felice was sound asleep. A crust was forming in the corners of the windowpane. The frost was settling in. She hurried back, stepped outside, and closed the door to behind her.

'Tino, why are you here? Should I worry?'

He laid a hand on her shoulder. 'Francesco's back.'

Concetta blinked at him uncomprehendingly.

'Francesco . . . ?'

'I walked *signora* Clara home.'

'Ah,' said Concetta. 'Francesco. Her son.' Her voice sounded tight. Not her own. 'He didn't send word. People didn't know if he would return.'

'He'd been taken ill as soon as he got over there,' said Tino. 'He had to wait three months to get his passage back. He didn't know about the earthquake. He didn't know about Peppe.'

Concetta nodded. 'No,' she said. 'He couldn't have known.'

'He was resting by the milestone on the main road from San Michele. He'd been walking for days. Could hardly stand. I helped him to the house and left them alone. He needed to rest.'

'*Signora* Clara?'

'She's revived. She could hardly believe her eyes.'

'It's like someone coming back from the dead. I told her not to give up hope,' she murmured half to herself.

Tino glanced over her shoulder at the door, and then back at Concetta. 'I thought you would want to know.'

After *signora* Clara had told her that Francesco knew who she was waiting for at the cemetery gates, she'd fretted that he may have told someone else in the village. Eventually, she'd confided in Tino, who had told her not to worry, that if there were any talk about the father he would find it out. Those in the village who might suspect her condition would simply believe that Felice was the father. Why else would a young man agree to marry a pregnant girl? But Concetta knew she had to be careful. Whoever knew the truth could ruin her still.

This news about Francesco arriving on her wedding night unnerved her. 'What if he says something?' she asked.

'He won't.'

Concetta bit her lip.

'I didn't want it to come as a shock, that's all.'

'I could speak to him,' said Concetta. 'I could ask for a name.'

Tino took a step back. 'It's not for me to tell you how to live your life.'

'No,' said Concetta. She shook her head. 'Better not to know.'

After Tino left, Concetta sat at the table and waited for sleep to come once more. It didn't, and she watched the winter half-light filter through the two small windows. The gloom hardly seemed to lift, though, and every so often she glanced over her shoulder at her husband as he shifted on the bed, swallowed and muttered in his sleep.

The room oppressed her even more now. Its strangeness was overwhelming. She'd always slept in a room apart from the main living room, with people to rouse her, the animals lowing and bleating for food close by, the sounds of hobnailed boots or a walking stick tapping along the street outside, the cheery hails of the people on their way to work. She closed her eyes, blocked out Felice, and listened. A bird cooed throatily. Its wings slapped and then there was a fluttering sound as it flew off. For a long time, there was nothing. With her eyes still closed, the world was blank.

When she opened them, she found Felice sitting on the edge of the bed. He had heaved himself up, but was still heavy with sleep and finding it difficult to focus. He coughed and ran a hand over his mouth. He glanced up at Concetta and, after a moment, when she didn't move but continued to stare at him, he spoke, his voice raspy.

'Is there any water?'

Concetta got up quickly from her seat and discovered a pail of water by the hearth. She dipped a cup in it and came over to hand it to him. She waited until he'd finished. 'More?' He nodded and she ran over and brought him back another cup.

'My head feels heavy,' he said. He cleared his throat and sank his head into his hands.

She didn't know what to say to this. She couldn't think what to say to him in general. She had never been on her own before with a strange man, one who was not a close relative at least. No, she closed her eyes briefly, and corrected herself. She had, of course, before the earthquake, but she couldn't remember it so that wouldn't help her now. She had no idea what a wife was supposed to say to her husband in the morning. She thought of her own mother and father and it seemed to her that they never spoke to each other unless they needed to. They said the necessary things, about food and work and getting the animals ready to take to the fields.

'I'm not used to the wine,' he said from his hands.

'I'll get you something to eat.' She looked around the room, but there was nothing, not even a crust of bread. 'I'll go out and get something.'

'No,' said Felice. 'My mother will come. She'll bring something. We can't leave the house until they get here.' He stopped and brought his face up again with effort. 'They're giving us some time alone.'

'Ah, yes,' murmured Concetta. She sat down again.

Felice glanced up at her. 'They've got to do the sheets,' he said. 'Hang them out. We can't leave the house until they do that.'

The morning after the wedding night, the mother and father-in-law had to be the first to enter the house to inspect the sheets for blood. The sheets would then be hung outside for those passing to see.

Concetta looked at Felice in horror.

'If we don't hang the sheets out, then people will know, won't they?' He broke off.

'So, after everything, everyone will know anyway.' She felt her cheeks stain. She couldn't help the shame rising up within her.

'No,' he said with a sigh, 'they won't.'

He eased himself up from the bed, tucking his shirt back into his trousers and adjusting the straps of his braces. He shrugged back into his jacket and walked over to the door and took his hat off the nail. He pushed his way out the door and made his way to the sty. There was a wire basket in there and a scrawny chicken inside. At the sight of Felice, it clucked forlornly. Concetta couldn't believe it hadn't perished in the cold. It must have been there all night. Felice grabbed the chicken by its legs and walked back indoors. He fished around inside his back pocket for a knife and, just before he slit the bird's throat, he looked towards Concetta. The chicken had begun to kick out in a dull kind of way and its squawk warbled and died as the knife went in. The strength went out of it quickly, it hardly flapped, and when the blood bubbled up Felice lifted the blanket away and scattered a few drops over the sheet. He stood away from the bed a moment to study the stain, which paled quickly into a pink smudge, and then took the chicken outside, its head flopping forward to expose the raw gullet.

Concetta didn't go out this time. Felice seemed gone a long time and then she realized that he must have walked a fair way from the house to throw the dead chicken. He wouldn't want to attract foxes or wolves as it was now the season for them. She knew, though, that when he came back in it would be time and she felt the light change, his shadow falling across the stone floor, and she watched him take his boots off slowly on the front step and hang his hat on the nail. He turned to the door and put the latch on.

He walked over to the bed, checked where the blood was, a faded bloom by now, and began taking off his clothes with great care. He didn't look at Concetta, but turned slightly away, his shoulder to her, and she could see that it was hard for him. It would be his first time. She wanted to say to him that it was her first time too, as good as, she had no recollection of any other, but of course she couldn't. Felice loosened his braces and took his trousers off, his legs were slender for a man's and they were covered in smooth, fair hairs, fine as silk. He unbuttoned his shirt, one button at a time until it gaped and he lifted it away from his body, folded it and laid it on the floor by his trousers. His chest was pale and hairless and he was slighter than she'd imagined, his ribs visible even from where she stood. He removed his socks, a woollen vest and underpants and turned away from her to slide beneath the sheets, careful to check again where the blood was.

Concetta stood up and walked over to the other side of the bed. She sat down on it heavily, her back to Felice, and unwrapped the shawl. She looked down at the wedding dress. She'd been wearing it for so long now it felt like it had become welded to her and she realized that she could not, on her own, get out of it.

'Can you . . . ?' She glanced shyly round at Felice. 'Can you help me out of this?'

Felice sat up on the bed and leaned forward, his knees knocking against her back, and she felt his fingertips, cold, fussing at her neck. The material was stretched taut and the buttons were difficult to work out of the holes. He picked at them until they gave and she felt the release of the dress opening up. She could breathe properly again. She felt her lungs expanding. She rubbed her neck and shoulders and, when Felice had finished, she peeled the dress away from her and stepped out of it. She still had her shift on, a plain cotton one, and she saw that under her pillow, there was a neatly folded blue nightdress, part of her *corredo*. She sat shivering a moment, wondering how she would get out of her shift and into the nightdress without Felice seeing her naked. She turned round, wanting to ask him to look away, but he was already sitting up now, staring at her through the shift, and his eyes had grown dark. Concetta had been dreading this moment: stripped of her clothes, her belly exposed, but he wasn't looking at her in that way, with scorn or curiosity. He seemed gripped by something else. Concetta thought that if she'd seen him at any other time with that look about him she would have been afraid. His eyes were fixed on her, unblinking, and he seemed wary of her, fearful almost. Her own dread had evaporated and she felt stirred to reach for him. She turned round to face him. She didn't feel the cold any more. Her hands were warm and she lifted them to his cheek. He closed his eyes at contact and, as she drew her hands away again, he opened them, sketching the ghost of a smile.

She turned back and lifted the shift off and, still shy of him, slipped under the sheets quickly. She turned round but his hand was already on her shoulder and he was breathing heavier now, panting almost. He climbed on top of her; she felt his weight press down and his hardness against her belly and she wanted to put a hand there to protect the baby, but stopped herself. She didn't want to bring that into it now. She lay there and watched him as he moved over her, rubbing himself against her, and it was as though there was a fire within him, an urgency, and he could barely keep his eyes on her now. He reached down, lifting the blanket off, and fumbled, then looked up at her a moment, almost a plea, and she had to shift her position and then she felt him digging into her until he entered. She'd not expected pain, so she cried out because it hurt her. He stopped a moment, but his uncertainty cleared swiftly and he carried on, and it still hurt her, and she couldn't relax or feel anything except the rub of it. She couldn't ask him to stop, though. She had no right.

He opened his mouth and fell forward, clinging to her breast like a child would to its mother. She looked down and saw that the hair around his ear was damp and matted. It appeared darker than its natural colour. His rapid breathing took time to calm and then he shifted his weight, flopping over onto his back. He didn't look round at her and she was glad; soon his breathing deepened further and he was asleep. She lay there for some time, and when she knew she could relax, she too closed her eyes and slept.

PART TWO

8

Felice's father, Giovanni, had given Concetta and Felice a strip of land to work further on from the village, an hour's walk away from their little house. It was close to a place they called the *mufita*, a desolate spot, other-worldly; a craterous hole which in winter filled with dark, clouded rainwater. In summer, it dried out to a dustbowl, just a trickle of foul-smelling mud deep within its cavity. On days when the wind changed, when bad weather was on its way, the sulphurous stink from the *mufita* carried all the way over to the village, and women would shutter their windows and retreat indoors.

People said that down there, in the hole at the bottom of the *mufita*, lay the way to hell. You could believe it: the smell of the place was rank and made your eyes water, and over time there'd been many who'd gone close to see and had fallen down dead on the spot, struck down by noxious fumes. Their souls, it was said, were sucked down the hole and straight into hell. It was true that on one of the few times Concetta had passed by there as a child she had seen the carcase of a donkey lying on its side, its legs locked rigid like the legs of a table, its flesh rotted away, the smell of death overwhelmed by a more powerful, acrid odour.

Because the *mufita* lay on this side of the village, Concetta had never had much occasion to go near and, even when the smell of it touched the village, she had hardly given this forsaken place a thought. Now that she would have to tend land close by, she was afraid. She would have to pass by there every day, morning and night, sometimes alone. Not so many people had land out this way and those who did planted olive or fruit trees that could be left untended most of the time.

A few days after the wedding, Concetta went with Nunzia and Immacolata to inspect the strip of land. Felice had already gone ahead with his brother Paolo. They found a few wizened olive trees, but they were ancient and broken and had not produced any worthwhile fruit for many years. It was decided that the men would chop the trees down and rip out the roots as far as they were able. Concetta and her sisters would start ploughing up the earth to plant cabbage and spinach, food that would grow quickly and be ready to eat in the early spring. The ground was softer now and it had become damp since the frost had loosened its grip. The winter sun, pale and low in the sky, brought some warmth, and the girls were able to shed their coats as they worked.

It was the first time Concetta had seen her sisters since the wedding. The shyness that had kept them from entering the house that night lingered. It seemed that it would always be there now. She saw that her sisters would be drawn together more and more and that she would have to stay apart. They didn't ask her about her life as a married woman and she didn't tell. There was nothing to say.

Concetta was glad that for the first few months, until the land was ready, she and Felice would get this practical help from their families. She would not have to come here and be by herself straight away. But they were all young and it was a new venture. The land, which had been untouched for so long, felt like virgin earth, so they went at it with vigour, and they were heartened in the way that comes from hard work and good progress.

Concetta could see that Felice was close to his brother. Paolo was several years older and the oldest of the brothers not yet married. He was protective of Felice and they often went around together as a pair. They looked similar, too, although Paolo was a broader, brighter version. It seemed to Concetta that Felice had a tendency to fade, as though he couldn't maintain interest in anything for too long. She had noticed it right from the beginning when he visited her family and she had mistaken it, this listlessness, for something more sinister, some hidden sickness. Paolo put the life back into Felice when he started to flag. He could keep him going. Concetta thought that she might learn how to do this, but then she wondered whether it was a thing that could be learned.

Some days later, Immacolata and Nunzia called on Paolo and together they stopped outside Concetta's house. They didn't come in, but sat chatting and laughing together, propped against a tree. Concetta had already prepared the day's food and hurried to put it together. She took half a loaf of bread, a jar of olives and a bowl of cooked spinach with *fagioli*, white beans, and wrapped them in a piece of cloth as securely as she could. She called out to Felice to get a bottle of wine. She tied a scarf over her hair, fastened it under her chin and then balanced the parcel of food on top of her head and walked out to join the others.

It was still early. There was a freshness to the light; everything – the colours, the trees, the hills – stood out sharp and clear. There was no trace of the mist that sometimes rose out of the forest first thing in the morning. Felice was carrying a spade and a couple of hoes and Paolo picked up the rear with the two goats that Concetta's parents had given them, hitting out at them with a cane when they set to munching by the wayside.

Almost from the first, Concetta noticed how the group broke into two parts. She and Nunzia would drop back to keep Paolo company with the goats and Felice and Immacolata would go on ahead together, their heads not turned towards each other, but nonetheless deep in conversation.

She liked Paolo. She had warmed to him quickly. The thought had entered her head that she might have married Paolo. He was the oldest of the unmarried brothers, after all. When this thought came to her, which it did more often than she liked, she reminded herself that she had no right to wish for anything. Her belly was showing now and she was lucky that she was mostly here, out of the way. It had hardly been noticed so far and she thought that if she stayed away from the village for long enough, people might forget and not get to calculating how and when.

It was downhill all the way and they walked briskly; Felice and Immacolata keeping a fair distance ahead. The path they took from the house passed at one point between some fields where grapevines were arrayed on either side, following the contours of the land as far as the eye could see. Here and there people were working, and the group would stop and shout their presence, hollering if the people were some distance away, and the workers would respond by hingeing back up from the ground, a hand to support their backs, with a friendly wave. From here, the path led down to an old fountain, where the women would sometimes bring clothes to wash, and then soon after it would meet a highway, a Roman road, the *via Appia Antica*.

It was once they had crossed this highway and plunged further downhill that they were in the vicinity of the *mufita*.

If there was no wind, it was only here that they would smell it, a prickle at the nose. Today the breeze was stiff enough for Concetta to need a hand at the parcel on her head. Almost as soon as they started out, she'd sniffed the *mufita* in the air. It was not as pungent as it could be, but the smell was ranker than usual, as though the gases were not releasing into the open but festering somewhere first. As they got closer, Concetta took a handkerchief from her pocket and pressed it to her face. She felt nauseous and her stomach turned over. She seemed to have escaped the sickness that women get when they first conceive and so it seemed strange to her that this place affected her as it did. The others would wrinkle their noses and moan about the stink of it but, on still days when it was at its worst, she would have to veer off to the side of the road and vomit her breakfast into the bushes.

Concetta stopped walking. She wasn't sure if she could swallow it down and go on.

'Sick again?' asked Nunzia.

Concetta gave a half-nod and put a hand to her belly. She stood for a few more moments staring at her boots. The nausea seemed to ease when she looked down to the ground. 'You go on. I'll catch you up.'

'I'm not leaving you like this,' said Nunzia.

'We can wait,' said Paolo and Nunzia nodded.

'I'm all right,' Concetta said after a moment. She looked ahead into the distance and, seeing nothing there, turned to the side of the road and spat. There was a bitter taste in her mouth.

A mile or so ahead there was a fork in the road. They always took the path to the right, which meant they didn't have to pass beside the *mufita*. The left path would take them very close and, with the low-lying trees and hedges that way, it was possible to glimpse it. When they arrived where the path forked, they stopped. Immacolata and

Felice usually stopped here to wait for the others to catch up, but there was no sign of them. Paolo cupped his hands to his mouth and shouted out their names, but there was no returning call. They hesitated for a moment, unsure which path to take.

'They must be walking more quickly than they thought,' said Nunzia. 'They'll soon notice and stop for us.'

'But which way?' said Paolo, eyeing the path towards the *mufita*.

'The usual one,' said Nunzia, surprised. 'Why would they go that way?' She made to go the usual route, but Paolo hung back and she stopped, too.

'I can't go down there,' said Concetta, nodding towards the left path. She felt hot again with the brightness of the sun, and her stomach was rolling.

Paolo looked down the path again, but then nodded and they started off down the usual one. Concetta felt the sickness rise and fall like a tide, and she tried to control her breathing and not let it show. She prayed for the wind to change. She didn't know that she would be able to work if it didn't. They emerged out of the path onto the fields that had become overgrown orchards; they now had their backs to the *mufita* and the air became less heavy with it. Concetta began to feel her breath come more easily.

Their field came into view and she saw the deep lines of furrowed earth and, in a far corner, a felled olive tree, its gnarled trunk and broken branches reaching up towards the sky as though there were still power in its unclenched grip. She swept her gaze up and down the field looking for Immacolata's red headscarf and, when she couldn't locate it, she turned to the others who were a few paces behind, absorbed in rounding up the two goats that had wandered across another field. Paolo was swishing at them in a playful way and Nunzia was putting herself in his path to protect them, but laughing despite herself.

Concetta couldn't remember when her sister was last like this, girlish and carefree.

Beyond them, she caught the fluttering headscarf out of the corner of her eye. Felice and Immacolata rounded the bend and came towards them. It seemed to Concetta that they were walking more slowly now, not hurrying to make up for lost time. She raised her hand high and waved. It was a few seconds before either of them reacted. Then, as one, they waved back. She could see that they were talking without looking at each other. She felt the sickness roll through her insides again and she gagged, her hands at her throat, and staggered over to the side of the path where she was sick. She stayed where she was for a few moments, putting a hand out to a nearby tree trunk to steady herself. She looked down at her feet, disgusted. She didn't even know what this sickness was now. It didn't make sense. She could hardly smell the *mufita* here.

She could hear Nunzia and Paolo still laughing behind her. They hadn't noticed she'd been sick. She walked back over to them and took hold of the goats by the scruffs of their necks. She didn't want them wandering off again. She waited an age for Immacolata and Felice to arrive. 'Guess where we went,' said Immacolata. Her cheeks were flushed.

'You went by that place,' said Concetta quietly. She still had hold of the goats and pulled them towards her.

'The stink of it!' Immacolata laughed. She put a hand to her nose as though to stop it up. 'It's ten times worse there than it is here.'

Felice laughed with her.

'You shouldn't go anywhere near that cursed place. Did you think we would follow you?' said Concetta, frowning. 'Half the day is gone waiting for you two.'

Immacolata looked stung and then angry. 'I'm sure we can go whichever way we want.' She looked round at Felice.

Concetta felt a heat rise within her. She turned to face her husband, but his eyes slid past her and he took a step back. She looked at Immacolata. 'Just walk with the rest of us.'

Immacolata stared. 'No, it wouldn't be right, would it? Going off with a man alone. That,' she said, smiling, 'would not be right.'

Nunzia put her hand out. 'Stop,' she said, 'right now.'

'She can't tell me what to do,' said Immacolata. 'Not after what she's done. She has no right.'

Concetta opened her mouth to reply, but nothing came out. Paolo put a hand on Immacolata's shoulder and drew her away and she allowed herself to be led towards the field. Felice stepped up alongside them and Nunzia, too, after a moment, moved off in their wake.

Concetta remained standing in the same place, unsure whether she would follow them or not. She wanted to turn round and go away, not back to the empty little house, but beyond the forest and the river, beyond San Michele even. Far enough away that she would never again have to sniff the *mufita* on the wind. One of the goats gave a muffled bleat and she realized she'd been half strangling it. She opened her hand to release the goats and they skipped away towards the fields.

9

Heavy snows had made the olive harvest late that year and now it would have to be done at the same time as the wheat. Some weeks after the year had turned, when winter was at its deepest, the wheat would need to be cleaned. The weeds, which threatened to choke it, would need to be plucked out and thrown away or burned and the soil would have to be turned over. It was still too cold to plant anything; they would have to wait for the frost to lift.

For the first time since they were married, Concetta and Felice would be separated during the days. Felice went to work alongside his brothers and Concetta made the long walk through the village every morning, to her parents' fields on the other side of the hill. There was more of a wind here and the air was clearer. She'd got used to the *mufita* and hardly thought about it now unless the lake was particularly stagnated, but here, away from it, she breathed more deeply, unthinkingly, as she had always done.

Concetta had hardly spoken to Immacolata since the day her sister had passed by the *mufita*. Nunzia had tried to get them to strike up talk, but they'd managed only the fewest of words before pulling apart again. Concetta guessed that Nunzia had taken Immacolata aside, asked her to take the words back, and that Immacolata had refused. Concetta often thought of what her sister had said and how she'd said it, and she saw that her husband often thought of it, too.

Concetta and Felice walked the short distance from their house to Giovanni Totila's in silence. As soon as he reached the path to his father's house, Felice mumbled a few words of parting, which Concetta didn't catch, and he turned away without looking at her. Concetta watched him, having an urge to call after him, make him look her in the eyes at least, but then the desire to do so passed. Her husband had little interest in her, but the truth was that she was finding it ever more difficult to feign any in him. She felt glad to leave him at the gate. She put her hands underneath her belly to support it and walked on.

Over the last few weeks, the bump had grown in a spurt and she had had to ask her mother to find new clothes for her. The child was moving a lot again. It seemed restless, fluttering around inside her, so that she couldn't concentrate on what she was doing, making her vague with people. She often just smiled at inquiries or greetings these days when she passed people on the street, prompting them to ask twice, and she felt herself retreating when in company, so that people hardly remembered she was there. Not so long ago, she had fretted that people would see her with her big belly and wonder. Now, if people stared at her, she couldn't find it within herself to care.

She walked slowly and arrived at the fields late. It was a warm day for the time of year and her brother, in shirtsleeves, whistled to her from the branches of an olive tree. She raised her hand in greeting. Her father and Immacolata were in adjacent trees, using canes to pull the branches towards them and pulling and shaking the olives away. Her mother and Nunzia had laid sheets out underneath and were bent down collecting the fallen fruit. Concetta wanted nothing more than to drop down onto one of those sheets and sleep. The walk had taken her nearly an hour and a half, and the sun was warm on her shoulders. She felt sluggish as though she hadn't properly woken up.

'Come on,' her mother called. 'You're late.'

Concetta knew the baby wouldn't win her special treatment. Her mother had worked each time right up until birth and it was either she or Immacolata who had been born under one of these very olive trees. She remembered her *comare* laughing about it, saying that her mother had simply wiped herself down afterwards and gone back to work, and Concetta knew that this probably wasn't far off the truth.

She went to the sheet underneath Immacolata's tree and, with difficulty, as she found it hard to bend, began to gather up the olives and put them into the basket. She found it easier to sink to her knees and pad around on the ground. Some of the fruit were still green and hard, some partly ripened to a darker colour. The work was tedious and time passed slowly. Occasionally she had to sit up and stretch, holding her back. Some days her family were like this, nothing to say to each other, keeping their thoughts to themselves. Now that she and Immacolata were not speaking, there was even less chatter while they worked. Her mother had noticed, of course – Concetta had seen her glance at the two of them – but she had decided to keep her counsel and for this Concetta was glad.

Lunch was a heel of bread scuffed with dried tomatoes and oil, and a withered apple that was half fermented and tasted strongly of earth and wood, of having being enclosed throughout the winter. Concetta reached over for the bottle of wine from her brother and took a deep slug to wash the food down. She could hardly keep her eyes open and, were it not for the chill creeping into the air now that the sun was sinking and the fact that she was standing on her feet, she really thought she would drop to the ground from sheer exhaustion. The desire for sleep spread relentlessly through her and she could feel her eyelids drooping. In the end, it was Immacolata who saved her by starting up some chirpy talk with Nunzia and her mother about *carnuale*.

Lent meant forty days of fasting and early mass before work. Just before it started, they celebrated *carnuale* to bring some cheer for the leaner days ahead. In the village, they dressed the children in makeshift robes as brigands or brides or sailors and took them round the streets in their finery to show them off. If it was not too cold someone would play a fiddle in the main square and someone else would sing and once people were warmed up a bit, they danced the *tarantella*. They heard of other villages and towns far away where *carnuale* was a different thing, wild, where anything was permitted for one night only, where men would roam, and the women too, because it was under cover of the night and they had masks to hide their faces.

Immacolata had the idea of going to San Michele for *carnuale* and was trying to persuade Tino and Nunzia to go. 'They'll have a proper dance in the main square, not like here, just Nino the carpenter on his scratchy old fiddle.'

'We'd have to start out early, after lunch, to get there by nightfall,' said Nunzia. 'We'd miss half a day's work.'

'We can work extra the week before,' said Immacolata. 'Eh, *Papà*? What do you say?'

Her father, seated high in his tree, released a branch he'd been pulling and the entire tree shook as it sprang back. 'What about the day after? You won't get back here until late and then you'll need sleep. Bah.' He broke off, shaking his head.

'Leave it be,' her mother said. 'We can't afford to lose a day for *carnuale*.'

Immacolata resumed her work and, after a few minutes, jumped down from her tree. She emptied out the olives from her apron pockets onto the sheet and then glanced up at Tino in the next tree. 'It will be market day in San Michele for *carnuale*, won't it?'

'Usually it is, yes.'

'We need salt and matches and' – she whirled round towards her mother – '*Nonna* needs some of that cream to put on her legs, so Tino has to go anyway.' She looked back up at her father and then down at her mother again, who shrugged.

'What do you say, Tino?' her mother asked. 'It's up to you.'

Tino dropped himself down from the tree. 'What about Concetta? She can't come in her condition. She'll be left here alone.'

Immacolata frowned. 'Not alone,' she said. 'She's married, isn't she? It would be me, you and Nunzia. Perhaps Paolo could come and some of the other brothers. We could get a group together.'

Tino looked across at Concetta.

Concetta turned towards them. 'Don't worry about me, Tino. Really.' It was a rare thing for girls to be allowed to go to San Michele for *carnuale*. For a moment she allowed herself to feel the thrill as if she were going too and she couldn't help but glance down at her belly. If it were not for this, she thought, surely Felice would have taken her, but then she remembered that if it were not for this she wouldn't be married to Felice. She gave her head a quick shake.

Immacolata ran over to Tino and pulled at his hand. 'Is that yes? Are we going?'

Tino shrugged. Immacolata squealed and ran over to Nunzia and they fell about laughing.

'Concetta.' Her mother beckoned her over. 'You're not looking yourself these days.'

Concetta gave her a smile to reassure. 'It's still all strange to me. You know' – she couldn't think of the words – 'you know, this, everything.' The vagueness was returning.

'You're eating?'

'Yes, yes,' she said, 'and sleeping a lot.'

Her mother nodded. 'You've got a long walk home,' she said. 'You go home now, a bit earlier, and get some rest.'

'But, *Mamma*,' started Immacolata.

Her mother gave her a dismissive wave. 'You're going to San Michele, now stop your yapping, and let's get on with this work. We've still got another row to go.'

Immacolata closed her mouth and, without looking at Concetta, bent down to pick up the sheet, then walked over to the next tree. She gave it a vigorous shaking-out and spread it over the ground where it lay uneven over the roots.

Concetta wondered at her mother. She never made exceptions when it came to work. She was strict about these things, and fair.

'On your way back,' her mother said, picking up a large basket of olives, 'take these to *signora* Clara. It's not too far out of your way.'

Concetta had put her arms out to take the basket, but now dropped them by her sides.

'What's the matter?' her mother asked.

'*Signora* Clara?'

'I said I'd send her some round. She wants to conserve them as they are, fresh.'

Concetta glanced up at Tino, but he was hidden in the midst of branches. 'I haven't seen her since the wedding.'

'Concetta,' her mother said, sighing, 'you'll have to start facing people. If she doesn't know about that, she soon will, and anyway she's got other things on her mind.'

'It's not that,' said Concetta. She couldn't think of any good reason to give to avoid going. Her mind was too slow. She took the basket and looked up again at Tino, but still his face was obscured, so she bid everyone goodbye and made her way towards the path that led up to the village.

The sun was pale and weak against a colourless sky and the cold was making itself felt, softly at first like the tips of delicate fingers at her exposed throat and ankles, and then, as she walked on and the light faded, it became more pressing, scouring her cheeks and bare hands. She'd balanced the basket of olives on her head, over her headscarf, and as she passed people she knew, bending down under trees or crouched on the ground close to the soil, she called and waved and they shouted back. As the day drained of light, they appeared as grey and obscure figures in the distance.

She took a longer route, circumventing the centre of the village so that she walked around the outskirts. Here there was wood smoke in the air and the sharp tang of pigs and, as darkness fell, through doorways and windows there was the soft sheen of light from oil lamps. These streets were mostly empty, people were still in the fields, but sometimes an old woman or a child peered out from a doorway or came the other way down the street and she spoke a greeting and they returned it, and then they were gone.

The night fell quickly at this time of year and, by the time Concetta had got to the road that led to *signora* Clara's, it was very black and she thought she might ask for a candle to light her way home. She approached the little cottage and prayed for *signora* Clara to be alone. A puff of smoke curled up and away from the house and some old clogs were propped against the doorstep. She rapped at the door and eased the basket off her head, holding it out ready so she could give it and be gone.

She heard the shuffle of feet against the floor, not the quick step of a young man, and she closed her eyes. *It's not him.* There were no voices and she rallied at the thought that *signora* Clara might really be alone. The door rattled a little as it was eased off the latch and then it opened, and *signora* Clara was frowning up, not quite recognizing her. Concetta lifted the basket and pushed it forward so that *signora* Clara's arms came out to take it. *Signora* Clara looked down, not comprehending, and Concetta removed the cloth from the top. 'My mother sent them for you.'

'The olives!' *Signora* Clara brightened with understanding. 'Is it Concetta? The married one?'

Concetta nodded.

'You're not stopping for something?'

'No, really, I can't.' She glanced back towards the path. 'I have to go. My husband is waiting for me.'

Signora Clara pushed forward out the door, the basket still in her hand. 'Your husband must come in, too. No use him waiting out there.'

'No,' began Concetta. *Signora* Clara was peering up and down the path. 'He's not here, with me,' said Concetta. 'I have to collect him on my way home.'

'Oh, he won't mind if you're a few minutes late,' she said. 'Listen to me; you need to keep them waiting sometimes. They appreciate you more that way.' She put a hand on Concetta's back and nudged her towards the door. Concetta didn't move at first and *signora* Clara turned to look into her face. 'I'll be offended if you don't at least take a glass of water.'

Concetta wondered at how this woman had changed since she'd last seen her at her wedding. She looked ten years younger and her mind that had been wandering and in such pain seemed to have returned intact. 'As long as I'm quick. I'm already late.' Concetta felt herself propelled in through the door and *signora* Clara bustled in behind her, still tutting.

Inside, a stout candle sat on the table. It gave off a wan light, steady in the centre but causing shadows to leap in the corners of the room. There were, here and there, the odd, careless signs of another presence in the house: woollen work shirts lying folded on a bench, a pack of dog-eared playing cards on the table, the nub of a pencil and a few sheets of paper beside it.

Signora Clara deposited a large carafe of wine on the table. 'Will you have a glass of wine or do you want something warm, *orzo*, barley water?'

Concetta clasped her hands together and eased them onto her lap away from view; they had mottled with the cold. She would have gladly accepted the *orzo*, but the water would need heating up. 'Wine, but just a small glass. I must be gone.'

Signora Clara made more tutting noises as she moved over to get a cup from beside the hearth. 'You young people, always in such a hurry.' A small fire was dying, the embers glimmering, and *signora* Clara bent over, sighing with the effort, to pick up some wood to drop on the fire. 'My son, Francesco, should be home soon, any time now. He went to talk to a man in the village about some work.' She mentioned the man's name, asking Concetta if she knew him and Concetta didn't, although she knew of him by reputation, a shepherd whom her father had occasional dealings with for wool and leather.

The fire was crackling now, beginning to flare up, and a warmth like a soft out-breath reached her cheeks. She hated the idea of facing the bitter cold again and then on to Felice and their echoing house that felt unloved and unlived in. She felt a twinge of guilt about not asking *signora* Clara more about Francesco, about the illness that had kept him from sending word, and how he had managed to get his passage back. She would have liked to say that she was glad he had come home, but she knew how *signora* Clara could talk away and she didn't dare risk staying any longer in case Francesco himself arrived.

She drained her cup and heaved herself up, the chair scraping against the stone floor, and *signora* Clara noticed her belly for the first time. 'My goodness,' she exclaimed. '*Complimenti*! That was quick work.'

Concetta mumbled her thanks and shrank down a little, wrapping her coat around her tighter.

'I didn't know it had been so many months since the wedding.' She frowned. 'It was the night Francesco returned to me, wasn't it?'

'A few months, not so long,' said Concetta vaguely and she picked up the empty basket and made for the door. 'My husband will be angry if I don't get back. Thank you for the wine, and for the fire.' She went out the door, and put a hand out to stop *signora* Clara coming out onto the step with her. 'No, you stay where it's warm. Don't let the cold in.'

She glanced back as she hurried away and was relieved to see that *signora* Clara hadn't come out after her. She reached into her pocket, took out her headscarf and tied a strong knot under her chin and blew onto her hands. She'd forgotten to ask for a light! It was too late. She wouldn't go back now. It was dark as pitch in the small yard that led up to the path and she had to keep peering down at her feet to see where she was putting them. She found the road, and the dark here seemed to have a different consistency, not so impenetrable but still murky. She could at least see her way forward.

She'd only taken a few steps when she made out a figure approaching in the distance. He seemed to come out of nowhere, as though he was part of the obscurity ahead of her that had broken off and become alive. For a second she wondered if she were seeing something supernatural, but then she saw that the figure had seen her and had altered his stride to walk more carefully now.

Concetta knew it had to be Francesco on his way home. She tugged the headscarf lower down on her forehead, pulled in her chin and walked more quickly, hoping that her hurried pace would deter him from mouthing any more than a formal greeting. She was almost a stranger to him, after all, and he may not even have seen her coming from his mother's house. She kept her eyes fixed ahead, and when he greeted her, she mumbled in return and continued on. She sensed behind her that he had stopped and was watching her, but she was so intent on keeping on that she didn't hear his approach until she felt the pressure of his hand at her shoulder.

'Concetta?'

She turned and nodded, suddenly uncertain since he knew her by name. She couldn't make out his features in the dark. A wide-brimmed hat, unusual for these parts, was pulled down low over his brow and he wore a thick scarf.

'Ehh,' he said. It was half-sigh, half-laugh. 'Concetta, how are you keeping?' There was a softness to his voice, and warmth. He took off his hat and she stared up into his face, feeling a small pull, a slight stirring of recognition, but at the same time the familiar frustration of not quite remembering. He was tall with wide, angular shoulders and his darkish hair was thinning slightly at the temples. There was a wateriness to his eyes, which made them appear bright, and they swam out at her.

He smiled at her then with a kind of wonder in his look. 'It's been a long time,' he said. 'God, so much has happened. Too much.' The words trailed off. His hands went up to her shoulders and he squeezed them. When he let go, she realized with a jolt that he was crying. He wiped his eyes with the cuff of his sleeve.

He shook his head. 'All those months I didn't know. Poor kid. He never had any luck.'

'Peppe,' she said as it dawned on her. 'Your brother.'

Francesco nodded. 'I only found out when I got back. I didn't know about the earthquake.'

'I knew you would be back. Your mother –' she hesitated. 'She was worried for you.'

Francesco nodded and she could see he was trying to gather himself. 'You are all right, though?' he said after a moment. 'They told me you'd been hurt, too, but that they found you and you're all right now.'

'They dug me out.' She shook her head at the memory. 'I hardly remember. It doesn't seem real. Like I dreamed it.' She gave a sad laugh.

'Ah,' he said. 'If only we could wake up and be back before the earthquake.'

They stood there in the road, not saying anything for a while. Concetta found herself reaching out for his hands and held them in her own, not wanting to let go even as slivers of cold pushed their way into the exposed openings of her clothes. She wondered what it would look like if someone walked down this way and she knew it wouldn't be right because this man was really a stranger to her. She released his hands, offering them back to him as if they were a gift, and stepped back.

'Come to our house,' he said, nodding up ahead. 'Have something to warm you. You'll freeze on a night like tonight.'

Concetta shook her head. 'I've just called in with olives for your mother. I'm on my way home.' She hesitated. 'I was married at the beginning of the year.'

'The night I arrived. The wedding.'

'Yes.'

'But you're too young to be married. When I think of last summer, it's like we were still children then, and now – seeing you again now. . .' He trailed off. 'That's the way it goes. But married, though.' He looked rueful. 'I haven't even congratulated you. *Auguri*.'

Concetta took another step back and glanced down at her stomach. 'This too.'

'Already? *Complimenti*.' She could see he was surprised.

Concetta looked away. She felt herself moulding the swell with her hands so that he could see its size and shape. Then she unbuttoned her coat and pulled it open. 'Last summer,' she said. She couldn't bring herself to look at him. She waited a moment before pulling the flaps of the coat together again, missing a hole as she buttoned it up so that it hung lumpily.

He tried to say something, but she put her hand up. 'I have a husband now.'

'This should never have happened. You didn't deserve this.'

'You know who he was.'

'Yes,' he said after a long time.

'A scoundrel in any case.' Her voice sounded strange, hoarse. She stopped herself from saying any more.

Francesco lifted his head, his eyes still bright. 'You were fond of each other. But you were children.' He shook his head.

Concetta spoke. 'I've lost my memory. Since the earthquake. Not everything. But this –' She broke off and cupped her belly.

Francesco stared at her, a hard look of disbelief, which gradually softened. He looked down at her holding her belly and then at a clump of trees nearby where a bat or a dark bird was flitting in and out of the branches.

'Peppe,' she said, the word barely audible. It all made sense: the cemetery gates were close to Peppe's house and he was there in the forest that time when Tino went eel fishing. Peppe, who'd died in the earthquake, could not have come forward when she was in a coma or claimed her when it was known she was getting married. The pieces fitted and, seeing Francesco, the half-remembered face of the brother, had sparked something inside her, something small and precious that had been snuffed out since the earthquake, and now it flared up again.

Francesco was still looking towards the trees. 'It wasn't right.'

Concetta touched his arm. 'It doesn't matter any more.'

He didn't react; it was as if he hadn't heard her and she let him be for a while until the cold and the lateness of the hour prompted her to touch him again, and this time he turned.

'I didn't know that he and you . . .' He paused. 'It was wrong of him. My brother was reckless sometimes,' he said. 'I should have done more. I should have stopped him.'

Concetta put her hand to his arm. 'I'm married now, a new life.' She shivered and adjusted her headscarf so that her ears were covered.

Francesco straightened and he readied his hat, bending back the brim.

Concetta took her leave. A few paces on, she turned round. 'You and I were friends.' It was neither a question nor a statement.

Francesco smiled and put a hand up to wave good-night.

10

Concetta spent her journey home in a whirl of thought. She brooded over Francesco's words and the fact that she had known Peppe, a young man, so well that they had stolen away in secret and done such things together. It was clear now that Peppe, whose face she could not remember but whom she had known carnally, was the father of her unborn child. As she walked on, she fell into a daze, unaware of where she was and what was around her. It was amazing to her that she would have done such things. She didn't remember Peppe, but she remembered herself even less. It was as if she was another person then, before the earthquake: reckless and bold and uncaring of those around her that she would dare to act as she had done.

She stopped a moment and saw that she was on the path towards home. The flour mill was ahead of her. She continued on. She realized that, bad as she had been, in many ways the news was the best that she could have hoped for: there could be no rancour in her heart against a dead man. She felt a stirring of hope. In the absence of the true father, she would try her hardest to persuade Felice to accept the child as his own.

When she got home, it was late and Felice, not finding any food on the table, had returned to his mother's for dinner and then stayed on late into the night.

The wheat had been plucked clean and the olives harvested, and they were able to turn their thoughts away from the fields and back to the village. *Carnuale* signalled the start of the new. It marked the proper end to the winter months. From here on in, the days would stretch out longer and warmer.

In the week before *carnuale* the *maestrale* blew in from the north-west bringing cold, luminous days. The low sun at the start of the day was as sharp and flashing as a blade. The wind left the leaves brittle and frozen, their veins sketched out in white. The soil, too, became encrusted with a frost that didn't melt.

A few days before *carnuale*, Felice roused himself earlier than usual, well before first light, and left the house. Concetta heard him in the dark dressing quietly so as not to wake her and he stole out, taking care for the latch not to scrape. She'd been sleeping deeply, dreamlessly, and once he'd gone, sleep returned to her but came this time in a whirring turmoil of images and fractured scenes. She was in the forest at night, running again with her lover, but when he turned it wasn't Peppe but Felice. The forest was silent and she realized that he was deliberately leading her towards the *mufita*, to the underworld, and she stopped running. He turned round again to face her, but it wasn't Felice after all, but a small child, an unknown face, curious and unsettling.

She awoke remembering the dream, as its last images ebbed away from her and only the prickle of anxiety remained. She lay there and tried to fish for the pieces again because she felt that the dream meant something and that perhaps her mother might be able to read it for her. She pulled back the blankets and sat blinking on the bed, her eyes bleary. She felt heavy and useless. She put her hands to her belly, feeling its contours as she did every morning as soon as Felice had left the room, and there was a dim glimmer of remembrance, that the child inside her was an estranged thing; something conceived out of the unknown. It hurt her to breathe, as though there were a thousand minute needles laid out across her chest, and she felt afraid and wished Felice were here. She wanted to throw herself on his mercy and ask him to return to her. She wanted him to be as he was the first night they were married, shy with her but pressed by desire. Then she thought again of her child's dead father, how he was both known and unknown to her, and the faces in her dream whirled round in her head and she saw them now as ugly and distorted. She put her hands to her head and stood up.

She couldn't stop trembling. She walked barefoot to the window and outside the world was shimmering into being, a new day, but the house felt dank and cavernous and full of her foreboding. Still in her nightdress, she pulled a coat off the hook and it caught, so she tore at it. It wouldn't come free and she knew she must look like a drunkard, swinging from the hook, and then it released and she toppled over. She scrambled up and pushed her way into the coat, then found some stockings and covered her feet with them. She searched for her boots, but they had been pushed right under the bench and, with her pendulous belly, she couldn't get onto her knees to reach them, so she left the house as she was, hatless and bootless, and she felt better with the wind on her face.

Concetta woke in a strange bed. The room was bright; sunlight streaming in through a window and dust motes rising and spinning in its path. She heaved herself up to a half-sitting position and tried to think where she was and how she'd got here. She glanced around the small room. Apart from the bed, there was a child's stool and on the floor a ceramic jug with a glass of water. She saw that she was wearing an unfamiliar nightdress, a thick cotton one, stiff with starch, and that her feet were bare under the blankets. Her own clothes were nowhere to be seen.

She felt light-headed, as if she'd been shaken upside down and everything emptied out. She lifted up her hands; they were trembling. She remembered leaving, needing to get out of the house, and how cold it was outside. There was that dreadful anxiety. She could still feel it now. She'd gone looking for Felice because he'd left the house too early and she'd been afraid it might mean he'd left her for good.

She eased the blankets away and lifted her feet onto the ground. The floor was smoother here than in her own house, the stone was grainier, more worn, and she knew that someone had spent hours on hands and knees scrubbing at it with a hard brush. She heard voices then, from another room, and she padded over to the door to put her ear to it. It was Franchina and the quieter, nasal voice of either Lucia or Mafalda replying.

She heard the outside door open. 'Where is she?' Felice had arrived.

Something heavy, a jug or bottle, was laid on the table. 'In there, sleeping.'

'What happened?' It was Giovanni Totila's voice. 'Is she all right?'

'She's got a fever,' said Franchina. 'I don't know what she thought she was doing. Wandering around like that, half naked, in this cold.'

Concetta heard footsteps and she ran back to the bed and got under the covers again. She shut her eyes and heard the door open a crack and then close again. The footsteps retreated.

'She's still sleeping,' said Felice. He sighed.

Concetta got up and crouched low on the floor against the door. Moving quickly had brought on the dizziness again. She felt like she was floating and made an effort to return to herself, to ground herself in the room. They continued to talk about her and she singled out Felice's voice. It sounded bland, unmoved. She put her hand to the door to steady herself and she was frightened to see that her hands were shaking even more now. The movement was violent, unnaturally so, and she prayed that she wouldn't lose her grip again. She didn't want to be here in this house with these people. She felt homesick for her childhood home and for that place in the bed between her sisters. She allowed the longing to wash over her and counselled herself that she must stay for a while longer, until she was able to walk on her own.

'What about her mother?' said Giovanni Totila.

'She's here now and our responsibility.' It was Franchina.

'The baby?' asked Felice.

'Nothing to do with that,' said Franchina. 'I have a feeling about all of this, though. If she gets worse . . .'

Giovanni sighed. 'Let's see how she is later. It might just pass.'

'Perhaps that's why she's, you know, having a child like that.' It was Mafalda. 'Do you think it's something to do with up here?' Concetta could imagine Mafalda tapping the side of her head.

There was silence. Then Giovanni spoke. 'The girl is tired and worried about the birth. She's only a child herself, for God's sake, and she's your wife, Felice. Remember that.'

'Yes, *Papà*.'

Concetta tiptoed back to the bed and climbed in. Her feet were rigid with cold. The baby was moving around more than usual. She put a hand just below her navel and felt a movement. She wondered if a child inside a belly had the same sensations as its mother: if she were cold, would the baby be cold; if the mother was anxious would the baby be anxious, too? Then she wondered if a child could share its mother's thoughts. Perhaps the child, once born, would remember. It made her want to cry.

The woollen blankets were heavy and scratched her skin. At first, they felt only oppressive, but slowly their rough warmth transferred itself to her, and the child inside started moving less and then she was aware of it sleeping, and so bit by bit she drifted off, too.

Concetta woke during the night, aware of another presence in the room. Her head felt woolly, as though it had lost its proper density. At first she wondered if what she sensed was the child's presence inside her own but then there was a dull clicking and she guided her gaze to the corner of the room by the door and saw Franchina, sitting on a chair, knitting, the needles tucked under her arms out of the way.

She watched Franchina's deft hands moving repetitively and purposefully, but the dullness of her head made even looking too hard. She would gladly have slept again, but she had a terrible thirst and she lacked the energy to sit up to look for the jug of water. She opened her mouth to speak and found her throat dry as ash; pushing sound out was an effort. She lifted her arm a fraction, but Franchina was too concentrated on her work and didn't look up. Concetta tried again and this time her weight shifting on the bed turned a spring and Franchina stopped and looked towards her.

'Water,' said Concetta. Her throat felt like it had been scoured.

Franchina came over and hovered above her. She pressed a cool hand onto her forehead and it made Concetta shiver.

'You're burning up,' she said. She bent down and came up again with a glass of water and then put it to Concetta's lips, cupping her chin to stop the water from dribbling. 'Careful now. Don't overdo it. A sip at a time.'

The water was cold and it tasted wonderful. She would have liked to drink on, but Franchina withdrew the cup. 'That's enough.'

'More.'

'Not yet. You'll make yourself worse. You've got a fever. You need to rest. Close your eyes and sleep.'

There was a searing pain at the back of her throat. She could barely swallow. 'Felice?'

'Gone home to sleep. He was here earlier.'

Concetta tried to speak. Franchina was pulling the blankets over her to still the shivering. Concetta tried again and Franchina looked hard at her because she didn't understand. 'Mother,' she said, finally able to make the sound.

'We'll get her tomorrow, if you're still like this. We take care of you now. You're not a child any more that needs her mother.' She picked up a rag from the floor and dabbed at Concetta's forehead. 'It's a nasty one, this fever. Try to sleep now.'

She couldn't sleep, though, because she felt the movements of tiny creatures marching across her body. First along her fingers, then in her scalp, and then at random points like on the tip of her nose or under her chin. She didn't have the will to scratch and she could hear herself moaning and trying to shrug them off. She lifted her hand up to see what manner of creature they were to torment her like this, but it was too dark and she thought they must be so small as to be invisible.

Then daylight seemed to arrive very quickly and in that long, suspended moment between sleeping and waking she marvelled that she must have been sleeping after all, because the time had flashed by. Felice was opening the door and putting his head in. He glanced quickly at the bed.

'She's been bad,' said Franchina in a low voice. 'Raving.' Her knitting was lying formless on her lap. 'Saying all sorts of things. Just before daylight she stopped and I went to check and the fever had lifted.'

'What was she saying?'

Franchina put a finger to her mouth and nodded over to Concetta. She got up, moved to the bed and saw that Concetta's eyes were open and staring. 'Feeling a bit better?' She put a hand to her brow, turned and nodded at Felice. 'Yes, it's definitely gone. She's back to normal.'

Concetta's head felt clearer and her body felt its normal weight again.

Felice approached the bed, cap in hand. As though visiting a stranger, Concetta thought. He looked a little sheepish standing there and didn't come close enough to touch her. He met her eyes and gave a half-smile. 'Better now, eh? You had us worried there.'

'I'm glad you came,' said Concetta. 'Thank you.'

'Don't be silly.' He sounded affronted. 'I sat with you earlier, too. I had to get some sleep last night. *Papà* needs me at the flour mill today.' After a pause he said, 'I knew you were all right. A touch of fever. That's all it was.'

Franchina left the room, closing the door behind her, and it felt suddenly intimate as though the proportions of the room had shifted and they were closer to each other. Felice took a step back from the bed and looked around the room with intense concentration, as though studying its corners and nooks.

'Did you used to sleep here?' asked Concetta. 'In this room?'

'No, Antonio did. He used to walk in his sleep, so he had to be on his own.'

He took another step backwards in the direction of the door and Concetta was afraid he was going to leave her. She felt weak but unburdened now the fever had gone. The heat that had passed through her seemed to have refined her mind. It felt clear and sharp. 'Please stay with me a moment.'

He looked up at her, doubtful.

'Just a few minutes.'

He picked up Franchina's chair, brought it over to the bed and sat down, still keeping some distance.

'What Immacolata said,' she began.

Felice had a stricken look about him. 'Concetta –' he began.

'She was right. I don't have any right to anything after what I did. I know this whole business has been terrible for you. This –' She swept a hand across the swell of her stomach. Tears leaked down her cheeks and onto her chin.

'Don't cry.' Felice fumbled around for the rag on the floor and handed it to her.

'Sorry, sorry,' she said, but now the tears were flowing and she couldn't stop them. 'You don't want to sit here and watch me feeling sorry for myself.'

'It's not that.' He looked down at the ground a moment and then put his hands to his face and rubbed at his eyes.

Concetta managed to stem the tears after a few minutes. Her eyes felt hot and raw. She knew there would be two red lines running down her cheeks. Crying always left its mark on her.

When she had finished, Felice looked back up at her. 'You didn't trust me with your sister.'

'It's not you. It's her I don't trust.'

Felice sat back in his chair and it seemed to Concetta that he was struggling with something inside. 'She's your sister.'

'We've been like this all our lives.'

'You don't trust her. You don't trust me. It boils down to the same thing in the end.'

'No.'

He hesitated before speaking. 'I trusted you, didn't I?'

'I know that. I'm lucky to have you. I wish I could prove it.'

Felice's eyes were on her own.

'I'll do anything.'

'It's not a test.' He looked away.

'No, no,' she said. 'Tell me.' She leaned forward and reached for one of his hands and held it to her.

'They've asked me to go to San Michele, for *carnuale*. Paolo asked me. Of course I said no because you weren't well. I wouldn't go.'

'Oh.' Concetta paused. She was taken aback that they would ask him, knowing that she couldn't go.

'I said no and I meant it. It wouldn't be right to leave you.' He looked away again.

Concetta gazed at his profile against the light from the window. 'But I'm better now. It doesn't seem fair for you not to go.'

'Your sister will be there. You don't trust her.'

'But I trust you.'

Felice considered her face. He put a finger tentatively to her cheek and traced the path of a tear. 'You're red here.' He withdrew his hand after a moment. 'No, I'm not going. A husband should be with his wife. It's not right.'

'Felice.' Concetta smiled and squeezed his hand.

He looked across at her again. 'We'll see. If you're really better, we'll see.'

I I

They didn't speak again of *carnuale* and it became clear that Felice would go. Concetta told Franchina that she would stay in their house only until the morning of *carnuale* and then she felt she would be strong enough to go home. She would have preferred to go to her mother's, she yearned to sleep in her old bed again, but she felt awkward saying this to Franchina. Tino had come to visit her the day before and Franchina had seemed displeased, as though he'd discovered some secret at finding her ill. She felt uneasy in her mother-in-law's house and yet Franchina had sat up with her for the whole night when she was feverish. The hours there passed slowly and her recovery seemed fitful. It was as if there was something sticky pulling at her feet and she couldn't wait to kick free of it and be away.

The morning of *carnuale* was damp and misty. Concetta rubbed the glass of the little window in her room and saw the wreaths of grey settling over the hills in the distance. She pulled on a capacious dark red woollen dress that Franchina had given her, an old-fashioned thing that reached down to her bootline, and she wound a heavy shawl over the top. She went through to the main room where Franchina and Giovanni were eating a breakfast of leftover swabs of bread in hot milk.

'What are you doing?' asked Franchina, rising from her chair. 'You shouldn't be up. You're not strong enough yet.'

Concetta still felt a little weak on her feet; under the skirt her legs trembled, but she couldn't bear to spend a moment longer in the bedroom. 'I'm well now. Really. I need to go and tend to things at home. I've been away for too long.'

'At least wait until Felice arrives,' said Franchina. 'You can't just walk off on your own.'

Concetta frowned. Felice might not be back from the flour mill for several hours.

'I'll take you then,' Giovanni said. 'Once you've put something warm inside you.'

Concetta knew it was of no use to argue. She made her way over to a chair at the table and sank into it. Franchina brought her some hot milk and bread and, even though she didn't feel hungry at all, she ate steadily, pushing the pieces of stale bread down with the back of her spoon to absorb the milk. She felt better when she'd finished, her belly warm and soothed, and she got up with Giovanni to leave.

Franchina insisted on tying a double headscarf on her and adjusted the shawl so that it covered all exposed skin. 'Keep that dress on over the next few days. You won't find another one warmer.'

'*Grazie*, Franchina,' said Concetta. 'I really mean it.'

'Don't be silly. We're family, aren't we?' She sounded brisker than usual.

'The state I was in. I'm sorry for everything.'

Franchina considered her. 'As long as all that business is over and done with now. You just look after my boy. Make him a good wife.'

Concetta nodded and leaned in to kiss Franchina. Her mother-in-law's cheeks felt cold and paper-dry against her lips.

Concetta and Giovanni walked to the cottage in silence and Concetta was thankful. He asked her once if she felt well and she said that she did and he didn't ask her again. Concetta's thoughts were with Franchina's parting comments. It was the closest she had ever come to speaking to Concetta about the scandal and there was something about the way she'd done it that didn't sit right. It was as if the matter had been brought up between them and Franchina had wanted to get the final word in. When they reached her door, Giovanni stopped and said he would go now, as he had to get back to the mill. He handed over a parcel of provisions: bread, a head of spinach, a jar of peppers in oil and a few shrunken yellow apples.

Concetta watched him make his way towards the trees and, as he was about to go out of view, she waved and he saw her and waved back. She continued watching the spot where he'd gone under the dark canopy of trees and then she turned her gaze around her.

It was a lonely spot. There was hardly a sound. She could just make out the looping whistle of a bird very far away. The world was mute, like a voice locked inside a throat. She could understand that. When there was nothing to say, why bother to speak? She thought of the spring and how she could feel its imminence, as though the world had quieted itself in preparation. She imagined the bleating of the newborn goats and the cheering voices of Felice's brothers calling to each other from the fields nearby and she tried to hear the sound that her own child would make when it arrived with the spring, but there was only that muffled silence. Even the far-off bird had flown on.

She entered the house and sat for a moment to take the weight off her legs. She could hardly look at the room. Felice had left the bed unmade and there were a few bits of crockery by the hearth to be washed, not many, as he'd nearly always eaten at Franchina's. She could see the room needed sweeping. In the few days she'd been absent, a fine dust had settled over the table and the chairs and even on the indent in the wall where the window sat in its frame. She gathered her strength and then set about these few chores. She moved around the room slowly at first, then with more energy and, as she got the heat moving within her, she wiped down the windows and the door, and cleaned out the poor chickens, too.

When she stopped, she felt very tired. She went inside with the intention of resting on the bed but, even as she stepped in through the door, she felt the familiar aversion coming back to her like a dull ache. She decided instead that she would walk to her parents' house and wait for them there until they came back in from the fields. She would steal in, while no one was around, and sleep in her old bed. The idea made her smile and it kept her going all the way there even though she was really too weak to walk that distance alone.

When she arrived, she was surprised to see the door open and, through it, the quiver of movement inside. She found her sisters in their bedroom and a great mess of clothes heaped on the bed. Nunzia still had her work dress on, but Immacolata was stripped down to her underthings and was sewing a piece of card into some fabric.

Nunzia put her hand to her mouth to stifle her surprise when she saw Concetta. 'I didn't see you there!'

'Should I have knocked?' Concetta smiled.

'I didn't hear you come in, that's all.' Nunzia looked down at the clothing scattered over the bed. 'Tino told us you'd been ill, but that you were better.'

'It was nothing. I'm well now.'

'I would have come today, but we hadn't prepared for *carnuale* and we're late. The others will be here any minute.'

'I'd forgotten that you were all going. I thought there'd be no one here. I was going to have a sleep in my old bed.' Concetta laughed.

Nunzia came over and wrapped her arms around her. 'Sorry, sorry. I feel terrible about not coming to see you and now you being here while we all go off to San Michele.'

Concetta looked down at her belly. 'Don't worry about me. I can't go in this condition, can I?' She looked over at Immacolata, who was sitting on the bed with her head down, sewing. 'Felice's going too.'

Immacolata glanced up. She had a needle in her mouth and she was pulling at a piece of thread.

'Is that really what you wanted?' asked Nunzia with her arms still around Concetta. 'Don't you want him to stay with you for *carnuale*?'

Concetta looked from one to the other. 'He needs to go and enjoy himself. He's still young and,' she said, glancing down at herself again, 'all of this, it's not of his making. In any case, I trust him.'

'Then everything is fine,' said Immacolata. She snapped the thread and picked up the piece of stiffened black cloth, a mask, and walked over to the other side of the room.

Nunzia took Concetta's hand and squeezed it. 'Come over to the bed and sit down.' She made Concetta lie down in her old place in the middle. 'How does it feel to be back?'

Concetta closed her eyes. 'Wonderful.' She lay there, not quite sleeping but drifting towards it, and she heard her sisters' voices, which sometimes sounded close and sometimes far away. She came to and sat up when she heard them both laughing.

Immacolata was holding a mask over her eyes with one hand and a mirror with the other. She stopped laughing and removed the mask. 'It doesn't sit straight. I'll have to redo it.'

'There's no time. The others will be here.'

'They'll have to wait,' said Immacolata.

'No one will see you in the dark,' said Concetta.

Immacolata ignored her and put the mirror down. She began to pick at the ties of the mask.

Nunzia came back over to the bed. 'You're getting big now.'

Immacolata turned to look at Concetta, her gaze travelling down the length of her. 'What a load to carry around with you.'

There was a loud rap at the kitchen window and Immacolata squealed. 'I'm not even dressed. You two, shut up now, stop distracting me.'

'*Ragazzine*, girls, are we ready?' It was Paolo calling from outside the door.

Concetta heaved herself up from the bed and stepped through into the main room. She could see that Paolo hadn't expected to find her there. He removed his felt brigand's hat and shifted to one side and Concetta saw that Felice was standing behind him on the threshold, one foot resting on the step. He had been looking down, but when Paolo moved he looked up at her and entered the house. A mask hung loose around his neck and an enormous black cape billowed out around him. Concetta had never seen these things before. She wondered if Franchina had made them specially or if he'd borrowed them from someone else. He came up to her and put a hand on her shoulder. 'You should be at home resting.'

'I can do that here.' His hand felt warm and she had a strong desire to rest her cheek against it.

Nunzia and Immacolata came through from the bedroom. Both of them carried their masks in their hands. Immacolata had put a heavy coat on and she was holding the lapels up to cover her throat. Concetta glanced down where the skirt of the coat gaped and saw the blue floral pattern.

'Ready?' Immacolata turned to Paolo and Felice.

Concetta looked outside. Some distance off from the house a group of people stood, well-wrapped, with masks dangling from their hands.

She felt Felice's hand press down and then he was waving and moving out the door. Nunzia kissed her on the cheek. '*Auguri*,' she said. 'You'll be fine with *Mamma*.'

'Tino?' Concetta had just remembered her brother.

'He's coming straight from the fields.'

Concetta walked to the door to wave them all off. The group had already broken off into pairs. She watched them as they turned the corner and until their voices were no longer audible, then she turned to go inside. She could still feel the pressure at her shoulder where Felice's hand had been. Almost imperceptible, but it was still there.

Concetta woke with a tug at her shoulder and she half rose towards it because she had been dreaming of Felice. It was her mother who had come to rouse her from the bed because it was late. She'd slept since noon. Dusk was gathering and the air felt thick and swirling with it. Someone close by had lit a bonfire.

Her mother had set out steaming plates of rabbit broth on the table for her and her father. The liquid was clear with just a few pieces of meat hanging from the bone. It made Concetta feel warm and lazy and she couldn't quite shake the sleep off her. She sat opposite her mother at the table and thought how rare it was for just the three of them to eat together.

They ate without talking. There were just the sucking noises of broth being eaten, sometimes blown on because it was so hot, and the occasional tap of a bone being laid on the side of the plate. Afterwards, Concetta went outside to sluice the dishes and the saucepan in water from the bucket and when she came back in, her father was already pulling on his coat to go. He was heading to the *Vecchia Osteria* to play cards.

'All right?' her mother said.

Concetta wasn't listening. She'd been musing about Felice and her sisters and how far along they were on their journey.

'So you've been sick,' her mother said, more loudly.

'Just a bit of fever. A day or so. Nothing to worry about.'

Her mother considered a moment and nodded. 'They looked after you then. That's what's important.'

'Franchina knew it would pass.'

'If she's like me, she'll know when something's serious.'

It was time for Concetta and her mother to leave the house and make their way to the *carnuale* celebrations in the main square. They rounded the corner of the street where she'd last seen the group on their way to San Michele and Concetta found herself wondering if her sisters, Tino, Felice and the rest of the group had already arrived.

She had only been to San Michele a few times, but she could remember each of her visits clearly. San Michele was set higher than their own village and there was a steep climb to its summit and the main square. The road started off gently and the land either side of it was part-cultivated and part-grazing land. As the first houses appeared, the road became cobbled and was much narrower and worn in parts because of the traffic. She remembered slipping once as a child and not being able to get her balance again. She'd been lucky because Tino had been walking just behind her and he'd dipped forward and caught her arms before she could roll too far down the street.

San Michele was always busy on market day and she could bring to mind the ringing voices of the people standing on doorsteps and hanging out of windows, and how they would try to catch your arm so you would look at their wares. She remembered the smell of tripe from a doorway where an old woman stood over an enormous cauldron of boiling liquid, stirring and glancing out to the street. Another woman with white hair and sad eyes stood on the step of the house, beckoning in a half-hearted way. Concetta would have liked to go in, to please the sad woman, but she didn't have the money and they always brought their own food.

At several points on the way to the top was a spectacular panorama overlooking San Michele itself as it sloped away and, beyond, the peaks of other villages. They always stopped at the place where there was a good view eastwards so they could locate their own village, a low, insignificant-looking crest where they would just be able to make out a cluster of squat buildings and, on clear days, the white bell tower of San Rocco. Concetta could never quite take in the fact that the streets and houses and people she knew so well were all crammed in there on a hilltop that was smaller, when she measured it, than the tip of her little finger. Beyond their village, the land rose and fell in ever-higher peaks and dips until, in the far distance, the green gave way to dark rock and the great mountains of the east.

Concetta always had to stop to get her breath back when she rounded the corner onto the main square at the top. The *piazza* was elegant, not wide, but a very long rectangular space with the castle and its ramparts forming one end of it and an imposing church in pink and white brick the other. A large rose window emblazoned the front of the church and there were grotesque, stunted-looking creatures carved into its façade. The houses on the square were taller than anything in Concetta's own village and constructed with the same pale pink brick. On market days, balconies were festooned with garlands; Concetta could never quite shake off the belief that in San Michele every day was *festa*.

The market traders and their stalls would spill out across the whole of the square. One time in particular she remembered, it was a livestock fair and she recalled the sharp whistles of the shepherds herding and retrieving and chivvying. The sheep had been so frightened that they had climbed on top of each other. She recalled the cows weighed down with clanging bells round their necks and the funnels of wet steam from a puffing bull as it was dragged along by a ring through its nose. There had been dappled horses, too, rake-thin and whinnying, and unable to keep their feet still amid the crowds, and there were cages and cages of rabbits and hares and all manner of poultry and game. The droves of geese had caused a great confusion by raising their long necks and flapping their wings to fly away, and she remembered how the men had beaten them down to ground again with sticks and she'd felt sorry for the geese then, and cried.

For those like herself who came from small and meagre places the *piazza* rose before them like a vision. She could see herself gazing left and right at the animated people and the humming talk and the flares from the torches that lit the place up once the daylight was gone. Sometimes she doubted San Michele was real and, if it was, then she felt sorry for herself and for those like her because it meant their lives really were hard and ordinary.

Her mother's touch on her arm brought Concetta back to the present. They'd arrived at their village's main square where a few people were already huddled in groups, talking among themselves. A large bonfire had been lit in the centre, a pyre of branches and broken furniture, and a ring of children in costumes, holding hands, was circling it and singing.

Concetta's *comare* shouted at them to come over because someone had brought a tray of *struffoli*, balls of fried dough drizzled with honey. Concetta spooned some into her hands, trying not to eat greedily, and when she'd finished she went to wash the stickiness away in the well at the side of the square. As she was flicking the water off her hands, she caught sight of Francesco standing beside his mother. She watched them pass in front of the bonfire, their profiles silhouetted, knowing that from where she was, just out of the circle of light, she couldn't be seen.

She caught herself smiling and glanced around in case anyone was watching her. After a few moments, she made her way back to her mother's side, careful not to look in Francesco's direction, and then she stood with her *comare*, arm in arm, while the fiddler, a young boy, walked over to his spot and began testing the strings of his violin. Eventually he tucked the violin under his chin and, balancing a foot against a wall, played the first halting strains of a formal piece. A group of men who'd been drinking began to talk over it and the song tailed off before the end. After much discussion, another young boy was dispatched to fetch a guitar, a pipe and a tambourine from a nearby house and Nino the carpenter and a couple of others took up position beside the young fiddler. They began by tapping out an introduction with their feet and then opened with a love song, to please the crowd, a fast *tarantella* and the tambourinist soon got everyone clapping and singing along.

Concetta spotted Franchina and Giovanni, and she and her mother went over to stand talking with them for a while because they were family. Franchina wasn't happy that the youngsters had gone off to San Michele for *carnuale* and that they would have to go straight back to work the next day without sleep.

'Going so far from home,' said Franchina, 'especially the girls. I'm surprised you allowed it.'

'Tino is with them,' said her mother.

'Paolo and Felice too,' said Franchina. 'I'm sure I would

worry, though, if I had girls.' She looked over at Concetta and smiled. 'Got some colour in your cheeks again. Feeling stronger?'

Concetta felt her mother's eyes on her and nodded.

'I didn't want to worry you about this one. She had a bit of a fever, but we took care of it, didn't we, eh, Concetta?'

Concetta's mother nodded. 'Good thing for Tino. He's my eyes and ears. This one can be shy about speaking out. You took good care of her, Franchina.'

The two women smiled at each other and then Concetta's mother turned to the bonfire, which was starting to fade, and saw a woman she knew feeding some sticks of furniture into the flames and went over to help. Concetta followed behind and she caught sight of Francesco, their eyes snagging, and she looked away, intending to carry on, but he was making his way towards her.

The song had come to an end and the musicians were consulting on what to play next. Some people had taken the opportunity of going home to get chairs to sit on. There was a general bustling around the square, a displacement as people shifted around to greet those they hadn't spoken to yet. Concetta had the dizzying sensation of being a fixed point in a turning landscape. Francesco put his hand on her shoulder to steady her, the place where Felice's had rested earlier.

'I saw you before,' he said, keeping his voice low, 'but you were standing with your mother-in-law.' He smiled down at her. 'Felice?'

'He's gone to San Michele. The others, too: Nunzia, Immacolata, Tino. A group of them.'

'Ah,' he said. 'Strange to leave you alone, though. Especially in your condition.'

'No, no. He didn't want to go, but I insisted. After all, if I could, I would have gone myself.'

'And he would have let you?'

Concetta laughed. 'Of course. My sisters and brother have gone. Why shouldn't he? No, he's a good husband.'

Francesco nodded. 'There aren't many who would have done what he did.'

Concetta hesitated. 'They owed us. Business from the past. Now we're even. Everything is as it should be.'

'Except for you maybe, eh?' His voice had fallen to a whisper and she could feel the heat of his hand through her coat. 'You've been unlucky.'

Concetta pulled her eyes away and towards the bonfire, which had roared into life again and was climbing higher. The sparks were hissing, flying off erratically into the night sky. Around her and above, the overarching blackness seemed to bear down on the square. An ember, a delicate grey sliver, winged its way down onto the back of her hand and she glanced at it, a soft husk that crumbled as soon as she moved her fingers.

'Not unlucky,' she said. 'I have a husband and soon I'll have a child.'

He looked up at the sky a moment and then down again. 'You were better off marrying this man than the other.'

'I might have married any man, if it comes to that. I might have married you.' She began to laugh at that, but then stopped.

'You might,' he said.

Concetta looked away again.

'You're happy at least.'

'He's a good man. I can't ask for more.' She took a step back and Francesco's hand dislodged itself.

The music had started up again, a sung *ballata*, and there was a flurry of arms and skirts around them and a general whooping. Francesco ushered her away from the centre of the square to stand to one side where they remained obscured.

'I was glad to see you tonight,' he said. 'I'll be going away soon. I wanted to tell you myself.'

Concetta had turned to go, but stopped.

'The *transumanza*. I'm joining the men who are already out there. I'll be back in the spring, when it gets warm again.'

The *transumanza* was the transport of sheep for the winter to lower, warmer lands. The shepherds had gone out several months ago on a two-week journey to the other side of the mountains in the east and they would return with the sheep for the summer. Concetta tried to think how many months he would be gone: three, four even, when the heat would bring them to higher ground and home again.

'It was my father's work. There's no other work to be found here and I don't want to go across the sea again. My mother is too old. If I had a wife and children, they could keep her company, but she's alone. Your mother is good to keep an eye out for her, but perhaps you could go sometimes. It would make me happy to think of you going there.' He stopped. 'When the baby is born, you could take it too.'

Concetta found her voice. 'How soon do you go?'

'A few days. They sent word that Giuseppe Di Leo has taken ill. It will take me a few weeks to get there.'

Concetta looked away.

'I'll only be gone a few months.'

Concetta knew that they were standing close, too close, and that even though they were in the shadows they might still be seen. She couldn't bring herself to walk away, not now she knew he was going. She'd been looking at him all evening, small glances, as though she were taking sips of a warming drink. Now, though, she wanted to take a good long draught. She tipped her head back and looked at the dots of stubble across his chin and the way his cheekbones jutted when he stood in profile and how his dark, liquid eyes seemed to hold everything, the square, the fire, her own face especially, in them.

After a while, she became aware of a voice calling her name and, looking round, disoriented, she stumbled back from Francesco.

It was Mafalda, Franchina's daughter-in-law. 'We've been calling you.'

'The music,' said Concetta, trying to regain her balance. 'I didn't hear.'

'Can you come?' Mafalda's eyes were on Francesco, as though it were really him she was addressing.

Concetta moved off after Mafalda, throwing a brief glance back towards Francesco. 'That was Francesco Di Rienzo. He knows my brother,' she said, trying to sound matter-of-fact, but the music had turned rowdy and Mafalda didn't hear. They had to turn this way and that through the mass of dancers, the women were lifting their skirts to one side so they could better stamp their feet and the men were clapping and whooping along with the tune. Franchina was clapping along, too. She smiled when she saw Concetta and took her arm and tucked it into her own. She continued to clap and gestured to Concetta to clap along, too.

After some time Concetta spotted her mother talking to *signora* Clara, but there was no Francesco and it came to her that he might have already gone. She brought her attention back to the people around her and, rather than look towards Franchina or Mafalda, she fixed her attention on a young man and woman dancing just in front of her. They were taking each other by the arm and whirling around one way, changing arms and then going round the other. They were focused on each other, their eyes trained on the other's face.

'Concetta?' His voice was so low at her ear that she almost didn't hear. She swung round to find Francesco by her side. Franchina turned round, too, and stopped clapping. Francesco removed his hat and introduced himself to Franchina and then spoke to Concetta. 'I wanted to say goodbye before I turn in.'

Concetta swallowed. She could feel Franchina's eyes on her.

Francesco turned to Franchina. 'I'm joining the men for the *transumanza*.'

Franchina untied and retied her headscarf revealing grey hair pulled back tight into a bun, causing the soft veins at her temples to bulge, and then glanced round to see who was behind her before she spoke. 'I don't want to speak out of turn,' she said, her eyes on Francesco, 'but it's not right that you two should talk together like this. My son is not here. It's not right.'

'Francesco knows my brother,' Concetta began.

'It doesn't matter,' said Franchina, pursing her lips. She looked down at Concetta's belly. 'It's not right.'

Franchina's meaning was clear. She knew, or had guessed, about Peppe. Francesco looked taken aback and stepped away from them. Concetta couldn't bring herself to look at him directly, but she saw him out of the corner of her eye replacing his hat, pulling it down low, and moving away.

Concetta shook her head. She had no recollection of saying anything about Peppe to Franchina. Her memory once again felt leaky, something that couldn't be relied upon. She looked up at Franchina, wondering how to form the words to ask.

Franchina took her hand. 'Promise me that you won't speak to him again. Promise.'

Concetta stood frozen, her hand in Franchina's. After a few moments, she looked round. Francesco had already passed into the darkness of one of the streets that led off from the square, and was gone.

12

Despite Franchina's offer to make up the bed for her again, Concetta insisted on staying overnight at her parents' house. She and her mother left the square a long time before the music and dancing stopped. The faster *tarantellas* were being played as they left and there were many shouts and shrieks of laughter. As they got further away, Concetta could just make out the sharp strains of distant violins and even voices, she thought, very faint, from other places, remote gatherings and nearby villages.

She woke the next morning with a crick in her neck because she had lain on her side all night, the only comfortable position she could sleep in nowadays. She was late getting up. Her mother and father had already come back from early morning mass and, as it was the first day of Lent, they'd had no food and were ready for their walk to the fields. Her mother had loaded the donkey and was shooing the animals out from the stable. The mist hadn't yet risen over the hills and everything looked vague and unformed: the faces of the animals, the trees, the sky. It seemed like a world half-made, one that was only now coming into being. It had rained overnight and the ground was sodden, so Concetta remained on the stone step looking out into the yard, still in her stockings and nightdress.

Her father emerged from the stable in his battered hat and padded winter jacket. He was carrying a pitchfork loaded with dirty yellow straw, which he dumped into the basket slung over the donkey. He looked up at Concetta. 'You up? Your mother couldn't wake you. We went to mass without you in the end.'

Concetta shook her head at her mother. 'I didn't hear you.'

'You're not a child that I can push out of bed any more,' her mother said.

'You helping Franchina out at the mill?' her father asked.

Concetta knew that she ought to have gone home with Franchina. Her duty, in her husband's absence, was to help there today. She shook her head. She couldn't face Franchina, Mafalda, any of them. 'The others will be late back. You'll need the extra pair of hands.'

'As long as Franchina doesn't mind.'

'No, *Papà*,' she said. 'She wouldn't want you to fall behind.'

'That sister of yours,' he grumbled, shaking his head. 'Only thinks about enjoying herself. They'd better be prepared to make up for it.'

'They'll be here soon,' said Concetta and she looked up towards the hills and wondered how far they were along the road home.

Her father continued to shake his head and headed back into the stable.

'Your father's right,' her mother said. 'Too much excitement. It won't do them any good in the end.'

'Oh, *Mamma*!' said Concetta. 'Can't they at least have one day in the year to enjoy themselves?'

'This is real life here. Not that over there.' She pulled the rope around the donkey's neck so that the animal stumbled forward.

Her father loaded the last of the straw and untied the dog in the yard, which yipped and jumped up. Concetta watched her parents as they made their way, trudging with heavy boots across the damp, uneven ground. Her mother was tall, but Concetta could see how she'd grown thin with age and her father, shorter and stockier, always appeared hearty but she knew that his hands, as he took the rope from her mother, were rough and gnarled at the knuckles. Her eye moved across the drab, antique clothes they wore, the practised way they herded the animals. She stood watching even after they disappeared from view and then she hurried in to get ready so as to catch them up along the way.

These Lenten days were the time to atone for past sins, to bring to mind the things you had done wrong and to pray for forgiveness. They were also a time for fasting and for the villagers that meant one meal in the evening of plain fare: no meat, no wine for the women and no sweet or fried foods. Some families ate their pasta *in bianco*, without condiment, just a knob of butter or a drop of oil and salt. No hunting or fishing was permitted, no music could be played, no singing and no card playing. The *Vecchia Osteria* would fall silent for these forty days.

Lent also marked the return to the fields. The earth, left fallow for the last few weeks, would need turning and the frost, a delicate white rime, would be starting to recede. The wheat, as always, would need to be cleaned of weeds that had grown in the meantime, and the rest of the land, stripped bare weeks before, had to be readied for the great days of sowing and planting that lay ahead.

The mist had cleared by the time they arrived. It was a bracing day of billowing high cloud and warm sunshine. As always, when they came back after *carnuale*, they noticed the signs of their absence. Animal tracks, fox and wild boar and wolf, had broken the soil and the prints criss-crossing to and fro seemed to mark aimless or frenzied journeys. A bucket that they used to get water from the stream had gone missing and the hedgerows along the path leading to the fields had to be cut back again. On the side of the field that backed up against woodland, a riot of brambles would have to be chopped and driven down. In a few short weeks, the edges of their land, left to itself, had begun to merge back into its surroundings.

Concetta watched her father lift an axe and swing out high and down, and she remembered exactly the same moment the year before and she thought of all the years in the future when he would arrive and pick it up and swing it in the same way. There would come a day when he wouldn't be able to any more and then it would be Tino lifting the axe and, after him, his own son perhaps.

She looked up at the sky and the hills around her and saw herself from above, a bird's view, standing in a bare field with a hoe in one hand, a heavy coat unable to conceal her protruding belly, an old headscarf to keep the hair out of her face. It was such a beautiful day, the sun catching the dew in the leaves and radiating its sparkle, but she couldn't help thinking back to Francesco the night before. He would be gone, if not today then tomorrow, and it struck her now that he hadn't, in the end, wished her luck for the birth.

Concetta and her mother and father worked right through the day, stopping only to go to the stream to drink when they felt thirsty. There was no food for lunch and as the sun's rays filtered through the trees late in the day, Concetta felt her first pangs of hunger. She levered herself up from the ground, holding her back for support and planting her legs wide. 'They said they were going to be here before noon.'

Her mother, bent over on the row to the side of her, pulled herself upright. 'They must have put their heads down somewhere for a few hours.' She glanced at her husband on the other side of the field. He was behind the cow, guiding the plough. The ground was hard in places and the plough had been sticking all morning. It snagged now and he stopped the cow and took out his spade, needing to push down with his full weight to open up the ground. 'He won't be pleased.' She looked back to Concetta. 'Tino wouldn't have let them stay out so long. It'll be those others, your husband and his brother.'

'Or Immacolata. She's the stubborn one.'

'She'll do what Tino tells her.'

She knew her mother was right. When Tino asked you to do something, you did it. She looked back over to the woods. The sun had sunk lower now, a burnished gold, and the light was hazy, dappling the trees. She could see fine cobwebs suspended between branches, tiny particles of dew strung out along them. She felt peaceful, tired after the day's exertions, and hungry, but the physical work had lifted her mood. They began gathering their things together; her father unshackled the cow, and Concetta went over to the clearing by the trees where they'd left the animals to graze and herded them out onto the path.

Just as they were about to set off, they heard a whistle. Immacolata and Nunzia were walking along the path further ahead, waving. As they got closer Concetta could see that they had the remnants of garlands, leaves and winter flowers, entwined in their hair, although they had changed out of their best dresses and put their work boots on. Concetta could see that their cheeks were flushed and that they must have run all the way from the house.

'*Mamma, Papà*,' said Nunzia, 'Sorry we're so late.'

'Tino?' asked her mother.

'At home,' said Immacolata. 'He said there was no point coming.'

'And he was right,' her mother said. She turned her back on them and went back to loading the donkey's baskets.

Her father led the cow over to where the girls stood. 'I only let you go on condition you were back before noon.'

Immacolata looked away.

Nunzia spoke. 'We didn't know what time it was, and then it was already late, and the others didn't want to go back, and we went as a group, so we had to come back as a group.'

'I'll speak to Tino. He was responsible. I don't care about the others,' her father said.

'It wasn't Tino,' said Nunzia. 'He tried to get us to go earlier.'

'But you didn't listen,' her mother said.

Her father smacked the cow on the shanks to get it moving. 'No use you two staying now. It'll soon be dark.'

'*Papà*,' said Immacolata, turning to face him.

'No more San Michele. That was the last time,' he said.

Immacolata had begun walking alongside her father and then stopped and turned to her mother. 'It was Felice and Paolo. They said we couldn't leave so soon seeing as we'd walked all the way there. It was true. You wouldn't believe the crowds in the square and the dancing and all the costumes. *Mamma*, please say we can go next year.'

'Not while you're under my roof,' her father said. He took the cow by the neck and pushed on ahead. Her mother moved off in his wake with the donkey, and Concetta and her sisters fell in behind her in a single file, as the path was narrow.

'I will go back,' said Immacolata.

'Don't be a child,' her mother said sharply.

'I can get married like her,' she said, turning towards Concetta. 'It won't be difficult to do.'

'And do you think your husband will let you go?' her mother replied from over her shoulder.

'I'll make him promise,' she said. 'Or else I won't get married.'

'You both look tired,' said Concetta. There were smudges of darkness under Nunzia's eyes.

'It was much better than market day,' said Immacolata, turning to Concetta. 'You couldn't put your arms out for the people. Everyone smiling and happy and coming up and dancing with you and it didn't matter that they didn't know you.'

'Dancing with strangers?' Concetta tried not to sound shocked. 'But did Tino let you?'

'He couldn't stop me.'

They were nearing the village now and the girls branched off to take a shorter route home. Without the animals, they could take a steeper path where someone had hacked through undergrowth.

'Did Felice go home?' asked Concetta.

'He went back with Paolo. The worse for drink and in a bad temper,' said Immacolata, throwing the words over her shoulder.

'Oh?' said Concetta, turning to Nunzia.

'He was just tired,' Nunzia said. 'It was a long night.'

'How would you know?' said Immacolata. 'You were too busy talking to Paolo.'

'That's not true.'

'Please yourself.'

'I was talking to the others, too.'

'If you say so.'

Nunzia opened her mouth to say something more to Immacolata's retreating back, but thought better of it.

She turned to link arms with Concetta and together they walked on to the house.

Concetta was anxious to get back to Felice, but she was feeling shaky from lack of food and so she stayed to eat with her family before walking the distance to the cottage. When they arrived back at the house, Tino was inside lying down on his bench. Concetta thought it strange that he hadn't come to the field with his sisters and it occurred to her that he might be angry with them. Nunzia and Immacolata disappeared into their room to disentangle the garlands from their hair.

They ate their evening meal in silence. It seemed to Concetta that each had their own reasons for not speaking. She kept thinking about Felice and wondered if he had perhaps fallen ill. It was an exhausting walk to San Michele and she'd always suspected his health to be delicate. He wavered in his moods, too: he'd spent weeks speaking to her only grudgingly and then when she was ill, he'd become kind again and gentle with her. She felt secure sitting here at this table with her father to the side of her and Tino in front. They were both strong men, men to depend on, showing affection only in the ways they knew; but then she thought that a husband was not a father or a brother and that she must remember this. There were so many things to remember, and her memory couldn't seem to hold them all. After dinner, Nunzia and Immacolata went into their bedroom to prepare for bed. Concetta found herself going in with them and then when she'd closed the door she turned, realized her mistake and laughed. 'I must be tired myself. I was about to undress.'

Immacolata sat on her edge of the bed, her eyes already shut, her hand feeling round to undo the buttons of her dress.

Concetta walked over to her. 'Here, move round. I'll do it for you.'

Nunzia was lying across the bed, her bare feet dangling off the edge. She propped her chin on her hands. 'Do you find it strange not being with us?'

Concetta nodded, releasing the last button and peeling the shoulders of the dress down. 'Sometimes it does feel lonely, just me and Felice.'

'The baby will be here soon. It will be different then.'

'I hope so.' Concetta sighed. It was time for her to go. They'd been slow getting dinner ready and it was late. She hoped Felice would be anxious about her, as she was about him.

As she went out into the other room and began to gather her things, there was a knock at the door. It crossed her mind that it might be Felice, come to fetch her home.

'Paolo.' Her mother stepped aside to let him in. 'We thought you would be resting after your journey.'

Paolo took off his hat as he came through and nodded at them by way of greeting. His thick fair hair had been neatly combed.

Concetta felt her anxiety grow. It struck her as unusual for him to call like this. 'There's nothing wrong, is there? Felice?'

'Asleep.' He accepted a chair from Concetta's father and lowered himself into it.

Concetta's mother took up another chair and sat down at the table.

'It's you, *signor* Salierno, I came to see,' he said, looking towards her father. Concetta had been standing, ready to leave, but she walked over to Tino's bench and sat by him. She looked at him to see if he knew anything, but she could see that he didn't.

Paolo cleared his throat. 'I've come to ask for your daughter's hand. Ever since our families came together,

157

I've got to know your daughter. I have feelings for her and would like to make her my wife.' He'd spoken without drawing breath.

'Which one?' asked her father. 'Things don't always happen in the right order in this house.'

'Nunzia,' Paolo said, reddening, 'your oldest.'

'Well,' her father said, looking round the room, 'I don't see why not.'

'Perhaps,' her mother interrupted, 'we ought to talk to her first. Does she know about this?'

The door to the girls' bedroom opened and Nunzia, then Immacolata, emerged. Nunzia came towards Paolo, her face stricken, and she shook her head.

Paolo remained in his seat. The high colour in his face had gone. 'I thought,' he said, 'I thought we had an understanding.'

'No.' Nunzia put her hands to her face and turned away from him. 'I didn't understand. I'm sorry.'

Her mother went over and put her arms around her. 'Nunzia, what is it? You like this boy, don't you? What's wrong?'

Nunzia just shook her head, her hands still over her face.

Tino went over to Paolo and put a hand on his shoulder. 'I'm sorry, Paolo. It's better that you leave.'

Paolo got to his feet and looked over at Nunzia again.

'Leave us to talk to her. She's tired. She'll come round,' said her father.

After Paolo had gone, it took a while before Nunzia would uncover her face. She'd been crying and she took out a handkerchief to blow her nose. 'I'm sorry,' she said after a long time. 'I didn't realize.'

'He's a nice boy,' said her father.

'I know,' she said, dabbing at her eyes. 'He's good company. He makes me laugh.'

'Then why?' her mother asked. 'Is it just the shock?'

Her father began to pace up the room. He looked over to Nunzia's mother. 'She's eighteen. It's time she was married. He's a good man. He's family. She should accept him, or I will do it for her.'

Nunzia shook her head. 'I don't want to marry him. I don't want to marry anyone.'

Her father laughed. 'What are you going to do if you don't marry?'

'Nunzia, *cara*.' Her mother took her arm again. 'Of course you want to marry. Perhaps not this man. But every woman has to marry.'

'Not all,' said Immacolata.

'Don't be silly,' her mother snapped.

Nunzia stepped away from her mother. 'I want to join the church.'

'What is she talking about? Has she gone mad?' Her father had stopped his pacing.

'I told them,' Nunzia said, pointing over at Concetta and Immcolata, 'that I wanted to join the church.'

'It's true,' said Concetta, turning to her mother.

'I told her it was a stupid idea,' said Immacolata.

'Enough,' her mother said, pushing her hair back from her face. 'No one is thinking straight. Concetta, you need to go home to your husband. It's late.'

Tino rose from his bench. 'I'll take her.'

They didn't talk for a long stretch until they were well past the house and onto the road that led into the centre of the village. Concetta put her hand on Tino's sleeve. 'We'll catch up with Paolo at this rate.'

'We can go another way. It's a shortcut.' Tino knew every route through and around the village, including some, Concetta felt sure, that he kept to himself. They diverted away from the main square and took a series of alleys between houses and through backyards. When they came across a dog that bared its teeth at them, Tino put a finger up to his mouth and the dog backed away.

'Does it know you?' asked Concetta.

'All the dogs know me,' he said with a short laugh.

Concetta smiled. 'Paolo didn't mention anything yesterday?'

Tino shook his head. 'He could have used me as a go-between, but he must have felt confident that she'd say yes.'

'Will she really turn him down?'

'She already has.'

They were nearing the end of the village houses and they started on the approach road to Franchina's house. Concetta was glad that she wasn't walking home alone tonight. Passing out of the confines of the village in the dark was like walking into a different atmosphere, a heavier one, which settled on you more and more the deeper into it you went.

'Why is everyone acting so oddly today?' she asked. 'Did something happen at San Michele?'

After a long time Tino spoke. 'Just some men hanging around the group.'

'Threatening?'

'I didn't like the look of them.'

'What about Paolo and Felice? Didn't they help out?'

'Paolo had other things on his mind.'

'Felice?'

He turned to look at her. 'The same.'

Concetta looked away. She could feel her heart bumping against her ribcage and it took a few moments for her to speak again. 'No one got hurt, though?'

'No.'

'But why did they pick on you?'

Tino shrugged.

'Immacolata,' Concetta said.

Tino's eyes were on the path ahead.

'Now I see why you didn't come to the field earlier. You were angry with her.'

They passed by Franchina's house and Concetta glanced over. There was a wan glow visible through the windows. The yard was silent and the house shut up for the night. Paolo must have walked back fast and already turned in.

They lapsed into silence and, as they walked on, Concetta thought of Francesco and wondered again if he had already started out for the mountains. They'd passed by the flour mill and had started on the path that cut through the fields. 'I spoke to Francesco Di Rienzo. The time I went to *signora* Clara's. The boy I was with in the forest that day was Peppe.'

Tino nodded.

'I still don't remember him, but it all adds up. Francesco is angry with his brother, embarrassed, but I can't feel that about him somehow.'

'You can't hate the dead.'

'No.'

'Did you tell Felice?'

'Franchina knows, I don't know how, so I suppose Felice does too.'

They walked around the bend that took them into the yard and Tino stopped. 'I can leave you here.'

Concetta glanced towards the house. There was no light leaking out from the windowpane. Everything was still and quiet. She turned back towards Tino, reluctant for him to go. 'What kind of man was he?'

Tino looked away for a moment, towards the dark outline of the hills. 'He was a boy more than a man. Rash, a bit foolish. He'd get into trouble for stupid things and Francesco always had to get him out of it.'

Concetta smiled. It was rare for Tino to say so much.

161

'He wasn't a bad person, but he didn't know what to do with himself.' Tino gave a quick lift to his shoulders. The moon was behind him and his face was shrouded. 'But Peppe's dead. Go in now and get some sleep.'

Concetta opened the door to the cottage as quietly as she could. Pushing against it felt like pushing against herself. The door was heavy on its old hinges and creaked, but once it was open, there was nothing to do but go in.

The next morning Concetta woke early, so early that she knew she would be better served by lying back down again and trying to sleep some more. There would be no light for several hours. The baby was restless, shifting and pushing against her as though trying to feel its way out. She thought it must be dark in there, and lonely, and she didn't blame the child for reaching out for company. She put her hands where she felt the movement, thinking this might give some comfort, but it seemed to agitate the baby more. Her mother had examined her the day before, looking at her belly, how far it had grown, whether the bump had dropped or remained high, and she had predicted at least another four or five weeks before birth. Probably longer, she had said, as the first child was often late.

As soon as there was light to see by, Concetta rose from the bed and set about finishing the sewing she had started days before and left to one side. There were some clothes for the baby and she had been repairing a tear in Felice's work shirt where it had snagged on an overhanging branch. Only a faint light crept in through the window, infused with mist, and she piled wood into the hearth to create some heat and sat close by, needing the fire's warmth and the light to get the shirt finished.

Some time later Felice stirred. He'd overslept and his smooth face was creased where he'd lain on it. He went outside and she heard him urinating against the back of the chicken coop and then splashing water on his face at the pail outside the door. When he came in again, he seemed out of sorts. She wanted to ask him about *carnuale* and his brother's proposal of marriage. But she saw he was not in a mood to talk, so she left him and went to milk the goats.

She came back into the house and found him shaved and dressed, but still he didn't say anything. She couldn't bear the silence any more. 'Did you know about Paolo?'

Felice blinked at her, not understanding.

'Paolo proposed to my sister.'

'He's going to ask her today.'

'He did it last night.'

Felice raised his eyebrows. 'He was keen.'

Concetta walked over to the wall and hung her coat on the nail. 'I wish he had said something to Tino first.'

'She refused him?'

'*Mamma* will speak to her today; see if she can talk sense into her. She was just tired last night.'

Felice shook his head as though marvelling at something and then brushed past her and went out the door.

Concetta reached for her coat again and followed him. He lifted a flask of red wine out of the hole in the ground they used for storage and he pulled out the cork and tipped it up to his mouth. Concetta watched him roll his head back and drink and it seemed to her that, since they'd been married, he had become cruder in his ways. After he'd taken his fill, he lowered the flask and wiped the wine from his mouth with the back of his hand.

'Nothing's ever good enough for you Salierno girls.' He dropped the flask into the hole and rolled the boulder back over it. He shook his head again. 'I saw them together at *carnuale*. It was what she wanted, too.'

'You don't know Nunzia like I do. She would never mean to hurt him.'

'Too late for that.'

'Yes, and I'm sorry for Paolo, but it's done now.'

Felice spat on the ground to his side. She could see that his hands were trembling.

'You didn't enjoy *carnuale*?'

'Who told you that?'

'No one.'

'Immacolata told you.'

'What if she did?'

He stopped when she said that as if he had been about to say something, but thought better of it. 'You don't know your sister as well as you think. She acts only for herself.' He looked at her then as if he felt sorry not for himself, but for her. 'She's lucky to have Tino as a brother. He can talk a man out of murder.' She stood there trying to think what to say and, after a moment, he walked away across the yard.

She moved off after him and when he bent down to collect some tools she laid her arm across his back and crouched down next to him. He didn't turn towards her, but he didn't push her away either.

'The father of the child,' he said, still looking down at the tools. 'When you had the fever, you spoke his name, called for him.'

'Peppe.' She spoke the name very softly. Now she understood how Franchina knew.

'You spent all your time at *carnuale* talking to his brother. Laughing at me, I suppose, the poor fool who married you.'

'It wasn't like that.' Concetta leaned her forehead against him.

'My father told me that by marrying you I would take the sins of the family onto my own shoulders. My mother took me aside afterwards and told me not to listen. She said that it was too much for one man to bear, that old sins stay in the past. She said that my father was willing to sacrifice me, but that she wasn't. I love my mother, but I came to your father's house and offered for you when I could see that you were carrying a child. I've tried to be good to you, to think well of you, but I think my mother was right. You were happy enough to take a husband to hide your own sins, but that wasn't enough for you. Then you make him out to be a fool. How many others know?'

'It isn't like how you're saying it.'

'How is it then? What happened with Peppe?'

'I don't remember.' She felt close to tears. She wished she could remember so she could explain herself, make sense of it all.

He wasn't listening to her. 'Now I look round at my brothers and at the other girls in the village and I think that I am a fool. My mother was right. I don't deserve this.' He staggered to his feet and looked towards the cottage and the grey outline of the hills and the goats that were bleating in the little outhouse and then back to Concetta, holding her belly. 'I don't deserve any of it.'

Concetta got to her feet.

He swung round towards her. 'If I could leave you, I would. But I can't. So we'll have to stay as we are. But there will be no more relations between us. We live together, but separate.'

'Felice, please listen to me.' She stepped forward and took hold of his sleeve. 'It will be a hell to live like that. We only have each other here.'

'My family is close.'

'Please, Felice, hear me out.' She pulled at his sleeve so he would face her. 'I don't remember what happened. It came to me only recently that Peppe was the father but, when I realized, I was happy because Peppe is dead.'

Felice snorted and pulled his sleeve away.

'Peppe can't touch us now. He can't come between us. You are the only father of this child.'

She could see that Felice was still resisting her but trying to make sense of it, too.

'I didn't mean to disrespect you. I was only speaking to Francesco because I was trying to understand more about Peppe and how it happened. I know that was wrong of me. I won't speak to him again.'

Felice looked past her, out towards the flour mill in the distance.

Concetta went on. 'We're married. There's no going back on that. We can make this house a happy one. We can have more children. Or you can choose for us to be miserable and bitter out here with just each other.'

Felice's eyes were still resting on something far away.

Concetta looked into them and, fathoming nothing, she moved off to the outhouse to untie the goats. When she came out again, she saw that Felice hadn't moved. She bent down to pick up an empty pail and stood waiting by the house until Felice was ready, and then they started out toward the fields together.

PART THREE

13

When Concetta's time was approaching, her mother sent word to Franchina that she would take care of the birth as she had experience of these things. It meant Concetta would move back to her parents' for the remaining days. Felice had gone to the flour mill that day to help his father and when he returned home, he told Concetta that his mother was not happy. 'She wants to take care of you,' he said. 'You're her responsibility now.'

'No one knows more than my mother about delivering babies,' Concetta said. 'She's brought hundreds of them into the world.' She saw that Felice was right about his mother, Franchina was just keen to help her daughter-in-law, but even so, Concetta was relieved her own mother would be taking care of her.

She had been worried, as the last few weeks had brought a radiating pain, slowly increasing, that seemed to shoot up from her back and along her arms and legs. She'd thought at first it might be the start of labour, but when it lingered and her waters didn't break, she decided it was just the effort of carrying around the extra weight. She had grown big, not just her belly but her ankles and wrists had bloated and her cheeks and arms had become soft and pudgy. She found it difficult to move around and wanted only to sit or sleep all day. Even her mother had told her not to go to the fields any more, but to stay indoors. 'There's nothing to do now but to wait,' her mother had said. Running her eyes over her daughter, she'd warned her she was carrying too much weight.

Concetta lifted herself from the chair and put a pan on the hearth to warm the *minestrone*. Felice went outside to wash his hands and came back in to sit at his place. 'That's what I told her,' he said. 'You need your mother at a time like that. It's only natural.'

'And what did she say to that?'

Felice tore a piece of crust from the loaf and put it in his mouth. 'She wasn't pleased, but she accepted it. She's not a bad sort. You just have to know how to handle her.'

'She's your mother,' she said. 'It's not the same for me.'

'No,' he said, 'but if you need to tell her anything like this, you can get me to do it, can't you?'

Concetta smiled. Since they'd spoken, several weeks ago now, she couldn't quite believe how things had changed between them. Felice hadn't mentioned Peppe or Francesco again, or their argument. He'd only said, later that day, that he'd meant to talk to his family about his problems, because it was the way they'd always done things at home, but in the end he hadn't, something had stopped him. Concetta had lain in bed that night brooding, trying to think what he might have meant, and she'd decided that when the time was right she'd understand.

After she'd cleared the dinner things away, she packed a bag with the baby clothes she'd made and a change of underwear for herself while Felice walked over to his father's yard to borrow the donkey. Concetta couldn't walk the distance to the other side of the village now; her legs ached too much and her feet had swollen. She had to borrow an old pair of boots from Felice as her own didn't fit any more. When he returned, he helped her clamber up onto the donkey and shifted her round to sit side-on, facing him. Then he took the bundle of clothes off her and gave the rope around the animal's neck a light tug so that it knew to move off.

Concetta glanced behind her as the donkey made its way across the yard and skirted the corner towards the field. The cottage, lying squat, looked different from how it had when she'd come back after *carnuale* just a few weeks ago. Puffs of smoke sat just above the chimney, not yet broken up by the wind, and Felice had left his spade and an old rake leaning against the back wall. A bit further along the same wall, one of the yard cats sat licking itself. As they rounded the corner and the house was obscured from view, she turned her head back towards it, trying to keep the picture fixed in her mind. It might be weeks before she would see her home again.

The fields either side of them had been newly ploughed and gave off the strong scent of fresh earth and animal dung. Concetta breathed it in. It felt good. Her lungs could expand again. She hadn't been able to leave the house now for several days and she'd missed the bracing feel of the open and the view of the hills, which could just be made out in the fading light. The new season had brought warmth, which lingered on even now after dark. The night-time chill hadn't set in yet. Around her, there was a feeling of newness and industry. The planting had started: straw for the animals, some early tomatoes, delicate vines in neat rows.

They stopped in at Felice's parents' house to say goodbye, and Franchina and Giovanni and the brothers clustered to the door to wish Concetta luck. Franchina stepped up to the donkey and clasped Concetta's hands. '*Nonna* Antonia knows just as much as your mother about these things. But I understand that you want her to do it.'

Concetta leaned down to kiss her. 'Thank you for that.'

Franchina stepped back and they started off again. Concetta turned to wave and, for the first time, noticed Paolo. She saw him turn away before the others and go inside and she brooded on this while the donkey carried her out of the yard and onto the uneven path that led into the village.

'I feel bad for Paolo,' she said. 'He still seems so sad after this business with Nunzia.' They hadn't spoken about it since the day of their argument. Concetta knew her husband was still angry at the way Paolo had been treated. Nunzia had remained true to her word and insisted that it was the church she wanted. If she joined the church, she would have to go to a convent far away, in Naples perhaps or Rome. She had cried, saying she didn't want to leave, but she wouldn't give up on the idea either. Her mother had called her stubborn and weeks had passed now and they had hardly spoken.

'He feels a fool.'

'There's time to talk her round.'

'No,' he said, pulling on the rope. 'He won't have her now. He's different to the rest of us. He acts like it's all a joke, but underneath he's soft.'

Concetta sighed. 'It's not about Paolo. It's being married, having children.'

Felice frowned. 'She's a woman. That's why she gets married. To have children.'

'She's afraid.'

'Of what?'

'Of everything. Men. Childbirth. *Mamma*'s always taken her round with her. She's seen what can happen. She's seen too much. Immacolata and I have always been more protected. It doesn't seem fair.'

Felice shook his head. 'She's nothing to fear from Paolo. He would make a good husband. But she's made her decision now.'

Concetta agreed with her mother. She couldn't believe that her sister really had made up her mind. Women of their type, peasant girls, only ever joined the church if they were very pious or if their families had failed to find them a husband. Neither of these was true of Nunzia.

They crossed the main square and she noticed how hushed it seemed. There were usually men standing in groups talking among themselves and sometimes, weaving in and around them, young boys charging after a ball of packed hay. Tonight, though, the village square was empty. A cold wind had blown up and Concetta wrapped her coat around her more tightly. Ever since they'd entered the village the pain in her legs and back had started up again, as the donkey kept slipping on the cobbles. She pushed a hand against her lower back to support herself and took comfort in the fact that she would soon be lying down.

'Nearly there,' Felice said, seeing her discomfort. 'It's quiet tonight. Like a ghost town.'

'Don't say that,' said Concetta; his words made her shudder. They took the narrow road that led to the house and Felice was careful to walk the donkey around the refuse that had collected there. Concetta was just able to make out a weak light from a window they passed. The glow was dim and hardly penetrated the street outside.

When they reached the house, Felice rapped at the door and then turned to help Concetta down from the donkey. Her mother answered, her face tired. 'I'd forgotten you were coming today,' she said and came over to help Felice lift Concetta down. When they had all withdrawn inside, her mother bolted the door and put her back against it. 'You came all this way alone, the two of you?'

'Where are the others?' Concetta sank down onto Tino's bench, letting the wall support her.

Her mother's hand was unsteady as she lit the candle. The flame jumped as she set it down on the table. The light threw the depressions and lines on her face into sharp relief.

Concetta stood up, her eyes on her mother's face. 'What's wrong?'

'Strangers,' her mother said. 'Marauders, perhaps. They were spotted earlier today out west by the ford. We left the girls to finish up and come back with Enzo and Renata. Everyone thought the danger was to the village.'

'They've probably taken refuge at someone's house.'

'No,' her mother said. 'Renata said she waved at the girls to come over, then she saw them putting the tools together and she stood speaking to someone else for a moment and when they didn't arrive she saw that they weren't there any more. The tools were left on the ground, but the girls were gone.'

'They wouldn't just go off without saying anything,' said Concetta.

'No.'

'What do we do now?'

'We wait. Your father and Tino have got a group together and they're out searching. They've been out for a few hours. You didn't hear anything?'

Concetta shook her head. 'The village was quiet. There was no one around.'

Felice roused himself. 'I'll go back and get my brothers.'

Concetta turned to grasp his wrist. 'On your own?'

'I'll be careful,' he said. 'Paolo will want to help.'

'She's right, though. You shouldn't walk all that way on your own,' said her mother. 'Rocco said a group would be going out beyond the cemetery and over the woods, in that area. You should go with them and then strike out alone when you're closer to home.'

Felice nodded. He reached into his pocket for his cap.

'I'll take you over. It's just a few doors down.' She put a coat on and wrapped a scarf around her head.

Felice laid a warm hand against Concetta's cheek. 'You get some rest. We'll bring them back.'

She took his hand into her own, holding it to her for as long as didn't seem awkward with her mother looking on. She let her grip loosen, the warmth from his hand was gone and she heard the door clatter shut.

Concetta stretched herself out on the bench and put a blanket over her legs. On the way here, she'd intended to go straight to her old bed and take her place in the middle, but now she couldn't face the idea of going into the bedroom. The more she thought about her sisters and the danger they were in the more it seemed as though her mother were talking about two other village girls. It didn't seem real somehow. Now, as she looked at her shadow on the floor, cast there by the candlelight, it appeared dark and lowering as if it were her fear become visible, growing and spilling out of her. She brought herself up to sitting again and, at that moment, her mother banged on the door.

'No one else seems to be missing,' she said, unbuttoning her coat and shrugging out of it. 'The first reports were of a group, but now it seems only two have been seen.'

'Some good news.'

'Doesn't change things, though, does it? For us, I mean.'

'They're probably hiding in a *pagliaro*. Just too afraid to come out.'

Her mother shook her head. 'Immacolata wouldn't sit it out. She's too headstrong, even with her sister to curb her.'

173

Concetta wished, for once, that her mother could be wrong. She had a knack of predicting what each of them would do before they did it. As a child, Concetta had wondered if her will was not exactly her own, if her mother made her do things, and then she would be puzzled as to why her mother would sometimes be cross with her. There was one thing that her mother hadn't been able to divine beforehand, though, one event that her mother had failed to see. She put her hands onto her belly and felt the slight trembling of the child inside. Her mother had been angry, but now she wondered if the anger had been directed not at Concetta but at herself for failing to have imagined such a thing.

They spent the next long hours without speaking. Her mother began by cleaning the table, odd cups and plates, and then she got down onto her knees, raked the ash out from the hearth and emptied it into a bucket. Then she took a chair and sat facing the window. The candle had burned down to the stub and gone out, but her mother made no effort to light another and they continued in darkness. Concetta had lain down on the bench again and was drifting in and out of sleep. Being awake and being asleep seemed to merge into one and she hovered suspended between reality and dreams that dissolved and pulled her in and then dissolved once more.

She awoke with a start. The dark was at its deepest and she thought that the beginning of dawn couldn't be far off. She pulled herself to an upright position and peered around the room. The chair where her mother had been sitting was empty. Concetta had a sudden fear that her mother had gone out to look for her sisters alone, but then she saw that her coat was still hanging on its hook. She manoeuvred herself off the bench and went through into her old bedroom. Her mother was sitting on the bed, still as a statue, her face turned towards the window. Concetta took a step closer.

'You're awake,' her mother said. Her voice was strange, not her own.

'What are you doing here, *Mamma*, in the dark?'

Her mother shrugged.

Concetta went to the bed and sat beside her. She put her arm around her shoulders. 'Why don't you lie down and get some sleep? I'll wake you if I hear of anything.'

'I want to stay awake.'

'Come into the other room then and we'll light a candle. The house is so gloomy.'

Her mother allowed herself to be led into the other room and Concetta set her down on Tino's bench. She went over to the hearth, found some matches and a new candle and she lit it, creating a ball of pale light in the centre of the room. Her mother sat without shifting her position, her eyes fixed ahead but not focused on anything in particular. Concetta sat on a chair and glanced over at her from time to time, but it made her fearful to see her mother so changed. Her presence seemed so slight that she had the sensation of not looking at her mother at all, but at the ghost she would become.

Concetta felt the prickle of nerves in her palms and in the soles of her feet. She stood up, feeling alert now, as though she needed to compensate for her mother's torpor. She moved around the room with briskness, tidying away a few objects and piling some wood on the hearth to get a fire going. Now they were awake, she could feel an icy chill rising off the stone floor. Her mother seemed not to notice. She stared ahead, beyond the candle flame, her body held rigid. Concetta couldn't bear to watch her any more and slid the bolt on the door and walked out onto the doorstep. She still had her coat on, she realized, and she pinched the collar to her neck to keep off the night air. She blew out a long stream of cloudy breath and watched it drift off and then stood there for a long time trying to identify distant sounds, voices perhaps, but there was just a bat fluttering against the eaves of a nearby house and, beyond that, the silence of the night.

When she went back inside, her mother had roused herself. She was looking about her, disoriented, as though she'd just woken from a deep sleep.

'Where did you go?'

'Out on the step.'

'What were you doing out there? It's cold.'

'Just listening.'

Her mother sighed and walked over to put some water in a pan to boil. She busied herself making hot camomile. Concetta was relieved that she had come back into herself again.

There was a noise outside, the scrape of boots against the ground and the ring of something metallic being propped against the wall. Sombre voices spoke quietly so as not to be heard. Concetta felt her heart leap and she ran over to put her head against the door. It was her father's voice and her hands shook so badly she struggled to loosen the bolt. She threw the door open and her father and Tino came in as they were, booted, bringing the sharp, briny scent of the river with them. She could see by their faces that her sisters had not been found.

'No sign?' her mother asked. She spoke with her usual brusqueness.

Tino shook his head. 'We tried all around the fields where they were last seen, through the cemetery, into the woods out west beyond the river. Nothing.'

'We're joining Pasquale's group once they come through the village and we'll start scouring the eastern fields,' her father said.

Concetta's mother nodded and looked away, then she remembered the camomile and went over to pour out two steaming cups. 'There are just two of them?'

'So old Giorgio now says. His wife thought she'd seen more of them, but now she's not so sure,' her father said.

'She's always been one to make things worse than they are,' her mother said.

Tino put a hand to the back of his neck and massaged it. 'We'd better go,' he said. His father drained his cup and rose to his feet.

'Wait,' said Concetta. Something had just come to her. 'Have you been to the *mufita*?'

Her father frowned.

'It would be a good place to hide,' she said. 'Immacolata has always been drawn to that place.'

'They'd be foolish to hide there,' her mother said. The gases that escaped from the *mufita* were invisible; sometimes too, if the wind was strong, the stink of sulphur could be blown away and so it was easy to be caught unawares, to be lulled into edging too close.

'We're keeping to the routes where the men might try to escape,' her father replied.

Tino put his head to one side. 'She's right, though.' He turned to his father. 'We should make sure they're not there.' He was in a hurry to go and already had his hand on the door. He opened it, waited for his father to go through and then nodded at them and left. They heard the crunch of heavy boots fade as the men rounded the corner of the street.

Concetta sat back down on the bench and after an hour or so she saw, through the window, the smudge of dawn. The cockerel in the room next door began to crow intermittently, its voice lusty but straining. The song was a cracked one. It roused the other animals and they shifted around with their early morning restlessness, impatient to get out into the open air.

Concetta stepped outside again, in part to wake herself up. She had to urinate, too, and went into the stable and pushed the cows aside and crouched down. The powerful smell of animal excrement rose up from the straw. Her head felt woolly with lack of sleep and the world appeared blurred. She'd just come out of the stable and had her hand on the front door, ready to push it open, when she heard the patter of hurrying footsteps. She paused and turned, certain that this person brought news.

It was her *comare*, Elena. In her haste, she had come out without a scarf, her hair was hanging loose and her coat was still unbuttoned. The door opened and Concetta's mother leaned out and when she saw that it was Elena, she pushed out from the step into the street.

'They've found them,' Elena said. 'They're safe.' She stopped to catch her breath.

'What happened?' Concetta's mother could barely get her words out.

'Those two men had them. The outsiders.'

'The marauders?' asked Concetta. She couldn't stop the awe creeping into her voice.

'I'm not sure they were marauders,' Elena said.

'Are they all right?' asked her mother. 'Are they hurt?'

'They're shaken. In shock. Nunzia is crying, but fine. Immacolata was shouting, but Tino's calming her down. She's better now.'

'Where are they?' asked her mother. 'I'm going to them.'

'They're all at Pippo's house. It was the closest place to take them. They found them by the *mufita*. They got the men, too. They're holding them there.'

Concetta's mother headed back to the door. 'I'm getting my coat.'

'I'm coming, too,' said Concetta. She turned on her heels and ran towards the house.

'Concetta, *cara*, are you sure?' her *comare* called after her.

Concetta hesitated. Pippo's house was several hours' walk away. 'I'll get the donkey.'

'Can you get on it?'

'I'll use a chair.'

They brought the donkey out and, with the women's help, Concetta managed to perch herself on top and they set off. Her mother walked quickly, Elena almost having to run to keep up, and Concetta was forced to keep slapping the donkey's flanks to get it to move faster.

They hurried through *Porta Vecchia*, and the few people who were up and about saluted them and looked mournful, as they hadn't heard the news that the girls were safe. They didn't stop to talk to anyone, but hurried across the main square and through the zigzag of little streets that took them to the road that led to Franchina's house. They passed the mill and Concetta's cottage, lying low behind its outcrop of trees, and then they were passing fields, with the highway up ahead.

There was no wind today and it wasn't until they arrived at the highway that Concetta sensed the presence of the *mufita*. The acrid air seemed to collect in her throat. Instead of going straight ahead towards the *mufita*, they took the highway for half a mile and then cut west down through a wooded area towards Pippo's house.

Pippo Caputo and his family worked on land adjoining their house. Pippo also worked as a woodsman and a carpenter. The house was a simple, white, two-roomed construction. An outer wall had been badly damaged in the earthquake and crudely rebuilt. It still bore its many scars; large cracks inside and out had been bolted with iron girders, giving the impression that the whole place had been patched back together again.

A tangle of bushes and stout olive trees camouflaged the house from the highway. The only way to approach it was a small winding path that brought them out into the yard by a brick well, which had become green and furry with moss. There was a large group of people milling about outside the back door, mostly men carrying guns and long staves.

As they approached, the men who had been standing in a loose group by the door removed their hats and moved to let them pass. One man hurried forward to take hold of the donkey's neck and a couple of others lifted Concetta off and set her down on the ground. It felt good to have solid earth under her feet again. It had been an uncomfortable, bumpy ride. She followed her mother and her *comare* into the house and was surprised at the controlled scene in front of her. There were no raised voices, no tears or signs of violence. Immacolata and Nunzia sat together on a narrow bed. They'd been wrapped in blankets and Nunzia had brought hers up so that it half covered her face. Immacolata was looking away from everyone. Her father was standing with Tino and Pasquale. Felice and Paolo flanked two other young men, who were pushed into a corner, one with an untidy growth of beard and a dull flush at his neck, and the other, shorter and wiry, with a fresh cut on his cheek, which he was attempting to stem with the back of his hand.

Her mother first went over to Pippo Caputo and his wife, Rosetta, to thank them, then she walked over to Immacolata and Nunzia and put a hand to each of their heads and began to stroke their hair. She didn't say anything and Nunzia shifted her head to feel her mother's hand better. Immacolata continued to look away. Concetta moved across the room, too, and sat down by Nunzia and took her arm.

They stayed like this for some time. Rosetta brought around some hot milk for the girls and camomile for everyone else apart from the *forestieri*, the outsiders, who continued to stand awkwardly, their shoulders pressed up against the wall. Concetta could sense the weariness in the room; her sisters looked as though they'd been wrung out, no energy to speak a word. It seemed wrong to her that they too, like the *forestieri*, were facing the room, their backs against the wall. Concetta laid her head against Nunzia's shoulder and allowed her eyes to close a moment.

The men, who'd been out all night on the hunt, looked tense, as though they couldn't find it in them to relax yet. Concetta could see why. The two men would have to be dealt with. Justice had to be done. There was no outward mark of violence on the girls, her *comare* had been right that they only looked shocked, and she prayed that her sisters hadn't been touched. In any case, her father had two girls on his hands who were now unmarriageable. No other man would want them after this, not even Giovanni would cede any more sons. That debt had been paid.

Concetta saw her father and Tino put their heads together and whisper. They said something to Pasquale and he turned round to them, a hand on each of their shoulders, and nodded. Felice and Paolo stood apart, closer to the *forestieri*, occasionally throwing a wary glance behind them at their charges. Time passed. A roaring fire was making the room stuffy and Concetta felt a wave of lethargy creep over her. The bed felt soft and yielding against her legs, which were chapped raw by the cold and the rough hide of the donkey. The room lulled and voices seemed to slur and distort. Concetta could feel her eyes getting heavy.

She felt the bed lift and she opened her eyes, looking up. Her mother was on her feet. 'So, what's been decided?' she asked, staring at the men in the corner.

Concetta's father walked over to her. He put a hand on her arm. 'Anna, it's not what you think.'

'Don't you men have it in you to do something?'

'These men know the girls.'

'It's not true.' Immacolata had roused herself. She flung the blanket aside and rose from the bed.

Nunzia put a hand out to calm her. 'We only saw them once, at *carnuale*.'

'They know them?' Her mother looked away from Immacolata and over towards Tino. He nodded. Concetta had never seen him look so sad.

Her mother gave her head a shake as though to adjust herself to the new situation. She turned towards the man with the beard. 'You. Which is the one you had your eye on?'

The man had quick darting eyes, close set. He held himself in a way that suggested he was ready to fight or to flee. He turned towards the bed, his eyes flickering towards Immacolata.

Her mother continued to look hard at him. 'What do you call yourself?'

'Famiglietti, Franco.'

She nodded over at the other. 'And him?'

'My cousin, Giulio.'

'Where are you from?'

'San Michele.'

She nodded again, as though satisfied. Then she turned to Immacolata. 'You said you wanted to go back to San Michele.'

Immacolata got to her feet. '*Mamma*! It's not what you think.'

Her mother turned to Nunzia. 'I never would have believed this of you.'

Concetta was stunned. All the girls in the village grew up in fear of *rapimenti*, or kidnappings. If a man knew a girl was unwilling to marry, he could hold her overnight and then have her to keep. Sometimes, though, it happened that a man and a girl wanted to marry, but that the girl's family had set against him, perhaps because he was poor or dogged by ill health or his family marked by misfortune. They knew of girls who'd gone against their families, secretly plotted to stay out all night, knowing it was the only way they'd marry their man. Concetta could see the way her mother was thinking.

'*Mamma.*' Tino walked over to her. 'They didn't intend to kidnap Nunzia. She wouldn't leave Immacolata. She thought by staying neither of them would be ruined.'

'Instead they both are,' Concetta's mother said.

'Franco is ready to marry Immacolata,' said Concetta's father.

Franco looked up from his boots and nodded in a vague way towards the room.

'He got what he wanted then,' her mother replied, then looked over towards Immacolata. 'They both did.'

'It isn't what you think,' said Immacolata. She got up from the bed and tossed the blanket to the floor. 'It was just silly talk. I didn't think he would really come.'

'There's nothing more to be done.' Her mother turned to her father. 'She marries him.'

Immacolata dropped back down onto the bed. She seemed dazed. After a moment, she craned her head round to look at her kidnapper as though assessing him for the first time.

Concetta could see that he had relaxed; his body was less tense. He's got what he came for, she thought.

Concetta's father looked grim. 'Anna, leave us to deal with this. The problem is not Immacolata, it's Nunzia. The other one doesn't want to marry her.'

'Why did he take her then?' said Concetta, unable to stop herself from speaking out. She glared over at the smaller man who had set his jaw. He was looking the room over as if squaring up to fight.

Nunzia seemed to come to then. 'It doesn't matter,' she said. 'I'm going to declare my intentions to *don* Peppino.' She shifted herself off the bed, ready to walk.

'It's too late for that.' Her father's tone was firm. 'They took both of you and they'll marry both of you.'

Nunzia stopped, stunned.

Franco put a hand on his cousin's shoulder and said something in his ear. His cousin's jaw appeared even more rigid. He shook his head.

Her father gestured at Tino and Pasquale to move over to the side of the room nearest the bed and away from the two men. Her mother followed them and Concetta walked over to stand beside her. She listened as they spoke in low voices.

'*Zio*, Uncle,' Pasquale said to her father, 'don't worry. I'll break him. He'll be only too willing to marry your daughter by the time I'm finished.'

Tino shook his head. 'We might get him to marry her, but then what? He'll either run off or make her life hell. I don't trust him.'

'Why can't she join the church?' asked Concetta. 'If that's what she wants.'

'Not even the church would take her now,' said her father. 'Especially if *don* Peppino hears that she knew her kidnapper. They don't want women who come to them in this way, desperate.'

'But she wanted to enter the church before.'

'Concetta, shush,' her mother said. 'She must marry. It's her only way out.' She sighed. 'We'll have to risk it with this man. We'll go to San Michele and find the family, see if we can talk to them, get them to persuade him.'

'Look.' Franco called over to them. He spoke gruffly. 'We didn't intend to keep the other one, but she stuck to us. Giulio doesn't see why he should marry her when she was free to go. But we don't want any bad feeling. We're going to be family, after all. Perhaps,' he said, looking round to check with Giulio, 'we can arrange something. If there was something extra, something to help him change his mind.'

Concetta's heart sank at the thought of this grubby man marrying Nunzia in return for something extra. She walked over to where Felice and Paolo stood and slipped her hand into Felice's.

'All right?' he said with a tight smile, glancing behind his shoulder at the two men.

She nodded and then looked up at Paolo, who looked doleful. 'Paolo,' she whispered.

'Yes?'

She searched for the right words.

'I'll do it,' he said, 'if she'll have me.'

Concetta closed her mouth. She hadn't really known what she was going to say.

'Wait,' Felice said. 'What are you saying?'

'She shouldn't have to marry him,' Paolo said. 'It's not right. She didn't do anything wrong.'

Felice turned round, his back to Concetta. 'Are you sure?' he said under his breath. 'You don't have to do this.'

Paolo looked towards Nunzia on the bed. She had her hands folded in her lap and was staring down at them. Immacolata had laid her head against her sister's shoulder and was stroking her arm, but Nunzia hardly noticed. 'Yes,' he said.

Concetta felt a little leap inside of her. She'd known that he still cared for Nunzia. She tucked her arm under Paolo's and moved with him across the room. She could see that her mother and father and the others still had their heads together and hadn't noticed them. They came to the bed where Nunzia was staring ahead, and she and Paolo crouched down beside her. Concetta turned to

Paolo, squeezed his hand, and then moved back again to Felice's side.

Felice was still doubtful. He shook his head.

'It's the right thing,' she said. 'Believe me.'

Paolo was sitting on the bed up close to Nunzia and he bent his head in such a way that it seemed as though he were pouring words into her ear. After a while, Nunzia turned towards him and nodded and Concetta couldn't tell whether it was a nod of acceptance or just to say that she'd understood. They both sat there then, not looking at each other, but taking stock of the room and the people as though contemplating the strange turn of events that had brought them there. Eventually, Paolo glanced over at Concetta and smiled. Then he took hold of Nunzia's hand and brought her up to standing. He coughed once to quieten the room and then spoke. 'She's marrying me. It's agreed. So there should be no more said about it.'

Concetta's mother turned in surprise and her father dropped his hands, which had been raised. There was a pause as everyone took in what Paolo meant by his words. Then Tino came over and embraced him. '*Grazie*, Paolo, and *auguri*.'

Pasquale slapped him on the back and pulled him forward to kiss him on both cheeks. '*Bravo*,' he said. 'It's a great thing you've done.'

Her mother came over to hug Nunzia. 'He's a good man,' she said. She turned to Paolo. 'We owe you.'

'No,' said Paolo. 'No more debts.'

Nunzia looked round wearily, but Concetta thought there was some relief, too. She must have imagined that this night would never end. Paolo's offer was better than she could have hoped for, thought Concetta.

After a while, as more people in the room crowded round her sister and Paolo, Concetta noticed Immacolata sitting on the other side of the bed. She had moved further away from Nunzia, as though wanting to put some distance between them. Concetta walked over to sit down beside her and, on impulse, leaned in to kiss her hair. She could still smell the *mufita* on her. It had penetrated the pores of her skin. She took her sister's hands and they were cold, so she rubbed them for her, noticing how her nails were bitten down to the quick, and dirty. Immacolata didn't speak or look at her, but she didn't push her away either. Concetta glanced up at Franco, her sister's abductor, and wondered what kind of man he really was. She could see that he was trying to remain apart, but couldn't help eyeing Paolo and Nunzia and the scene of festivity around them. Immacolata, she thought, would have to make the best of it.

14

The marriages were to take place together and quickly, a few days after the kidnapping. Paolo was not happy. He didn't want his own marriage to be further tainted by the stranger from San Michele, but Concetta's father said it was a question of time and cost. Even though the days were longer now, there weren't enough hours of light for the work that needed to be done. This was the season for sowing and planting, their busiest time of the year.

After the events at Pippo's, they had returned home in exhaustion and there could be no work done that day. Only Tino had disappeared from his bed to make up for the lost time while everyone else slept and he had returned early, shortly after nightfall, and without his usual cheerful whistle to signal his approach.

Concetta had never seen her mother so angry. She carried herself around the house stiffly, hardly speaking a word. She never turned in Immacolata's direction. It was as though she wasn't there. Immacolata stayed to her room at first and refused food. She wouldn't be consoled and when the fury had finally swollen within her she said she would run away and threatened to strike out at anyone who dared to stop her. Her father had her shut up in the bedroom and they secured the window with rope tied to a slab of stone.

'She's a stubborn girl, and stupid,' said her father. 'Not to marry would be worse. Why can't she see that?'

'She wanted to choose her husband,' said Concetta. 'There's nothing wrong with that.' She turned to Nunzia for support, but her sister looked away at her mother instead.

'She made her choice,' her mother said, standing up from the table.

'We'll make sure she's at the church,' her father said. 'Then I wash my hands of the whole business. No more girls to marry,' he added. 'Thanks be to God.'

Concetta heard a heavy thump from the bedroom, and after a long pause, it came again. A few seconds later, they heard the window rattle in its frame.

Concetta mused a moment. 'Perhaps you should let her see Franco. He could talk to her about San Michele. She wanted to go back there more than anything. Now she's going to live there.'

'But won't she be sad,' said Nunzia, 'to leave us?'

'No,' said her mother. 'She knew what she was doing. I only hope he turns out to be a decent one.'

Concetta frowned at her mother. She didn't want to believe that Immacolata had known about Franco's intentions. She turned towards the bedroom and listened. After a moment, there was another bump on the door.

The next day when their parents and brother went out to the fields Concetta and Nunzia were left to keep an eye on their sister. When she heard the others leaving, Immacolata railed and screamed to be let out and then the noise stopped all at once. It sounded like the silence of resignation and Concetta wondered if her sister had finally come round to her fate. Nunzia tiptoed over to the door and laid her head against it. 'She must be sleeping,' she said.

'We'd better let her be. Once she's calmed down, we'll go in to speak to her.'

Neither of them said anything for a while. Nunzia had her ear cocked towards the door, listening out for movement from the room within.

'That night.' Concetta paused, unsure how to go on. 'Did they hurt you?'

Nunzia looked down at her hands on the table. 'When they jumped out at us I started screaming and kicking and that one, the cousin, hurt my arm when he tried to pull me away. But, after that, once we'd got to the *mufita*, no. They kept a close guard, though. There was no way we could get away.'

'You could have gone free.'

'I wouldn't have left her.' Nunzia sounded fierce. 'Even though,' she broke off and looked down again at her hands, 'she'd told me to go. She was worried I'd ruin everything by staying.'

The thoughts were turning round fast in Concetta's head. 'It was her idea to go to the *mufita*. She knew no one would think of going there.'

Nunzia nodded. 'She told me they'd make me marry him, but I didn't believe her.' She looked up. 'How could I leave my sister alone with those men?' She shook her head. 'But she was right. They did try to make me marry him.'

Concetta reached for her sister across the table. 'You're still getting married.'

Nunzia nodded. 'Not to him, though.'

'Paolo is a good man.'

Nunzia turned away to hide a smile.

'The other one, Franco. What is he like?' Immacolata had many admirers in the village, but she had always kept herself aloof from them. None had been encouraged to come calling.

Nunzia considered. 'He isn't afraid of her like a lot of other men. I think she liked that in him. There was this dance at *carnuale* where everyone had to swap partners. Tino said that we shouldn't dance it, and Paolo and Felice too. They worried they wouldn't be able to recognize us with our masks on. But Immacolata got upset at coming all the way to San Michele and not joining in and she insisted. I don't think she was wrong, not for that. She was only trying to enjoy herself. Franco was one of the few not wearing a mask and when he got to Immacolata, he wouldn't release her for the next man but hung on to her. He wanted her to remove her mask, but she didn't. Not then anyway.'

Nunzia looked down again. 'After the dance, he went back to his friends, but he had his eyes on her all night. Later we left to get some water from the fountain and suddenly he was there, too, asking her if she would dance with him again. She said no, but he wouldn't be held back. He wanted to see her face. I tried to bring her to Tino and the others but she sent me away. I left her for a few minutes only, making her promise that she wouldn't take her mask off. After, she swore she hadn't.'

'Is that why Tino was angry?'

Nunzia shook her head. 'Not for that. She was only gone a few minutes. It was later. On our way home. Midway down the hill, there is a church there, a small chapel, only fits a handful of people.'

'I remember,' said Concetta. 'It's hidden by trees. You can't see it from the road.'

Nunzia nodded. 'They must have been hiding in there. Franco, Giulio and some others. Some of them were masked still and they were carrying sticks. It was just the way they appeared, like they'd been following us, hunting us down. Tino asked them what they wanted and Franco, he gave Immacolata a good long look, and asked Tino who we all were and why we were in the area. Tino told him and he sized Tino up, then gave Immacolata another look and said that Tino ought to keep more of an eye on his sister as he could see that she was beautiful and that a man with certain intentions might try to take her.'

'What did Tino say?' asked Concetta.

'That a man with those intentions could try.'

Concetta leaned forward in her chair.

'Franco backed off then. He laughed and tried to shake Tino's hand, but Tino wouldn't have it. Franco told us of a shortcut he knew, but Tino said we'd keep to the main path as we'd set out to do. Then they left us.'

'You must have been afraid.'

'I felt bad for Immacolata. She was sorry then. I told her that she couldn't have known that he'd come after her.'

Concetta looked over to the bedroom door. There was no sound from within. 'Is that why Felice was angry too?'

Nunzia nodded. 'He told her she'd nearly brought us all to a bad end and that she was never to be trusted again. It took a lot for Paolo to calm him down. I think it was just the nerves, the fright, coming out.'

Concetta remembered how he was the day after, although it had seemed a spent anger by then. She glanced towards the bedroom door. 'Why is she being like this? She got what she wanted.'

Nunzia considered a moment. 'I don't know that she has.'

Concetta frowned. 'It sounds as if she knew Franco would come for her, or as good as knew.'

'Perhaps she felt she had no choice. Perhaps she can't have what she really wants.'

Before Concetta could ask her what she meant, Nunzia got up from the table and craned her head round to the bedroom door. 'I can't hear anything in there.'

Concetta went to the door and tapped on it. 'Immacolata! Are you still in there?' There was no answer.

'Open it,' urged Nunzia.

They slid the bolt and pushed the door open. The room was empty. They saw that the window had been forced. Concetta ran towards it and pushed it open but she knew, even without looking, that there would be no sign of Immacolata in the yard.

Concetta was forced to wait at the house while Nunzia ran off to alert their mother and father. She wanted to go with her, but she would only have slowed her down. After several hours passed without word, Concetta's uneasiness grew so much that she knew she couldn't sit alone any longer. She stood up from Tino's bench and paced about the room and realized she had to get out of the house. The waiting reminded her too much of the night when her sisters had been taken. There was no donkey in the room next door, her mother had led it away earlier to the fields, so she would have to walk.

She pulled her coat off a hook on the wall, pushed her feet into Felice's old boots outside on the step and struck out along the street, not quite knowing in which direction to go. She walked towards the main square as fast as her body would allow. She'd had the idea of coming here first to ask if anyone had seen her sister, but instead she crossed the square, just nodding at the people she saw, a few women returning from the oven with trays of bread on their heads.

She found herself on the road towards her own house. When she got close to Franchina's, she stopped. There was an upturned tree trunk lying by the side of the road and she walked over and sank down onto it. She remembered that the tree had been felled in the earthquake and that Felice had told her that he and his brothers had had to push it out of the way, as it had been blocking the road. She felt very tired even though she'd walked slowly and she reached down into her boots to massage her calves. They were pulling from the exertion. There was no sign of activity at Franchina's house. It was mid-afternoon and she knew Franchina and her daughters-in-law would be working at the mill and the men out in the fields. She relaxed back on the trunk and closed her eyes. She could feel the sun on her face, and the heat gathering on her shoulders. Around her there was birdsong, shrill cries in the distance and, closer, the flute-like warbling of a blackbird. Beyond was the sound of the wind as it moved through grass.

After some time she felt her strength return and she pushed off the trunk and took the road again, walking past Franchina's and the flour mill, and turning into the fields that led to her own house. She walked along the ridge of ground that cut between the fields and when she looked up at the little cottage surrounded by its outcrop of trees it appeared to her perfect, as if in a picture. There was a parting in the clouds and sunlight was streaming down onto the roof, causing the dull red of the tiles to glisten and the white of its walls to appear very bright. She made her way into the yard and it seemed that she moved easily then, as if she were gliding rather than walking, her feet hardly touching the ground. Even before she rounded the house, she heard voices, which sounded both familiar and strange.

She stayed back behind the wall, scarcely daring to breathe. When she was calm enough she inched forward to look. Immacolata and Felice were standing very close, as close as it was possible to be without touching. They weren't speaking now, but Concetta could see that something had been said that had affected them both. Immacolata, just a little shorter than Felice, had her eyes raised while Felice was looking away from her in the other direction so that

Concetta couldn't see his face. They stood like this for so long that it struck Concetta that they might have heard her and stilled themselves. Felice eventually turned to look down at Immacolata and she saw that his face was damp. Concetta knew she should close her eyes, not look any more, but stronger still was the impulse to see, to get the measure of what was between them. Immacolata felt for Felice's hand and raised it to her lips.

'It's no good,' he said, shaking his head.

Immacolata tried to kiss his hand again, but this time Felice set her away from him and took a few steps back. 'Stop.' He said it as though he'd said it many times before.

Immacolata looked down at the ground. 'They'll come looking soon.'

'They won't come here,' Felice replied.

'Why not? They'll search everywhere.'

'You shouldn't have come.'

'Maybe not.' Immacolata looked up at him and then around her. As her gaze travelled to the house, Concetta dipped back behind the wall and held her breath.

'You didn't want me to?' she heard Immacolata say in a mocking tone.

Concetta couldn't hear Felice's reply and she edged forward again, her back as flat as it could go against the wall, and looked round the corner. Felice had his hands in her sister's hair, half freeing it from her plait so that it fell about her shoulders. He appeared seized by a wild energy and began to kiss her on the neck, his hands pushing into her coat.

Concetta drew back. She put her hands on the wall to steady herself and then pushed off from it and began to walk the way she'd come. She felt heavy and cumbersome as she made her way through the yard, her progress hampered by boots that were too big and which caught in the weeds.

Concetta took the long route home, veering off the path towards Franchina's and crossing fields and acres of scrubland to get to the village. By the time she got back home, Immacolata had returned and the house appeared calm again. Immacolata was sitting in the main room with Nunzia and their mother but Concetta couldn't bring herself to sit in the room with her sister and told her mother she felt ill and went straight to bed. She slept until late the next morning, not hearing a sound from her sisters when they joined her.

A few days later, on the day of the marriages, Concetta roused herself from bed and told herself that she had to remain calm. For Nunzia at least she couldn't ruin this day. Immacolata was quiet that morning and allowed herself to be dressed by Nunzia almost as a child might; her arms were lifted and pushed into a borrowed wedding dress. The lace trim at the hemline and at the sleeves was beginning to yellow with age and her mother had to take a needle to the matching veil, which was torn in a few places. Tino had gone out very early and returned with some white flowers, late snowdrops, and her mother pinned these through Immacolata's hair before she hung the veil over her face. She used the rest of the flowers to make up a small posy and handed it to Immacolata, who stood in the corner of the bedroom without speaking while her mother and Concetta turned their attention to Nunzia.

Franchina had offered Nunzia her own wedding dress to wear and insisted on adjusting it herself. Nunzia had gone over to have it fitted the day before and Felice had brought it round earlier that morning. He had stayed for a while in the kitchen by the fire, but when neither Concetta nor Immacolata emerged from the bedroom, he'd got up and left.

Franchina had sent sprigs of rosemary and green leaves for a bouquet and a parcel of brown paper tied with string. When Nunzia opened it to find an antique silver crucifix, she sat on the bed and began to cry.

'What's wrong?' asked Concetta.

Nunzia shook her head and showed her the crucifix.

'It's lovely,' said Concetta. 'It looks very old. She really does mean well.'

Nunzia dabbed at her eyes with a scrap of cloth.

'She'll love to have you with her,' said Concetta. Nunzia would be moving into Franchina's house with Paolo, in a large room with its own fireplace. 'You're the daughter she's been hoping for.'

Nunzia reached for her hand. 'She's already got you.'

'I'm not like you,' said Concetta. 'You'll make her happy.'

Concetta saw that her mother had turned away from them and was busying herself by unfolding Nunzia's veil on the bed. It struck her that her mother would be losing all of her daughters. She had depended on Nunzia most of all, though, had willed her to be like herself and in this she had failed. Nunzia was not like their mother. She had never wanted to be a healer or a helper and had only ever been a witness, a helpless bystander in the darkened rooms of birth and death. Concetta thought her sister would finally find her place in Franchina's household. She would be content to be told what to do and she would do it because it would be simple enough work, commonplace duties in the fields or at the mill. For herself, Concetta couldn't help feeling happy that Nunzia would be so close to hand.

She steeled herself to look over at Immacolata who, unlike her usual self, stood mute in the corner. Concetta remembered the way that Felice had kissed her at the place where her coat gaped at the neck and the sound he had made, something between a moan and a cry, and she let her eyes fall away. Soon, she thought, she would be far away, among strangers, wedded to a man who had shown himself to possess a sly and ready violence, and for this Concetta was sorry.

There was a knock on the front door and Concetta went through to open up. Her *compare* had arrived with two chickens dangling upside down in his hand. 'You'll be on your way to the church soon,' he said, 'but I brought these for the wedding meal.'

'*Grazie, compare.*' She took hold of the chickens by their feet. 'Come in.'

'No, no,' he said. 'I'll go now. I didn't want those two to go without after what happened. I can spare these. It's the least we can do.'

Tino and her father were not yet back from the fields. They'd taken the animals out to graze, so Concetta could take the chickens into the stall to kill them without frightening the other beasts. She took one of them into the house and put it under a cage her mother had made from plaited rushes. It squawked, made a show of ruffling its feathers and then quietened. She took the other into the stall and quickly, before it knew enough, she pulled its head to her chest and gave it a strong wrench. She felt the resistance of the bone before it snapped and then the neck, loose now, yielding. In a clean twist, she pulled the head off. She lifted the bird by its legs and let the wings flap until the life drained out of it.

She disliked killing more than one bird at a time because the second would always be able to smell the death on her hands from the first. She scrubbed her palms with a hard brush in the pail of cold water outside the door, but as soon as she came back in she could see the bird glaring at her, a beady eye from behind the rushes. She moved towards it and sought to empty her mind of what she was about to do. She remembered the quiver of fear when, as a child, her mother had taken her hand and wrapped it around the gullet of her first bird. She'd placed her own over the top and squeezed. Concetta hadn't been able to help looking into the eyes of the bird, seeing the moment when its life expired, and afterwards in her mind she'd often relived that passing from life to death.

She looked at the cage to see where the bird was and then lifted it swiftly, but was unable to stop the bird dashing forward and under Tino's bench. It backed into a corner and began to squawk in a low, urgent way. She walked over to the bench and tried to lower herself, but it was useless with her bulk and she stepped away, reached for a broom and poked it underneath. The animal fell silent and she bent down, feeling around with her arm for its soft mass, but couldn't locate it and she dipped her head to see. Then it came at her, stabbing at the skin just above her ankle, above the boot line, and she staggered back across the room until she felt the table against the back of her legs. The sensation at her ankle was hot and sharp, like a warmed needle and she called out for her mother more in surprise than in pain.

The bedroom door rattled on its hinges and her mother emerged, followed by Nunzia. 'What's all the noise?' She saw Concetta backed against the table. 'Are you all right?'

Concetta shook her head, trying to get her breath back. She could see her mother feared it might be the start of labour. 'The chicken escaped from the cage. *Compare* brought them. I've killed one. This is the second.'

'Be careful,' warned Nunzia.

'I was trying to be.'

Her mother dipped under the table and caught the bird in one hand and brought it hard against her apron. Its neck twisted and it fell limp. She turned to Concetta. 'I'll take care of this. Get dressed or you'll be late.'

Concetta nodded and turned to the bedroom door. Immacolata was standing in her white dress and veil. A shaft of delicate light came in through the window, falling across her. Despite the drabness of the dress, the contrast between the white cotton and her sister's dark complexion was stark.

'You are beautiful,' said Concetta, not as a compliment but as though it was the answer to a riddle. Immacolata seemed not to hear. She continued to look steadily into the room and then, as if she'd lost interest, she stepped away from the window and out of the shaft of light.

Concetta and her mother didn't go on ahead as was usual but walked with her sisters, their father and Tino to the church steps. As the ceremony was about to begin she slipped inside and found Felice on a pew at the front, his hands clasped together in prayer. From the back of the church, as she approached, she saw that he kept inching round to look out for her. When she neared, he reached for her and, a hand under her elbow, guided her to his side. It came back to her how his hand had often been at her elbow during their own ceremony, too.

They were joined on the pew by Franchina and Giovanni and Felice's brothers and then her father was walking down the aisle with Nunzia, and Tino followed on with Immacolata. Paolo stood at the front with one of his married brothers, Pietro, and Franco was beside Giulio, both of them holding themselves stiffly in the midst of strangers. Concetta was surprised at how different Franco looked with his face scrubbed, his beard shaved off and kitted out in church clothes. Immacolata looked like she had at home when the shaft of light had illuminated her. The white dress seemed to reduce her proportions, made her appear slighter, and the lace at her throat and over her hair gave her a fragile air. Nunzia, she could see, didn't think it proper to seem too joyful. She ignored Paolo's eyes and kept her attention on the priest.

The day had clouded over and the light through the rose window was barely strong enough to light the church. It brought no warmth. The service, a double one, was long, the vows were made and repeated, and the voices of the marrying couples sounded so weak as to seem doubtful.

Later, while she was waiting in line for Communion, Concetta noticed the brooding Madonna of the Pomegranates to the left of the altar. It seemed so long ago that she herself had been standing shivering beneath it and fearing that it might be an ill omen. Immacolata was the one seated closest now and she only needed to turn her head a fraction to stare straight into it. Her eyes were trained ahead, though, on the congregation and she was heedless of the mother and her baby.

As Concetta edged forward, she could make out the lines of the portrait better and it seemed to her now that the Madonna was more composed than she remembered. Her fingers were long and elegant, as would befit a lady of high rank, and they held the child tightly so that he wouldn't fall. A mother's clasp of fierce protection. She frowned. It seemed strange that she could have seen it so differently. Ahead of her, Felice stepped to the side and *don* Peppino was already bending forward, the host raised in his hand. She opened her mouth to receive it and closed her eyes in prayer.

The wedding feast was a simple meal of pasta in broth, roast chicken, spring vegetables and salad. Franchina and Giovanni had organized another celebration later for Paolo and Nunzia, but Franco had wanted to leave before nightfall for San Michele. It was decided that Tino would go, too, and stay for a few days, as Concetta's mother did not like the idea of Immacolata being alone all at once.

Nunzia took Immacolata into the bedroom to help her change out of her wedding dress and after a moment, because it would seem rude for her not to, Concetta joined them.

'Which dress do you want to put on?' asked Nunzia, searching through the chest. 'The cotton print one with the blue flowers?'

'That will do,' said Immacolata.

The door opened and their mother came in. 'That dress is a good one to wear,' she said, taking it from Nunzia's hand. She beckoned Immacolata forward. 'Come here. Let your mother dress you for the last time.'

When they went back out, Tino had prepared a sack of Immacolata's belongings, some gifts from relatives and neighbours, a few items of clothing, jarred olives and *conserva*, concentrated tomato sauce for pasta. Franco was outside the door drinking *orzo* and deep in conversation with Giulio, and when Immacolata emerged from the bedroom in her travelling dress, her hair freshly plaited and a new red handkerchief tied over the top, he moved away from Giulio and came inside to say his own goodbyes.

Immacolata had gathered herself and was no longer as listless as she had been during the ceremony and the meal. Concetta knew that all day her sister had been careful not to look at Felice but she did so now, coolly, her eyes sweeping him up and down, before turning to her mother and father and Nunzia in turn to give them each a cursory embrace. She did the same to Concetta and they both pulled away from each other, then looked away. Immacolata was impatient to start on the journey, and her new life. Even before she had left, Concetta could see that she didn't want to dwell any more on her old existence.

Concetta watched the four of them set off down the street and it seemed that it was done with the same unconcern as if they were setting off for the fields. She stood by her mother and father at the door and watched as Immacolata's head twitched slightly as she rounded the bend, as though she were about to look back, but had thought better of it. Concetta glanced back inside the house and saw that Felice had sat down on Tino's bench, his eyes on the floor. She moved off the step then and walked as fast as she was able, and when she rounded the corner, she called out to Immacolata. Her sister stopped and turned, thinking something had been forgotten. Concetta walked over and gripped her sister's shoulder and she could see that Immacolata hadn't expected this and had stepped back from her. 'Before you go,' said Concetta.

Immacolata pushed her hand away. 'I've nothing to say.'

Concetta looked over at Tino and he nodded and indicated to Franco and Giulio that they should walk on and leave the girls alone.

Immacolata watched them for a moment and then turned back towards Concetta. 'I've got nothing to say,' she repeated.

'I saw you,' said Concetta.

'What do you want from me?' Immacolata deposited her bag on the ground and looked back up.

Concetta held her sister's gaze and then looked away. The dusk was gathering and, out of the corner of her eye, she could see the dark outlines of birds flitting across the sky.

Her sister's voice had a strange tone to it when she spoke. 'He loves me.' She said it again as though the words might not have penetrated the first time. 'He loves me.'

After a long time, Concetta noticed the darkening clouds. Day seemed to be shifting into night before her eyes 'And you?' she asked finally.

Immacolata gave her a tight smile. 'It's hard not to love back sometimes.'

Concetta nodded. She wondered why it was that the important things only came to you when it was too late. She found it hard to speak, her throat was closed, and she had to force the words out. 'I thought you wanted Franco to come. I thought it was what you wanted.'

'I knew he would come for me. *Mamma* knows me better than anyone.'

Concetta shook her head. 'Why have you done this to me?'

Immacolata made a noise between a laugh and a shout. 'Poor, poor Concetta, eh? How many times have I heard that?' Despite the bite in the air, Immacolata's face had begun to flush. 'I'm tired of hearing about the baby, the earthquake, the whole lot of it.' Immacolata spoke in a rush, the heat rising in her cheeks. 'I'm just sick of it all.' She bent down to pick up the bag and looked back up again. 'Look after yourself,' she said, then turned to follow the others.

15

A week or so after the wedding, on washday, Concetta insisted on accompanying her mother to the river, even though her father had the donkey and she found it burdensome to walk any distance at all. Her mother hadn't wanted to take her and told her to remain at home and make *fusilli* for the week, but Concetta longed to get out of the house. She'd been feeling out of sorts and fidgety since her sisters had left. It made her melancholy to sleep without them and she couldn't bring herself to say much when Felice called to see her.

The women washed their clothes in the river downhill from the village, a place where the banks were wide and easy to access and where the water was high enough for them to tie their skirts at the waist and wade in to their knees. Some wide, smooth slabs had been laid nearby and there was a stone fountain with a grooved scrubbing board, which they'd pummel the clothes onto to beat out stubborn grass stains and dried blood.

There was a great deal of wind that day. It came in fierce gusts that tugged at their scarves and whipped their skirts up from the ground. It made the journey even harder for

Concetta as she couldn't balance the load on her head, but had to hold it out in front where it knocked up against her belly.

'It's a good day to put the clothes out at least,' her mother said, wrapping her shawl around her, its tassels jumping and splaying in the wind.

Concetta felt better being out here, away from the village, amid the greenery. The wind revived her spirits, knocking the solitude of the night out of her. She found it hard to walk and her mother wouldn't slow her pace, but the day was so clear and bright that she soon forgot her swelling feet and the extra weight she was carrying.

By the time they got there, later than usual, dozens of women were already hard at work slapping wet cloth against the slabs and thigh-deep in the water wringing clothes out first one way and then the other. Concetta loved washdays because she could catch up with the other women in the village. There was a feeling of camaraderie, all women together, and they liked to joke and make light of any hardships, and she needed this kind of solace today.

They made their way along the riverbank until they found a space to deposit their baskets of clothes, all the time saluting and waving at women they knew. Concetta couldn't remove her stockings, but had to get her mother to peel them off for her. She hitched her skirts up to her waist and waded in and the water was as cooling as balm on her poor feet. She touched the bottom where the ground felt silky and the sand gave slightly so that she sank down a little. Close to the bank, there were long, slippery reeds that wrapped themselves around her ankles and she felt the tug of them at her feet as though the river itself was trying to pull her deeper. She waded a bit further out and began to soak the whites, unfurling the sheets and dipping them into the water. She worked like this without thinking of anything in particular, only now and then sharing a few words with some of the women near by. She felt buoyed by the water and light again; her body almost felt like it had been before the baby started growing inside her.

When she had finished, she slapped all the dripping clothes together, squeezing some of the water out, and she had to get help to clamber back onto the bank. She took a bowl and, from a jar, poured some water and ash mixture into it and put in the stained clothes that needed soaking. She sat back on her heels to get her breath back and thought to herself that washing was heavy work but that today, more than any day, she'd done it with gladness. She sat until her legs and feet began to pucker in the wind and then she picked up the basket of dark clothes and plunged back into the river.

Her mother had walked off to talk to a woman whose child had fever. Concetta saw *signora* Clara in the distance and gave a wave, but she didn't see her and turned away. She thought then of Francesco and how so much had happened since he'd left and how he had slipped from her thoughts. She wondered if he ever thought of her, but then she thought how lonely it must be for a shepherd with only his flock for company and she decided a woman would not slip from his mind. She'd promised Felice she would never speak to Francesco again, but so much had changed since she'd made her promise.

The wind had strengthened, scuffing the surface of the river, and Concetta bent over to draw one of her father's shirts out of the water and, in a repetitive movement, dipped it back in and out again. She stood up to straighten her back and felt an overwhelming need to urinate. She gathered the clothes so that she could make her way to the bank. But as she stood up water gushed out of her and she dropped the clothes, confused at her loss of control. She turned to a woman who was standing a short distance from her in the river and, not knowing what to say, she looked back down at the water, greenish-brown in colour, still running out of her and into the river. She heard her mother calling and looked up and saw that she was at the edge beckoning her over. All the women near by had stopped working now and had turned to look. A small group gathered on the bank to pull her out. Concetta reached up for them and was lifted up out of the river by strong, work-roughened hands.

'The waters have broken,' said her mother.

Concetta nodded. The water was still trickling out of her. She felt a relief at being among the women. They all knew what was to come and yet they were laughing and patting her on the shoulder.

The woman who'd been near her in the river gathered up the wet clothes and laid them down on the bank.

'Am I really having it?' Concetta asked her.

'Don't be in too much of a hurry.' The woman laughed. 'You'll know soon enough.'

'It might not come yet,' said her mother. 'But better to set off now.'

'Take deep breaths,' said the woman. 'You'll know what to do when the time comes.' She leaned over and kissed her on the cheek.

One of her aunts, Rosina, her father's sister, appeared. 'Has it started?' She turned to Concetta's mother. 'What a week this has been for you, eh?'

Concetta and her mother left the washing to be finished by Rosina. The news had already run along the river bank so that, as they walked past, the women stopped what they were doing and waved, shouting '*auguri*, good luck' and 'we'll be thinking of you'. Concetta waved back and, once they had left the women, they took the route along the riverbank as it was flatter and easier to pass through. Concetta could feel her drawers sticking to her, as she'd not had time to dry herself off. They proceeded in silence and the wind stayed brisk. Concetta felt overawed by the thought of what was about to come, but serene too, because it was what she had waited so long for.

They turned away from the river and struck out along a wide, stony path that was the gentlest route back up to the village. There were orchards of apple and peach trees in blossom on either side and the air was fragrant with them. The wind had swept the clouds away and the spring light made the colours of the landscape cleaner and the lines sharper.

'All right?' asked her mother.

Concetta turned to her and nodded.

'It might be a while yet. I remember Rosina took three days after her waters broke the first time.'

'I hope it's sooner than that.'

Her mother reached a hand across Concetta's belly. 'There,' she said. 'Can you feel that?'

Concetta felt a tightening, a tiny movement, that lasted just a few seconds in the place where her mother's hand lay.

'That's good,' her mother said. 'That means you've started. It still doesn't mean it will be quick if the baby has a mind to stay in there. Sometimes they get too comfortable.'

They walked on again and Concetta put her hand where her mother's had been. She felt the pressure herself, small but insistent. She began to feel a light cramping in her stomach as she touched it, and she thought to say something, but decided it wasn't strong enough yet to be worth mentioning. She felt reassured to know the baby had started to make its way out.

They entered the village, where the roads were steeper, and Concetta felt the first twinges of weariness. They'd started off from the river slowly, but it was almost a forced march now. It hadn't been her mother increasing the pace. She'd done it herself. A sense of urgency was starting to seize her. It was difficult to walk over the cobblestones. Her body had felt buoyed in the river, but now she felt its proper size and weight pulling her down so that she had to stop at the side of the road. She put a hand to her stomach and doubled over. She breathed out a long moan, something like a lowing cow. It sounded muffled to her, as though it were someone else far away making the noise.

'Bad?'

Concetta nodded. She couldn't speak. She closed her eyes to try to block the pain from her mind. Her mother didn't seem alarmed that the pain was so strong and she took some comfort from this. 'I don't think I can walk,' she managed to say.

'Let the pain go, and then try to walk a bit further. We've still got some way to go. It's come on much quicker than I thought.'

Concetta waited until the cramp subsided and then bent herself back upright again.

'All right?' Her mother put a hand on her back and looped the other under her arm to support her. 'Let's go faster.'

Concetta pinched her eyes together. She could just make out the main square in the distance. She sent a silent prayer. *Let me get home before it starts again.* The thought of having the baby in the street panicked her and she started walking quickly, pulling her mother along.

'Take it steady. Try to stay calm.'

'I want to get home.' Concetta could hear her voice fraying. She tried to divide the distance up: how far to get to the square and how far from there to the house. But really her mind was full of the pain in her belly. Something soft and vital felt like it was being shredded up. The shock of it halted her.

'You didn't tell me it would be like this,' she cried and broke off again. The pain came over her in a surge and she stumbled to lean against a house front. The noise rose up again from her throat.

'Better not to know.' Her mother spoke kindly and put a hand to Concetta's hair to move it out of her eyes.

Concetta hardly heard her. Her underarms were sticky and her feet felt as though they were boiling up in the boots. All she could hear was the moaning in her ears. This is what pain sounds like, she thought.

Her mother twisted the lapel of her coat round. 'Bite on this,' she said. 'It will make you feel better. Rest until it passes.'

Concetta bit down into the fabric, grinding her teeth against it. The noise rumbled in her throat. After some time, she felt the pain lift. She unclenched her hands, which she had been holding against her chest, and released the lapel from her mouth. She could breathe again.

'Has it passed?' her mother asked.

Concetta nodded. She pushed away from the wall and they walked with as much speed as Concetta could manage. She was surprised that she could move like this when only a few moments ago she had hardly been able to stay upright. She fixed her eyes on the square ahead and willed the pain not to return until she got to the house.

It came back, though, as they were entering the main square. Concetta had just enough time to see that the square was busy before shrugging her mother off and veering to the side. 'I can't take it any more,' she said.

'It's started,' she heard her mother say and she felt herself drop to the ground. There was a confusion of faces around her. Her own face was sopping wet and she put a hand to her hair, which was damp too, the tendrils at her forehead sticky. There were voices around her, warm breathing against her face and she felt her limbs being gripped and pulled in different directions. She fought for air and tried to scream for everyone to give her space, but only the animal sound came out. She began to feel an urge to push and, grunting, tried to bear down.

'Not yet,' her mother said. 'It's too early.'

She opened her eyes, searching for her mother's face. 'It's coming.'

'Hold on.'

Her mother spat into a rough piece of cloth and dabbed Concetta's forehead with it and then scraped it round her mouth and her chin. 'You're doing well,' she said. 'We're going to carry you. I need you to help us. Look at me.'

Concetta felt her face being shaken and she opened her eyes again. 'Keep breathing. Try not to push until we get home.'

Concetta met her mother's eyes and nodded. She inched her legs back together and felt stickiness there.

'There's blood on the ground,' someone said. 'Spots of it.'

'Concetta?' Her mother's voice sounded harsh. 'Say something.'

The hands were all over her body again and then she was being lifted and she could hear the ringing of nailed boots against the ground. The cramping was still in her belly, but there was something different about it now. It was just the movement, the muscles working. There was no pain.

'Nearly there.' It was her mother's voice again. Cold hands pressed into her jaw and then it was being shaken hard. She could hear her teeth rattling inside her head. 'Can you hear me?'

She wanted to speak, but her mouth wouldn't open. The lowing noise was trapped inside her now and she thought that it must be the sound of the baby crying. She wanted to speak to it, cry with it, but she was mute.

16

S he recognized the stillness from the first time, after
the earthquake, and it was so peaceful, only her own
voice inside her head. She was amazed that she should
have returned to this place again; it felt familiar to her
and she had no fear. She sensed another presence with her
and she realized it was the baby and she was happy that
it was with her in this tranquil place.

After the earthquake, she had tried so hard to search
her memory for the time she had lost, but in this place
she could remember everyone and everything as clearly
as the day it happened. She could hear her own voice in
her head recounting it all and she realized that she must
be telling the child because it was right that it should
know. Now and then, while she was remembering, she
surfaced into the world again and she heard the voices
of her family around her once more, although their
words eluded her. A few times, she was able to force her
eyes open and see her old bedroom, but the light was so
sharp, like a blade on her eyes, that she would have to
close them again and sink back down to where it was
safe.

She returned instead to the hot and dusty days of that summer, before the earthquake. She remembered how the heat had built up, each day hotter and drier than the one before, and how the sun blazed as soon as it rose in the mornings so that there was no let-up by day or night. By midsummer, earlier than usual, their father broke the working day up and they returned home at noon to sleep within their shuttered house because there was no shade to be had under the trees. They started out earlier in the morning, with the owls still up, and worked into the night and they spent many of their nights out in the *pagliaro* so that the working hours became longer and the sleeping hours shorter.

Nunzia had been right about it being hotter that summer. Concetta could feel the scorching sun even now, her hands blistering, the skin reddening and bubbling up. She saw herself gripping the handle of a spade ready to push down and felt the effort it took because the earth crumbled on the surface, but was hard as brick below. She felt herself itching under her clothes from the sweat, but having to keep her arms and legs covered to shield them from the sun. Only her hands remained exposed on the spade, a winking sun reflected in the dull shine of the blade.

That night, she put her swollen hands into her mother's lap and her mother had pursed her lips and turned to Nunzia. 'She looks like she's run into a swarm of bees,' she said. 'That sun is too much.'

'We've never had heat like it,' said Nunzia. She'd just come back from the oven where it was all anyone could talk about. 'They say the sun is getting closer.'

Her mother unrolled a ball of white crêpe for bandage. 'There was another summer, when I was a young girl. It was worse than this.'

'Hotter?' asked Concetta.

Her mother shook her head. 'There was no sun. Day after day. The plants hardly grew and the animals didn't breed. That was worse.'

'They were talking about that summer at the oven,' said Nunzia. 'They said it was when the last earthquake hit.'

Her mother tore a piece of crêpe off with her teeth and began to bind Concetta's hands. 'People have too much time on their hands,' she said.

Nunzia looked away. 'It's what everyone is saying.'

'Let them talk,' her mother said.

The heat had continued, though, and there were those who insisted that it was no hotter than usual and they pointed to the fact that the river had hardly dried up, which was true, and they said that the summer was bringing not an earthquake but a kind of madness to the village. 'People just want something to talk about,' Concetta's father had grumbled one day on their way back from mass.

'Or to worry about,' her mother added.

It was early morning, after the first mass on a Sunday, and already the humming of the cicadas had started up. Concetta, mindful of her mother's reply to Nunzia, hadn't dared to say anything although she shared Nunzia's way of thinking. It was not just the heat. Other things were making people unsettled. At mass, *don* Peppino had made an appeal for anyone to come forward who knew the whereabouts of sant'Emidio, their protector against earthquakes. No one could believe that someone would steal the statue and there was a general whispering about what it might mean, although they were careful not to talk of earthquakes in church.

After mass, before they started for home, Concetta had been standing with Tino in the main square when two men had stopped to talk to him. She could see by their faces that they were brothers. They were tall and rangy, their shirts hanging loose over their frames as though they weren't quite getting enough to eat. Both had dark hair that curled slightly at the nape. The older one was starting to recede a little at the temples and he had dark, expressive eyes. Concetta hadn't known their names at the time, but she knew them now to be Francesco and Peppe Di Rienzo. She'd remembered afterwards meeting Francesco, but had forgotten that Peppe had been with him. Walking home from mass, she'd asked her brother about them. He had shrugged. They were not people he knew so well, he said.

There was a disruption to the stillness around her. Her voice stopped its recounting. The other presence was no longer there with her and Concetta felt herself come up again into the bedroom. Now she could feel the baby, its head was down and it was fighting. She could feel it pummelling and at first she thought its fists were being used against her, but then she realized it was only trying to feel for a way out. The moan that came out of her throat threw her forward and she opened her eyes.

Her mother and Nunzia were in the bedroom beside her, with her *comare* on the other side. Her mother was bending over her and she could see streaks of blood on her mother's face and in her hair and, when she stood up, a huge quantity of it splashed on her apron. She had her hands on Concetta's face and it was as if she were saying a prayer and it took a moment for her to realize that her mother was repeating her name over and over again.

'Her eyes are open,' shouted Nunzia.

'Look at my face,' her mother was saying. 'Stay with me.'

Concetta jerked her head in answer. Her throat rasped. There was liquid there, clogging it.

Nunzia put her head into her hands and turned away.

'Listen to me,' her mother was saying. 'The baby is trying to come out. You need to push. Can you do that?'

Concetta wanted to speak, but she didn't know if she could push. Her mother and Nunzia lifted her up, propping her against the pillows.

Concetta looked down at the sheets. They were sticky with blood. She felt waves of heat pass through her. She was racked by a contraction and she felt herself pushing down with all her might. After a time, when it subsided, she felt her body fall back against the pillows.

There was a sharp rap at the door and her mother said something to her *comare* who nodded and went out of the room. A few minutes later, she returned with Franchina and a solid-looking older woman whom Concetta didn't recognize, who flung her coat onto a chair and rolled her sleeves up. Franchina stayed back, but the older woman joined her mother and Nunzia. There was a bowl of steaming hot water by the bed and the old woman dipped strips of material in it and began to help Concetta's mother staunch the blood.

'Felice?' Her mother turned to Franchina.

Franchina nodded towards the door. 'Outside with the others,' she said quietly.

The older woman came up to Concetta and looked hard at her. 'How much blood?' she asked. Her mother leaned in to her and said something that Concetta didn't catch.

She felt the woman pull her eyelids open and after a moment she let them fall shut again. A cold hand pressed against her forehead and then below her breast, feeling for the heartbeat. The woman lifted Concetta's hand and rubbed the palm to get the blood flowing and then laid it down again on the bed. A spasm passed through her like a splinter piercing somewhere deep and then she rocked forward, a deep groan knocked out of her, and she felt herself gasping in the air like a fish thrown out of the water.

*

A few days after Francesco and Peppe had stopped to speak to Tino after mass, Concetta's mother sent her over to *signora* Clara's to drop off some salad from their field. Her mother had taken Nunzia with her to tend a dying man and Immacolata was at home preparing food for their father and brother, who would be staying out all night again. Concetta had only been to *signora* Clara's a few times before on occasions when her mother or sisters weren't able to go. It was mid-afternoon and as Concetta walked over to the east side of the village she saw all around her only parched fields and plants that were wilting, weighed down by the heat. She glanced up towards the sun, but it was too strong and she closed her eyes and looked away. The imprint of it burned there under her lids: a hard, bright ball.

She arrived at *signora* Clara's small house and knocked on the door. When there was no answer, she walked over to the window and peered in. The house was dim inside and, because of the sun's glare, she couldn't see anything. She caught a vague movement and returned to the door and was about to rap on it again when it opened and the younger of the two men she'd met in the square stood on the step, yawning. He had a work shirt on, but it was unbuttoned to the waist and she took a step back.

He rubbed his eyes and looked her over. 'I know you,' he said.

Concetta took the basket off her head and lowered it to the ground. She thought him rude.

'Ah,' he said, hitting his forehead with his hand, 'Tino's sister.'

'Salierno, Concetta,' she said.

'Who is it?' a voice called from inside.

'Salierno, Concetta,' Peppe parroted over his shoulder. 'She's brought something for us.'

'Let her in,' Francesco called. 'Don't keep her on the step.'

She could feel the afternoon heat on her back and wanted more than anything to enter the cool interior but she hesitated to go into a house occupied by two half-dressed men. 'The *signora?*'

Francesco appeared at the door. He was tucking his shirt into his trousers. 'She's gone to Vincenzo's to help out.'

'Ah.' Concetta nodded. The dying man. She held out the basket to Francesco. 'My mother sent this.'

'You're not coming in?' asked Francesco.

'At least a glass of water,' said Peppe.

Concetta thought of the long journey back. 'I won't come in,' she said, eyeing Peppe at her side, 'but if you have a glass of water, I'll have it here.'

'Look,' said Francesco. 'I'll feel bad if you don't come out of the sun. You've walked a long way. My mother would be angry with us.'

Concetta hesitated. She still didn't think it right to enter, but there was no one to see her and Tino knew them after all. 'I can't stay long,' she said.

'As long as you like,' said Peppe, following her in.

Francesco shot his brother a look. 'My brother hasn't learned his manners yet.' He drew a chair out from the table for Concetta and poured her a glass of water. Peppe went over to the corner of the room, took a clean shirt from a nail on the wall and slipped it over his head.

'You're not out working?' asked Concetta.

'Only when somebody asks for us,' said Francesco. 'We don't have any land of our own.'

'Day-labourers,' said Peppe.

'Ah,' murmured Concetta. It made even more sense to her now why her mother sent food to *signora* Clara. The father had died some years before and, without land of their own, these people had to scratch a living on the land of others. It seemed to her that work would be even scarcer with this heat.

'It's hitting us hard,' said Francesco, 'but it's the same for everyone.'

'What can anyone do, though?' asked Concetta.

Francesco shook his head. 'We're in God's hands.'

Concetta nodded and then realized that she had been looking at him for longer than was proper. It had taken her no time at all to feel at ease. She rose to her feet. 'I should go.'

Peppe got up, too. 'I'll walk you back to the crossroads,' he said.

She didn't really want to leave. There was something about the way the two of them sat and looked at her, a kind of gentle awe, that made her feel as though she'd been singled out for some special attention. She thought it must be because she was by herself and not with her sisters for once.

'There's no need,' said Concetta. She turned to Francesco. 'Pass on my regards to your mother, and thank you for the water.'

Peppe moved towards the door. 'I'm going in that direction anyway,' he said.

She hesitated. People might talk if she were alone with a boy. But if he were walking there anyway, it seemed rude to not walk with him.

'All right,' said Concetta.

It was Peppe who first told her about old Paolo's dog. 'The wolf-dog?' Concetta stopped walking.

Peppe laughed. 'A bad-tempered thing. Old Paolo forgot about him yesterday. Left him tied up all afternoon while he was out and when he got back, the dog was lying there, stiff as a log, covered in flies.'

'That dog pretended to be bad-tempered, but he wasn't really.' Concetta looked away from Peppe a moment.

Peppe stopped smiling. 'I didn't really think it was funny. I was sad about it, too.'

'It doesn't matter,' said Concetta. 'He's dead now.'

They walked on in silence. Up ahead was the crossroads where they would take their separate ways. She thought she might have been too abrupt with Peppe about the dog and wanted to say something else before they left each other. She saw that he had a rifle slung against his shoulder.

'Can you use that?'

'Of course.' He laughed. 'Rabbits, pigeons. I hunt most things.'

'Isn't it hard?'

'For some people maybe. I've got a good eye, though. Better than Francesco even. Don't you know how to use one?'

Concetta shook her head.

'Hasn't Tino shown you?'

'I've never asked.'

They arrived at the place where the paths crossed and they stopped walking. 'I'll show you,' said Peppe. 'I'm good at things like that.'

Concetta had heard of women protecting themselves against marauders with guns. She'd never seen her mother handle one, but she knew she could use a gun if she needed to. She knew she would never be able to go out alone with Peppe so she just waved her leave and took the narrow path that led out towards the fields.

A few days after, the weather turned and the air became charged with the static of approaching storms. The *mufita*, too, made itself felt throughout the village; the air was heavy with it, and the women were quick to bolt windows to keep its fetid odour, worse with the terrible heat, from gathering in their rooms and stables.

When Concetta and Immacolata went to do the weekly wash the following Monday, they stood with all the other women to stare at the cracked expanse of mud that only a few weeks ago had been a fast-flowing river. There was just a brown rivulet trickling down the middle of the riverbed. The women gave thanks to the darkening sky that rain was finally on its way, but the days passed and the clouds gathered, and still there was no rain. Sometimes, in the distance, over San Michele or some other nearby village, they would see a break in the clouds and the smudged grey of falling water.

'If it's raining there,' asked Concetta, pointing at the distant clouds, 'why doesn't it rain here?'

Her mother stopped to look across the hills. 'The clouds are out of rain by the time they get here. There's no water left.'

'But why would we live here then?' Concetta asked, turning to her mother.

'Silly child,' she said. 'We've always been here.'

That evening, Concetta's mother went with Nunzia to stay overnight with the men in the fields. She sent Immacolata to sleep with Concetta in the house and Immacolata, exhausted by the heat and the tomato harvest, went straight to bed. She was sleeping like the dead but Concetta, beside her, couldn't drop off. She lay there, her eyes open, listening to the rasping of the cicadas.

She heard a rustling noise outside her window and sat up. There had been talk that the drought was driving wolves into the village at night and Concetta thought of the pig and the chickens, which were outside because it was too hot for them in the stall. She turned to Immacolata and tried to shake her awake, but she only muttered and turned the other way. Concetta waited a few minutes longer but then she thought that her mother would not have waited at all.

She got up, found a nightdress and pushed it over her head before going through into the other room to get a candle. She opened the door, stepped outside and peered around. The pig was moving in its pen, snuffling the ground, but beyond that she could hear nothing except the cicadas. She waited to make sure and then, just as she was turning back, she heard her name called. In a fright, she ran behind the door and half closed it, putting her ear up against it. 'Who's there?' she asked.

'It's me, Peppe,' she heard. 'Don't be afraid.'

Concetta inched the door back and saw him standing against a tree, his gun slung across his shoulder. She went back onto the step. 'What do you want?'

He approached the door, stopping a few feet away. 'I've been out hunting.' He turned to show her and she saw that he had a couple of rabbits hanging down his back, eyes glassy in the darkness.

She crossed her hands over her chest. 'What are you doing here at this time?'

'I was passing,' he said. 'Are you alone?'

'My sister's inside. If you're not careful she'll wake up and she'll be sure to tell my father that you were here.'

He moved a few steps closer. 'I'm sorry about what I said about old Paolo's dog.'

'You've said sorry already.' She sounded impatient with him again and said, more gently, 'It doesn't matter now.'

'I promised I'd show you how to use a gun. You ought to know how to defend yourself.'

Concetta stared at him. 'Now?'

'Yes,' said Peppe, smiling. 'It's too hot to sleep anyway.'

'I don't know,' said Concetta, biting her lip. 'I'll get my brother to show me. Tino would do it. He's good like that.'

Peppe's smile faded. He stepped back. 'If that's what you want.'

'What if someone saw?'

'No one will see us. I'm careful. We're not doing anything wrong.'

Concetta thought a moment. Peppe was just a boy. Someone she could talk to like she talked to her sisters. She turned her head to the door. Immacolata was sound asleep inside and there was no one else around. She could slip out for an hour or so. 'Wait a moment then,' she said. 'I'll get dressed.'

She tiptoed back into the bedroom, flung on a dress and tied a handkerchief over her hair. She fished under the bed for Nunzia's mirror and brought it up to check her face was clean. She glanced to the bed where Immacolata was sleeping on her side, her head burrowed into the pillow.

It was a relief to be out at night, so much cooler than during the day. All around her windows and doors were open to let in the air and there was something thrilling about passing so close as people slept. They made their way out of the village and Peppe said the woods would be a good place to practise as it was far from the village and the fields where people would be sleeping in their *pagliari*. 'We just have to be careful of those out fishing,' Peppe said. 'The river runs through the forest.'

Concetta nodded. She hadn't spoken much while they'd been walking. Being out late and alone with Peppe like this made her feel heady, but she didn't want to show this to Peppe for fear of seeming foolish. After a while, though, she had to speak. 'You're lucky to be able to go out like this. You don't know what it's like to be a girl.'

Peppe shook his head. 'It's difficult being a man. My father spent his life living away from home, just the sheep for company.'

'That must be hard.' Concetta nodded.

'Francesco is going away to earn some money so we can buy land.'

'Where will he go?'

'A long way. To America. Some men from San Michele will put him in touch with people there.'

'But how will he get there?'

'By ship. You borrow the passage and then you work it off when you arrive. They say there's money to be made as long as you're not afraid of hard work.'

'What about you?'

'Francesco says I have to stay to look after my mother. She's not been well since *Papà* died.'

They had reached the forest, the outer ring of trees, and Concetta halted. She wondered then if she had done the wrong thing in coming here with someone she hardly knew. She felt a prickle of danger and shivered, but it wasn't Peppe she was afraid of. She was made nervous by the darkness and the late hour and the sounds that came from deep within the forest, snapping branches and animal noises that sounded almost human.

Peppe was listening too. 'We have a gun,' he said, holding it up. 'I've shot wolves before.'

'But what about brigands?' she said 'Or wandering spirits? What use would a gun be then?'

'My father was once chased by a spirit,' Peppe said. 'He'd been out hunting and night had come down quicker than usual. He'd taken a different route to go home and had found himself in unfamiliar land on the other side of the forest. He began walking along a path, which he hoped would lead to the village, and after a time he heard a clanking sound behind him, of heavy metal being dragged. At first he thought it was just a man, a living man, behind him, dragging a wheelbarrow or a spade and he called out to him because he couldn't see in the dark.'

'Don't tell me now. I'm afraid,' said Concetta and shuddered. But she continued to look up at him and Peppe put his arm round her shoulder and they entered the forest.

'There was no answer to his call so *Papà* decided that perhaps he had imagined it and continued on his way.

He'd only taken a few steps when he heard the noise again, louder this time, and when he turned around, he saw the silhouette of a man some way behind him. It was hard to make out in the dark, but he looked like an ordinary man of about his own age and height, but hung with heavy chains, which were wrapped all around his body even up to his neck, so that he could hardly stand upright. The man called out to my father to help him and my father stopped and was about to go to him when it came to him that this wasn't a man at all.'

Concetta stumbled against some gnarled roots on the ground and stopped a moment to regain her footing. Peppe drew her closer and they walked on.

'There was only one way forward so he began to walk a bit quicker, reasoning that the man in chains wouldn't be able to run as fast as him.'

'Spirits can move quickly.'

Peppe frowned slightly at her interruption. 'As he was walking he could hear the chains behind him and they were getting closer, so he looked back and the spirit was catching up, so he started to run and still the spirit was getting closer, and my father ran the fastest he'd ever run in his life, and all the time the spirit was gaining on him and the chains were getting louder and the spirit was calling out to him to stop. *Papà* was drenched in sweat by the time he entered the village and still the spirit followed him through the streets and he went out down that road that leads to our house and the spirit was getting so close that it was almost touching him.' Peppe stopped to draw breath.

'Did he make it?'

Peppe pushed a branch out of the way of their path. '*Papà* came round the corner to our house and he put his hand on the door to open it and, as he was about to go through, he knew it would be foolish and lose him time, but he couldn't help himself. He wanted to look the spirit in the eyes.'

Concetta put her hand out to halt their movement forward and they both stopped and looked at each other. 'What happened?'

'It put a finger against my father's ear, just like this.' Peppe put a hand to her ear and she felt the squeeze of his finger. 'In the place where shepherds nick the ears of their lambs to mark them.'

Concetta stood still and Peppe's hand dropped away.

'A few days later he was off to do the *transumanza* and he died out there, across the mountains. We don't know how. They told us different things, but Francesco says it was the loneliness that killed him. My father hated being away from the village.'

'I'm sorry.' Concetta reached out for his hand.

They walked on in silence for a while. They were deep in the forest now, and it was densely wooded. Ahead there was a clearing, and this is where Peppe indicated they would stop. It was so dark that Concetta wondered how he would be able to see to shoot. Peppe laid the rabbits on the ground, unslung his hunting rifle, and took out a leather pouch tied around his waist. 'See,' he said, showing her the contents. 'Gunpowder.' He brought out the gun then. Concetta could see that it was a very old one. It had a dark, wooden handle and the barrel had worn smooth. Peppe went over to a nearby tree and took a knife from his back pocket. He scratched a circle with a cross in it and came back to where Concetta was standing. 'Can you see that?' he asked.

She squinted at it. 'I think so.'

'Today you just watch,' he said. 'Learn how it works before you use it.'

Concetta wanted to say that there wouldn't be a next time. It was risky enough that she had come out with him tonight. She didn't say anything, though, and instead watched Peppe preparing the gun. He propped the rifle on its butt and poured a small quantity of powder down the muzzle. Then he tapped the butt lightly on the ground and took out a round bullet, snapped open the rifle and placed it inside, pushing it into the muzzle.

'It has to sit in the powder,' he explained, showing her the inside of the barrel. He closed it and then lifted the gun, pointing it at the tree. 'Stand there,' he said, pointing to a space just behind him. He put an eye up against the lock and took aim. There was a sharp crack and he lifted the gun away. 'How did I do?'

Concetta made to go towards the tree, but he caught her arm.

'Never run in front of a gun, even if it's been fired.' He glanced up at the circle. There was a mark just inside it. 'Not bad,' he said. He showed her again how to load it and he allowed her to stand closer to him so that she could see how he squeezed the trigger.

She flinched when the bullet hit the tree and looked away.

'That's no good,' he said. 'You need to keep your eyes on the target. Pretend the tree is a man. You may have missed or only injured him and he might still be coming after you.'

Concetta nodded. It was harder than she thought. He was right when he said it would take practice. She glanced up at the trees and, beyond them, she saw that the darkness had lifted a little. It wouldn't be long before dawn. 'I have to go back,' she said. 'My sister will be awake soon.'

They left the forest and went along the path towards the village. Her legs felt heavy, but she felt elated, as though she could walk for ever. As they neared the village, they stopped at a broken tree; an ancient, twisted oak that her mother said had been felled by an earthquake many years before. This was where their paths would separate. Concetta didn't want to risk Peppe coming back into the village with her.

'I can teach you to use the gun yourself,' he said.

'I don't know. I have to be careful.'

Peppe gave her a brief smile. 'Being a girl, eh?'

Concetta nodded. 'If I can come, I'll leave a sign for you.'

'How?'

Concetta tried to think. 'I'll tie a scarf to one of the branches of this tree. You'll have to pass this way every day to see. She turned to look towards the village. The sun's rays were just starting to come over the horizon and she could already feel its heat on her face. She turned back to him and gave a little wave with her hand. 'Until next time.'

He stepped over and kissed her on both cheeks like a good friend or a brother would and, with a salute of his hand, turned away.

17

It was only a week later that Concetta's mother and Nunzia again arranged to sleep out with the men in the *pagliaro*. The weather still hadn't broken and her mother and father were worried about the crops. They had decided to start harvesting early, even if the vegetables weren't fully grown. The tomatoes at least could be ripened off the vine.

During the day, Concetta tried to keep her mind from wandering. Her mother had to speak to her a few times, as she stood gazing out across the field, her hands stained purple with the beetroot she'd been pulling up. She should have been more tired. The humid heat made the work harder and her clothes were drenched with sweat by mid-morning. Instead, she hardly minded the work and felt herself to have plenty of energy, but she couldn't stop her thoughts from slipping to Peppe and the forest.

Immacolata was in a bad mood all the way home and wouldn't stop complaining about the heat. Nunzia was accompanying them to get food for the others. 'You said it was no different this year,' she snapped at Immacolata. 'So what are you complaining about?'

'Leave me alone.' Immacolata walked faster to get ahead of them.

Nunzia turned to Concetta. 'I'm glad it's you staying with her and not me. As if she's the only one suffering.'

Concetta saw the broken tree up ahead and when they got closer she said to Nunzia, 'You walk on. I need to stop for a moment.' She shifted from one foot to another.

'It's a bit open here, isn't it?' said Nunzia.

'I'm going behind those trees.' Concetta made her way over to the nearby clump of trees and saw that Nunzia, so as not to catch up with Immacolata, had only gone on a few steps and then stopped to wait for her. Concetta waved at her to go on and Nunzia raised her eyebrows and turned to trail after Immacolata. Concetta waited a moment and, when she could see Nunzia's back to her, she quickly untied her handkerchief, ran to the toppled trunk and fastened it to one of the lower branches. Nunzia was just turning as she was making her way from it.

'So modest!' said Nunzia. 'You must be growing up.'

Later that evening, when Nunzia had gone, Immacolata continued in her sullen mood. 'What's up with you today?' she asked Concetta.

'Nothing.'

'You're acting strange, like you're happy about something.'

Concetta took up a piece of her mother's embroidery, a blue pillowcase, thinking she might finish it for her. 'I'm not like you,' she said. 'I can't see the point in moaning. It's the same for everyone.'

'There's nothing to smile about, though,' said Immacolata, eyeing her. 'You're either mad or in love.'

'I must be mad then.'

'So it's love.'

'Aren't you tired yet?'

'I won't go to bed unless you tell me who he is.'

Concetta flung the embroidery down. 'Who would I be in love with?'

Immacolata considered this. 'I think you like somebody.'

'Even if I did, I wouldn't tell you.'

'So it's true.'

Concetta got up from the chair. She walked into the bedroom, stripped off her clothes, and got underneath the sheet. She could hear Immacolata in the other room humming to herself, but she couldn't tell how much time was passing and she began to fret that it would be too late. Peppe would only wait for so long and then go. Much later than she usually did, Immacolata came into the bedroom, undressing noisily. When Concetta heard her sister's breathing deepen, she got up from the bed, put her dress back on, and tiptoed out to the door. She walked out into the yard and put her hands to her mouth to whistle.

Peppe materialized from the darkness. 'It's about time.'

'Where did you come from?'

'I've been here waiting. Come on, let's go.' He took her hand and they ran together and she was almost falling to keep up and trying not to laugh. Peppe was laughing, too, but he made a show of putting his finger to his lips to shush her. 'Do you want us to get caught? People will think I'm stealing you away.'

'Oh stop. You're making me laugh.'

They took the same route to the forest, running fast this time. The moon was full and very bright and the air rushed by like hot breath against her ears. Every so often, as they ran together, Concetta stole a look at Peppe: the way his cheekbones were set high, giving his face an angular look, and how his hair curled up at the bottom of his neck. She was conscious of Peppe's hand around hers and she felt that this might be the most wonderful moment of her life so far.

They didn't stop when they got to the outskirts of the forest, but burst through, Peppe out front, his hand tight on hers. The ground was bumpy and Concetta could feel twigs and nutshells and fallen berries crunching and mashing underfoot. The fragrance of the forest was pungent and woody; it was like passing into a dream, a place that had a different texture from her real life, out of time and enchanted.

They arrived at the clearing and Peppe made to continue on, so Concetta pulled at his arm to stop him. 'Isn't this the place?' she asked, catching her breath.

'It's where we were the other night.' He walked over to the tree where he'd carved the circle and traced his finger over it.

'Where's your gun?' Concetta only now noticed that he wasn't carrying it.

'I didn't bring it.'

'You were going to teach me.'

'There's plenty of time for that.' He saw the disappointment on her face and picked up her hand again to pull her to him. 'We've got all summer.'

Concetta twisted her hand away. 'That was the reason I came.' She crossed her arms and walked back into the clearing. 'I want to learn.'

'I thought it was me you wanted to see.'

He'd come to stand in front of her, very close, and he was looking into her face and she couldn't help but look back. His eyes appeared black in the darkness and a lock of his hair had fallen across his forehead. He put a hand to it and pushed it back, then smiled at her. His smile seemed to say that both of them were foolish to be standing like this staring into each other's eyes. She stepped away.

'You promised. I wouldn't have come if I'd known you would trick me.'

He reached over to her arms and pulled them so she was forced to step forward again. 'Don't say that, Concetta.'

'Take me home.'

He put a hand to her hair and she let out a small scream and turned to run away. She felt his hands on her arms, digging into them, and she was brought up short.

'Did I hurt you?' He examined her arm and then rubbed it hard. 'I didn't mean to scare you. You're not bruised?'

Concetta looked down at her arm. 'No,' she said. 'You didn't hurt me.'

Peppe pushed a hand through his hair, the same gesture as before. 'I'll take you home. I don't know what I was thinking, bringing you here. I'm always doing things I shouldn't.'

Concetta wished she hadn't screamed like that. She could see that he hadn't meant to harm her. 'What were you going to do,' she asked, 'if you weren't going to teach me to shoot?'

'I don't know,' he said. He lowered his eyes. 'No, that's not true. I thought I could persuade you to let me kiss you. I've been thinking about it a lot. I didn't think you'd let me, though. You're not that type of girl.'

They stood facing each other in silence. Concetta felt she was standing on a threshold and she could either step further in or step back and leave. The moment was powerful in her – she could feel the turmoil of it inside – and all of her senses were sharpened. It was as though she could see and hear everything around her as it was happening, all the tiny movements, the faint breathing of nearby creatures, the lightest of breezes brushing against the leaves. She closed her eyes and thought of all the reasons why kissing him would be wrong, and there were so many that came to her, but when she opened her eyes they fell away.

'I'm here with you, aren't I?' She spoke so softly that at first Peppe didn't seem to hear her. He'd looked down again and she thought he seemed sad and she wanted more than anything to soothe him. She put a hand to his cheek and he looked up at her and she saw that it wasn't sadness at all, but wonder. She moved forward. His lips were soft against hers and he took tiny bites at her and she did the same; and they did this for a long time until she felt him against her more pressingly and she smiled against him, to hold him back. He put his arms around her and at first it felt awkward to do the same, but when he started to push at her teeth with his tongue, she held onto him then. He broke away from her and caressed her hair, then he took her hand and guided her against the tree so that her head was just below the target he'd carved. He stroked her cheek, then his eyes grew more thoughtful and he started to kiss her like before, breaking away often to look into her eyes. She was concentrating so much on the feel of his mouth against hers that she hardly noticed the rest of her body and she felt a kind of shock go through her as his hand went first to her breast and then further down to between her legs and she felt the wetness there and she wondered where it had come from. She opened her mouth to speak and she felt him move forward so that her spine was hard against the tree and his tongue on her own. She realized that soft sounds were coming from her and it took some effort to find her voice to speak.

'Peppe,' she said, moving her mouth to one side so that his tongue trailed wet against her cheek. 'I can't.'

Peppe stilled, his mouth at her neck. He nodded and after a moment he pulled himself upright and Concetta moved away from the tree, too. She brushed her dress down and put a hand up to sweep her hair away from her face. She felt shy looking up at him. He took her hand and they walked back across the clearing.

'I promised to teach you to shoot,' he said. 'I'm going to keep my promise.'

Concetta frowned. 'With no gun?'

'We'll run back to my house and get it.'

'It's too far, and it's too late.'

'Can't you stay out a bit longer? We don't know when the next time will be.'

She knew it might be weeks before they could be together again. She thought of those long days stretching ahead. 'Let's do it.'

Once they were out of the forest, they ran along the road hand in hand, turned at the broken tree and came along the path that led to Peppe's house. They got to the cemetery where the wooden gates had been drawn shut for the night and Peppe told her to wait a moment here, a little way from his house.

'I don't want anyone to hear us,' he said. 'My mother barely sleeps and is always up and about. I'll get the gun and come straight back.'

Concetta eyed the gates. She thought of the last time she'd come, a few months ago, with her mother and sisters to put spring flowers on her grandfather's grave. There was no headstone, just a simple wooden cross among the hundreds of wooden crosses. They had laid the sprigs and stayed for a moment in silence. Concetta had tried not to tread on the other graves, but it had been impossible to see where one grave began and another ended.

She watched Peppe make his way down the road to his house and, even though it was the dead of night when no one would be around, she stepped back into the shadow of the gate so that the moonlight wouldn't fall across her. To the side of the gates a small row of cypress trees had been planted and she decided to sit under one of these. She looked again towards the house: there was no movement. All was still. Tiredness was beginning to creep up on her now and she felt her eyelids beginning to droop. She tried to keep them open and trained on the road, but she felt drowsiness overcome her.

After what seemed like a few minutes, she felt her arm being shaken and she looked up to find *signora* Clara bending over her and, just behind, Francesco, a rifle in his hand.

'What are you doing here at this time of the night?' *signora* Clara said. 'Does your mother know you're here?'

Concetta scrambled to her feet, disoriented by the shock of coming out of sleep, and she swayed back against the tree. She glanced round for Peppe but there was no sign.

'Please don't say anything to my mother.'

'Are you waiting for someone?'

'No, no,' said Concetta. 'I'm alone. I was just out for a walk. I couldn't sleep and then I got tired and decided to rest a while.' Her voice petered out. She knew it didn't sound right.

Signora Clara turned back to Francesco. 'Her mother would be furious if she knew.' She turned back to Concetta, her tone still hard. 'Do you care anything about your reputation?'

'Please don't tell anyone,' said Concetta, shrinking back against the tree.

'I'm sorry for you,' *signora* Clara said. 'But your mother has a right to know. She has done a lot for me over the years.'

'*Mamma.*' Francesco had stepped forward. 'She looks frightened enough as it is.'

'It's not right for a girl to be here at this hour,' *signora* Clara insisted.

'She made a mistake,' said Francesco. 'That's all.'

'How will she get home?'

'I'll take her,' said Francesco. 'She can't go by herself.'

'But what if someone sees you?' *Signora* Clara looked unhappy.

'I know a way. We won't be seen.'

The shock at being discovered began to wear off and, now she knew she was going home, a malaise settled over her. The journey was a long one and she felt bone-tired. She craved the comfort of her bed.

Before *signora* Clara turned back to the house, she seized Concetta's arm. 'If you were my daughter, you'd get a thrashing for this. Young girls don't wander around at night.'

Concetta couldn't bring herself to say anything as they walked down the road towards the village. After some time, Francesco spoke. 'I'll talk to to her when I get back. She won't say anything to your mother.'

Concetta mumbled some words of thanks.

'It was a stupid thing to do, though.'

She glanced up at him and nodded. The less she spoke of it, the better. She didn't want to get Peppe into trouble, too.

'I saw Peppe,' he continued.

Concetta felt the heat rise in her cheeks.

'My mother doesn't know Peppe had come in looking for the gun. She was already out in the yard and saw you moving around at the cemetery gates.'

'Why didn't he come to help me?'

'I stopped him. If my mother knew you had been with him, she would have blamed you, not him. That's the way she is.'

'We didn't do anything bad,' she said. 'He was going to teach me how to shoot the gun. That's all.'

Francesco shook his head. 'You ran a great risk. Anyone could have seen you. Once you get a reputation, you never lose it.'

Concetta felt sick. She'd been foolish to think she could do what she liked. She wanted to put her face into her hands and cry at her own foolishness.

'Don't let him talk you into it again.'

'I won't,' Concetta said with vehemence.

They heard the pad of fast-approaching footsteps. It was Peppe sprinting towards them. 'Sorry I didn't come for you.' He stopped in front of her, bending over to catch his breath.

'I know why.'

Peppe glanced up at his brother and then back to Concetta. 'I had to wait until my mother went back to bed. I came as soon as I could.'

'I just want to get home now.'

Peppe put a hand out towards her, but she stepped away so that he couldn't reach her.

'Leave her alone, Peppe.'

'What have you said to her?' Peppe turned to his brother.

'It's my fault,' said Concetta. 'I should never have gone out with you alone.'

'We wouldn't have been seen. I would have made sure.'

'Peppe.' Francesco put a hand against his brother's chest. 'You're forgetting something. You *were* seen.'

'*Mamma* doesn't count.'

Concetta turned to face him, too. 'We were lucky that it was her and not somebody else.'

Peppe pushed up against Francesco's hand. 'I knew you'd do this. We weren't doing any harm.'

Concetta dropped her face into her hands. 'I don't want to talk about it any more.'

'Go home, Peppe.' His brother's tone was still composed.

Peppe's eyes moved back to Concetta. 'Is that what you really want?'

Concetta uncovered her face, turning away from him. 'Go back and get some sleep. Francesco will take me home.'

Peppe let his hands drop and, glancing back up at his brother, he turned and walked away.

Francesco and Concetta walked on until they reached the outer edges of the village and then Francesco indicated to her that he knew a way through an underground tunnel that connected the old gates of the village. He heaved up a rusty grate in the ground and dropped himself down what seemed a fair distance. He called to her to do the same, his voice echoing up. She positioned her hands on the edges of the hole, took a deep breath and then let herself drop down. Francesco's hands came around her waist just in time to break the fall. Concetta put her hands to him to steady herself and gazed around in amazement. She had landed in a cavernous place, a narrow passageway carved out of white rock. 'What is this place?'

'Very few people know about it.'

Concetta moved across to one of the walls. There were crude markings etched into the stone. She put a finger to them and it came away chalky. 'What are these?'

'Wait.' Francesco lit a match. It flared purple. 'See. They're crosses, pictures of saints, some writing, names and dates of people who were down here.'

'But why would they come here?'

'People hid here, in case of attack or siege.'

Francesco moved off and she followed behind, as there was only enough room to walk in single file. She continued to look around her in awe. On the walls, at intervals, were rusted iron brackets, which Francesco explained were to hold torches. They walked on for a while and then they came to a wider section, the size of a small room, and here Concetta could see that there were deeper etchings, still crudely executed but more elaborate. She made out some hooded figures in robes, which appeared to be saints, or religious figures. She recognized a rough rendering of the crucifixion scene and leading away from it, in the opposite direction, the *Via Crucis*, the Stations of the Cross. One of the walls had an indent cut out of it to create a low bench.

'This part was a church. Some men, churchmen, hid down here for many years. Some say they were heretics, but I don't know if that's true,' said Francesco.

Concetta was studying the vague outline of a female figure. She laid a hand against the halo, which was so faint as to be almost indistinguishable. 'I wonder who this is supposed to be.' She coughed, the dust collecting in her throat.

'This area is underneath the main square. That's where we are now.'

'We've walked all that way?' She was surprised. It felt like they had walked no distance at all.

'You travel quicker down here. No houses or corners in the way.'

They moved out of the church and Concetta followed Francesco once more along a narrow passage. There was the incessant dripping of water from all sides. 'Wells,' Francesco said. 'A lot of them pass close to here into the ground.'

Concetta had a thought. 'Does my mother know about this place?'

Francesco shook his head. 'Tino knows.'

Concetta nodded to herself. It explained how her brother could move so quickly at times in and out of the village.

A little further on, Francesco put his hand onto a flat piece of stone that jutted out from the wall. To the side and a bit higher up, there was another, worn smooth in the middle. 'Put your foot on the first ledge and your hand on the ledge above and move up like I do.' He demonstrated, stepping from one to the other, stopping at each level to reach down to help Concetta up. Above them was another iron grate. He put his head to it, glanced around to make sure no one was coming, and then lifted it using his head and jumped out onto the street. He pulled Concetta up and she brushed herself down. She was surprised to find herself only a short distance away from her house. 'It's only round the corner,' Francesco said.

They arrived at the house and Francesco stayed back, not stepping into the yard. 'I'll leave you here,' he said.

She put a hand up to wave and he merged back into the dark, his footsteps fading.

She was back in her bed and, in the darkness, she put a hand out to touch her sister. She wanted to feel her solid presence beside her, but there was nothing, just an empty space. When she opened her eyes they were flooded with light when she'd been expecting darkness, so she closed them again. There was a gentle pressure at her arm; someone was shaking her. She obliged by opening her eyes again.

Her mother was there and Nunzia, her *comare* in the corner, an old woman and another woman of about her mother's age, with weather-worn features. A boy with a delicately moulded face and soft fair hair was the one shaking her. He looked pale and unhappy, and for a moment she wondered if he were an angel come to take her away. He seemed to know her because he was calling her name. A part of her knew she must be very ill and that her grip on body and mind was weak. There was pain, but it felt familiar as though she'd long got used to it. The boy brought her a glass and she sipped a little from it, enough to wet the insides of her mouth, and she sank back against the bed.

Her mother put a hand on the boy's arm. 'You understand?' she said.

The boy nodded. He looked back to Concetta and put a hand to her forehead and kept it there a moment, then he turned away and walked to the back of the room where Concetta couldn't see him any more. She heard low voices and she could hear the woman speaking, her voice ragged. Nunzia's eyes were red and she had twisted her face away towards the wall.

Her mother addressed the boy again. 'We don't have much time. We can try to save one or the other.' She hesitated a moment, seeming to struggle to form her words. 'You are next of kin. It's for you to decide.'

Concetta couldn't see why her mother would be consulting a young boy, a stranger, in her sick room. He approached the bed and half crouched down and laid his head against her stomach. He stayed there a few seconds, then rose again and came close to her face and leaned down to kiss her forehead. Before coming away, he sought her eyes and opened his mouth to say something, but then thought better of it and turned away.

Concetta heard something, a wet cloth, being slapped around in a bucket of water, and she could see the steam rising from it. Nunzia disappeared from the room and came back in with a bottle of clear liquid. She poured a small amount into a cup and came over to Concetta to administer it to her. Concetta spluttered. It was pure spirit and it singed her throat. It made her feel light-headed again and she felt a sudden sharp stab of anxiety. Her grip was weakening. She stared at all the faces around the room and wondered why they would make it worse for her.

Her mother came over and gave her another drink, hot water mixed with something that tasted sour like yeast, and she felt the panic leave her. Her own presence was retreating but she didn't mind any more. She gave up the fight.

PART FOUR

18

Concetta woke before first light. She tried not to stir and wake Felice before time. It was hard on him these days, late spring and one of the busiest times of the year, without her to help him. Today, like every day for the past weeks, she would have to remain at home to do light chores or walk to the village, or to Franchina's. She was still not strong enough to go back to work.

She lay there in the silence that was still the silence of the night and said her daily prayer for her dead child. She knew he was in that place they called limbo because she had been there, too, for a while and he had been with her. When she recalled that place, it seemed so real and her feelings were so vivid that it sometimes made this place fade, as though the colours here, of the sky and the flowers and the sun, had lost their vitality. Her mother said that this was what grief was: she was mourning and that was how it should be. She knew her mother was right because she was always right and so she trusted that the colours and the brightness would return to her one day.

When Felice rose, she roused herself too and he told her to stay abed because she was still weak, but she wanted to feel useful and it gave her some pleasure to prepare his food for the day and warm the milk, and any pleasure that there was to be had she took. Ever since she'd come round after the birth, Felice had been so attentive. He'd treated her as though she were a fragile child, easily broken, and he'd looked at her with a kind of awe from which she knew she must have suffered greatly. She remembered the pain, but only as a distant memory, and only in part. She knew what her mother would have said if she'd asked her about that, that there was no use remembering, that it was best forgotten. She wasn't sure her mother would be right about that, though, and so she hadn't asked. She didn't want to forget the child, and the pain and the child were so closely bound together in her mind that to forget one was to forget the other, and so she held onto both, but only for a short moment, and only on first waking.

She went to the door with Felice and she allowed him to kiss her on the cheek and then she stood on the step and watched him as he rounded the house to take the road. It was such a beautiful day that she walked forward into the yard and looked out over the fields and up at the hills in the distance. There was no moisture in the air and the lines of the horizon were sharp and the colours clean and pure. It was a perfect spring day. She stood for a few moments more and then turned and went back inside.

Today she got through her housework quickly because she had an errand to run. She swept the floors with a new broom, changed the sheets on the bed, milked the goats and collected the eggs, then fed the small pigs that had been given to them as a gift. Then she cleaned the windows and wiped down the front door. She'd become fussy over her chores and house-proud since she'd been able to get up and about, partly because the house had been neglected while she'd been away and she felt bad that Felice had suffered too.

She took the black handkerchief her mother had made for her and placed it over her head, tying the ends under her chin. Then, after a moment's consideration, she walked around to a reed basket by the hearth and took out a quantity of *fave*, broad beans, that Felice had brought back the day before. She tied them in another handkerchief and balanced them on her head.

She started out on the path across the fields and waved at some of Felice's brothers working nearby. Paolo was there, and he feigned a military salute at her, and she felt obliged to smile. He was standing knee-deep in ears of wheat, which were moving slightly in the breeze, and he was plucking the weeds out, a job which they had to do several times before harvest. His father, Giovanni, had his back to her on an adjoining field, but she could see that he was planting seeds and she knew it would be potatoes, tomatoes or corn because of the time of year.

She rounded the flour mill and walked past Franchina's house, hoping she wouldn't be spotted by Franchina herself or one of the other daughters-in-law. Nunzia, she knew, would probably be inside as she hadn't been with Paolo, but she wouldn't stop today even for her sister. At the outskirts of the village, she took the road that led out to the cemetery and, beyond that, to *signora* Clara's house. The evening before, after he'd got in from the fields, Tino had come to visit and brought the news that the men from the *transumanza* were due to arrive during the night. She hadn't wanted to waste even a day before coming. She'd waited long enough already.

She kept on straight at the cemetery gates and at the small cottage she gave the door three short raps. She heard the shuffling sound of soft house shoes against the stone floor and then the lock scraped as it was being pulled back and *signora* Clara was squinting up at her.

'Ah, child,' she said. 'Come in. Come in. It's good to see you out and about. So sorry to hear of your loss.'

Concetta entered the dim interior. Francesco was at the table rising to his feet, taken aback to see her.

Signora Clara went round to Francesco and laid a hand on his arm. 'Concetta had a sad loss recently. Her child.'

Francesco shook his head as though he couldn't make sense of it all.

'You're still not well,' said *signora* Clara. 'Sit down, please.' She drew out a chair from the table.

'I feel like I've spent too long recovering from one thing or another. I prefer to stand. I am here to speak to your son.'

Signora Clara seemed puzzled and turned to Francesco.

'*Mamma*, please leave us for a while.'

Concetta kept her eyes on Francesco. It pained her to remember how so alike the brothers had been.

After a moment *signora* Clara spoke. 'If that's what you want, son, then I'll go into the yard to tend those lambs.' She shuffled to the door and went out.

Francesco sank down again. He had dark circles under his eyes and he was far too thin. The bones at his neckline jutted and his face was gaunt. He seemed too exhausted even to look up at her and she didn't say anything for a while. She took the parcel of beans and placed it onto the table. 'It will kill you like it did your father.'

She waited until he had lifted his head before she spoke again. 'My child is buried close by,' she said, indicating the cemetery with a nod of her head.

'You didn't deserve this.'

'I remember it all now. Everything.' She met Francesco's eyes and held them. 'It wasn't Peppe. You mustn't think that any more.'

The chair scraped against the floor and Francesco moved away from the table.

Concetta looked away. 'I wanted you to know that.'

Francesco walked round to her and held her hands.

'I cared for Peppe, and he cared for me.' She pressed her eyes shut and brought Peppe's face to mind: the angular cheekbones, the slightly crooked smile, the trail of his lips, wet against her cheek that time in the woods. 'He did care for me.' Remembering had brought her only sorrow, which was a different kind of pain, one that numbed but wouldn't pass easily. Her grief, she knew now, was so great because it was twofold: for Peppe and for her child.

She felt Francesco's pressure on her hands. 'Who?' he said. 'Who was it?' His voice was low.

'No.' She said it almost to herself. 'This ends here. No more debts to pay.' She moved away from him and over to the window. *Signora* Clara was putting water down for the lambs. A makeshift pen had been constructed to house them. After a moment, Francesco walked over to the window, too, and she felt his hand on her shoulder. They stayed like that without speaking for a long time.

For several weeks after *signora* Clara had caught Concetta at the cemetery gates, the weather remained unbroken. One day, the sky packed with clouds and thunder rolled in from over the hills and it was as though the air itself had turned to water. They willed the storm to bring them release.

Her mother had declared that Concetta and her sisters would stay in the *pagliaro* that night while she returned home with their father and Tino, who had spent many nights in the field and needed a proper rest. Immacolata had protested because, when it rained, water leaked through the roof of the hut, but their mother had considered the sky and shaken her head. 'Don't count on rain,' she said.

Immacolata looked at the lowering sky in amazement. 'How can you say that?'

'It's a false promise,' her mother said.

The thunder rumbled on and, beyond the hills, the storms flashed and cracked, and then, as their mother had predicted, they drifted away, the noise and the light fading and the heat returning even heavier than before. Everywhere now there was the sweet and insinuating smell of decomposition: stored meat and fish on the turn, sick and dying animals, the build-up of gases from the *mufita* hanging in the air and festering.

Concetta and Immacolata, out in the field together, began to argue about which of them had done a particular row of potatoes and they bickered for a while until their mother stepped in. She pointed out a different row to Concetta, a shorter one. 'You were over there.'

Concetta glowered. She was ready to pick a fight even with her mother. 'I don't want to stay out here tonight.'

'Your sisters will be here,' she said.

'I don't care.'

'She's been like this all week,' their mother said to Tino. She shook her head. 'If it's not one of them moaning, it's another.'

Concetta felt something boiling up inside her at that and she looked away at the clouds that had retreated to beyond the line of the hills and tried to calm herself. She still felt the burn of shame at being caught at the cemetery gates, but she felt it less hotly now. She hadn't seen Peppe or Francesco since that night and she wondered about Peppe and what he was doing and whether he thought of her any more. She thought now that perhaps she had been too harsh towards him. After all, she had chosen to accompany him into the woods. He hadn't forced her. She sighed and turned to the ground again, back to the potatoes.

Later that evening, after her mother and father had left, Tino sat with them for a while by the *pagliaro* while they ate a frugal supper of fried peppers and potato under the dark branches of the fruit trees.

'All right?' Tino turned to Concetta when she'd finished eating.

She shrugged.

'What's wrong?' Tino asked.

'Just the heat,' she said.

'It's getting all of us down,' said Immacolata.

'It will break soon,' said Nunzia. 'It has to.'

Concetta turned to Tino. 'Are you going back?'

'The river first, if it's not dried up,' he said, nodding behind him in its direction. 'See what I can catch.' He considered Concetta for a few moments. 'I won't if you don't want me to.'

'No,' she said, shaking her head. 'You go. We need all the food we can get.'

When they slept out in the *pagliaro* they went to bed earlier than if they were in the village. It seemed to grow dark a lot quicker out here and their mother said there was no use wasting candles. They threw a blanket onto the floor, over the rushes, and bedded down for the night. Concetta knew that sleep wouldn't come to her easily and so she lay there listening to the sounds of the birds as they swooped and cried before quietening and the more distant animal calls from the forest and the river. She hoped sleep would steal upon her, as it often did. She heard her sisters' breathing deepen and then Tino, who'd been sitting outside, put his head around the door. After a while, he whispered, 'Concetta?'

She squeezed her eyes shut. She felt foolish for trying to stop him going fishing, so she stayed silent and, after another long moment, he backed out of the hut and she heard his boots walking away on the dry grass.

She tried not to toss so as not to wake her sisters, but she was aware of how uncomfortable the floor was and the more she thought about it, the more she felt she could never relax enough to sleep. It irked her that her sisters had fallen asleep so quickly. She wanted to speak to someone. The need became more pressing, so that she very nearly put a hand to Nunzia to shake her awake and let everything that had happened with Peppe spill out of her. She knew how shocked her sister would be and that stilled her hand. She couldn't stop turning around on the bumpy floor and it became stuffy in the hut and the smell of earth was overwhelming.

She sat up and sighed and told herself that it was only sleep and what did it matter if she missed a night, she'd done it before. She couldn't lie down any more, though, so she rose and, since she was still in her underthings, she slipped on her dress and stepped out of the hut. It was a little less dark outside, and the cicadas sounded gratingly loud and close, which she supposed they were. She felt restless and couldn't keep still in one place, so she paced about a bit by the *pagliaro* but there wasn't much space and she couldn't walk over the tilled soil itself, so she turned around and took the path that led from their field out towards the forest and the river.

She thought she would just walk along it for a few minutes to stretch her legs and then turn back, but she found herself walking on further and there was the lightest of breezes, just the same as the night with Peppe, and the air was so much more pleasant out here than inside the hut.

She could hear the gurgling of the river and she knew that up ahead there was a series of stepping-stones where the water was at its shallowest and, beyond that, an outcrop of forest that came right up to the water's edge. She reached the stones and the river was so dry that there was only a brown trickle that flowed onwards to the deeper waters further along. She hesitated because she knew she should turn back now, she'd already come too far, but the stones were so easy to make out in the dark and were dry, not slippy with moss, and she couldn't help but to jump from one to another. She hadn't even needed to take her boots off.

On the other bank, the forest began. She decided not to plunge into it, but to stay close to the river and to follow it round. She reasoned that this way she would not get lost. She had only walked a short while when she heard voices close by. She stopped and listened. Her heart was like a drum in her ears. All of her senses were attuned to try to understand where the voices were coming from. She realized that the men were probably only a few feet away, just around the bend of the river. She closed her eyes and felt the wind moving her and she heard the voices again and recognized first Peppe and then Francesco. She backed away then, her heart thumping, and realizing that she was exposed on the banks of the river, she turned on her heels and went into the forest. She walked on and tried to remember which trees she had passed and how many, but she knew as she was walking that she was losing count, and being lost felt like an inevitability.

Concetta walked until she was exhausted and, seeing a small clearing, she turned into it and sank down to the ground. She wanted to weep, but she didn't have the energy and so she crouched there like a wild creature, her eyes and ears alert and searching. She lost all notion of time, of how much had passed, and of what was left until daybreak. She closed her eyes, but fearful thoughts came to her, of restless spirits like the one that had followed Peppe's father, and the one that her mother had seen in the branches of the tree. The moon was full and she knew this meant that *li lupi pampanari*, werewolves, would be about, and witches too.

She stayed close to the ground; the smell of the earth and pine leaves was intense and familiar and gave her some comfort. Soft noises came from all parts of the forest and she concentrated on each one to identify what it might be. She heard the branches of the oak tree behind her creaking in the wind, and there was a rustling noise of some small creature scampering over the undergrowth close by. The cicadas were singing here, too, although not as loudly as by the *pagliaro*.

After a time, she heard another noise from a distance, footsteps, approaching. She felt so scared that she could hardly lift herself off the ground, her legs were shaking, and she started to moan to herself under her breath. She calmed herself down and concentrated on where the footsteps were coming from, then when she was sure they would pass close to her, she hid herself behind the oak tree and prayed that whoever it was would not hear her breathing.

The person was getting close, heavy boots crunching along the path just by the clearing, and still she dared not move in case she was heard. Once she knew the person had passed, had his back to her, curiosity overcame her and she couldn't help wondering then if it were man or spirit. She inched around the oak tree and saw that it was a man and that he had stopped to tie his bootlace. Something about the shape of his head seemed familiar to her and she moved away from the tree towards him. She must have made a noise because he shot up and turned, his hand on his gun, and there was shock in his eyes when he recognized her. 'Concetta? What in hell's name are you doing here?'

'Pasquale.' It was her cousin. 'Pasquale, I'm so glad it's you. I'm so frightened.' She started crying with relief, unable to control herself.

'What are you saying? Calm down.'

She took hold of his shirtsleeve and spoke through her tears. 'I got lost. I was in the *pagliaro*. I couldn't sleep and

I went for a little walk and then I crossed the river and I heard voices so I came into the forest and I didn't think I'd ever find my way out again. I was so frightened. Thank God I found you. Thank God.'

Pasquale took a dirty handkerchief out of his pocket and handed it to her and she blew her nose. 'Don't worry. You're all right now. That was a silly thing to do. Wasn't your brother with you in the *pagliaro*?'

'He went to the river and then back home to the village.'

Pasquale considered this for a moment. 'I'll take you back, but I don't want to be seen taking you. We have to be careful.'

Concetta dabbed at her eyes. 'But you're my cousin. They wouldn't say anything, would they?'

'Your brother might.' Pasquale shook his head. 'He's protective of you girls. He would jump to the wrong conclusion.'

'I'd tell him you helped me.' She felt a prickling of anxiety. 'You're not going to leave me here, are you? At least take me back to the river.'

'Of course I'll take you. Just don't say you saw me.'

'I won't tell anyone.'

'Good girl. Right. Let's go then.'

Concetta felt then a little afraid of her cousin. He was close to her brother in age and they had grown up together although in later years they'd drifted apart. Concetta had always thought that it was because Tino was so solitary, but now it occurred to her that they were very different. Pasquale was bigger and broader than her brother. He had a mass of dark curly hair and often grew a beard. He was closer to her father and her uncle, Pasquale's father, in that he liked sometimes to drink and play cards, and he had a loud cheerful clap of a voice that, as a child, she had adored. She hadn't seen him for a few months before tonight, and it occurred to her, walking beside him now, with her nerves fraught, she felt differently towards him than she had as a child.

They took a winding path, not the one that Concetta had taken into the forest. They seemed to walk for miles. The fatigue she had felt earlier returned, but she dared not ask him to stop for fear of him abandoning her. After some time, she heard the rush of water that indicated the river was near, and she put a hand to Pasquale, and smiled. 'This is where I came from.'

Pasquale shook his head. 'It's a different part of the river. Further downstream. Be careful here because there are a lot of men out fishing tonight.' He put a finger to his lips and she nodded and stayed quiet.

They walked on and skirted the river for a while. She wanted to ask him if they were getting closer to the part with the stepping-stones but she was mindful of not speaking out loud, and he was intent on the journey. She'd remembered him as talkative so she thought he must be like this, moody, because of her. She'd put him in an awkward position.

They reached a small wooden shack and Pasquale stopped here. She understood that the hut belonged to him, that he'd constructed it and that he slept out here in the summer months. She could still hear the silvery sound of flowing water and realized that the shack was well hidden, but still close to the river for fishing at night. Inside there was just enough room for one person and she could see that it was lined with rabbit hides, but it was really a rough place, a place for a wild man.

'We'd better stay here for a bit,' he said, entering the hut.

Concetta felt the tears again and pushed them away. She couldn't believe he wasn't taking her straight back. 'Can't we go back now? I'm really tired.'

'It's too risky. Anyway, if you hadn't gone wandering around on your own, you wouldn't be here now, would you?'

Concetta bit her lip and remained standing just outside.

'Come in and sit down, for God's sake. We'll have to stay here for a while. There are too many people by the river.'

She sat down on the floor where she was, and Pasquale looked over at her and shrugged. 'Up to you, but it's much more comfortable in here.' He patted a small place beside him on the skins. She shook her head and looked away.

'If you want to go home, I'll take you.' His voice had changed. It was more cheerful, more as she remembered it.

'I do.'

'Only if you do something for me.'

Concetta waited a moment before responding. 'What?'

'Come here and I'll show you.'

She didn't move.

'Come on. Then I'll take you straight home.'

She pushed up from the ground and walked over to the shack.

'Sit down.'

She let herself drop to the ground.

'Now smile, for God's sake. Take that sour look off your face.' Before she had time to react, his hands were on her mouth, pulling it. 'Smile.' His fingers were like pincers. She grimaced. 'That will do.'

She knew she should rise as fast as she could and run, but her legs felt heavy as stone and she couldn't move them and instead she began to plead with him. 'Please,' she said.

'Please what?' He had moved his hand to her wrist.

'Let me go on my way. You don't need to take me back any more.'

He sighed and turned away from her. 'You're like your brother. Never need anything from anyone. But I've done you a favour. I've brought you here, close to the river again.' He looked at her expectantly.

'Thank you,' she said.

'No one does anything for nothing in this world. Family is family, but there's still what's owing. Do you understand me?'

She nodded.

'It's not the first time you've been out when you shouldn't. There have been other times, other men.'

She shook her head.

'I saw you a few weeks ago with young Peppe Di Rienzo late at night. You were on the edge of the forest and you'd stopped because you heard something. You thought it was an evil spirit but it wasn't. It was me, close by, watching.'

'It's not what you think.'

'I saw you the other time too,' he paused and studied her face more intently then, 'kissing him by the tree. Your family would be ashamed if they knew. A cousin of mine. It brings shame on me, too.'

She put her head in her hands and began to sob. After a moment, she felt him tug at her hand, but she resisted and the pressure became stronger so that he peeled her hand away from her face and guided it towards him. With the other hand, he unbuttoned his trousers and she watched in horror as he pushed her hand down there and she felt something soft which seemed to grow, getting harder. He began to breathe as though with difficulty and then he took hold of her face again and smiled up at her. 'I promise I'll take you back, and we won't speak about what happened with Peppe.'

She had her eyes on his face, which was contorted between a smile and something like pain, and she pulled away from him and got up and as she was about to turn to run, she was knocked to the ground and then she felt his full weight on top of her, pressing into her. He was grinning now, and Concetta remembered how he and Tino would wrestle in sport when they were boys, and it looked like that was what they were doing now, except that his hand was pulling at her underthings and his nails were sharp, scratching at her skin.

He was breathing heavily now and pushing against her, grinding into her, and he finished off undoing his trousers and the ground felt rough against the back of her legs, grazing her, and then she felt something hard up against her intimate place, and she couldn't breathe any more but only watch his face in amazement. He caught her face with a hand again and looked into her eyes a moment and then pushed and there was brief pain as something resisted and she felt stupefied and lay there like a block. After a while she realized he was rocking up and down and grunting and saying words which were disgusting to her, part tender, part blasphemous, and all she could think of was would there be an end to this night.

Some time later, he groaned and stopped as though he were deadly tired of it all and he lay on top of her and it was agony. She tried to close her eyes and pretend that she was lying in her own bed. There was a slippery sensation of the thing that he'd put into her coming out, then he sighed and sat up and didn't look at her in the face, but busied himself putting his clothes in order. Once he'd got off her, she pulled her clothes down with difficulty, because there was pain, and she got up off the ground. She felt fluid, blood she thought, running down her leg.

'I'm going now,' she said without looking at him, and she began walking away.

'Wait. I'll take you.' He slung his gun over his shoulder and ran up alongside her. 'I said I would.'

They walked on towards the river and it occurred to Concetta that she didn't care if anyone saw her now. She only wanted to get back and to drop down by her sisters and sleep. She'd never been more weary. Tomorrow she'd wake and she would go back to work in the fields. There were still the potatoes to pull up.

'I won't mention you and Peppe Di Rienzo and you won't mention this.' He sounded less certain of her now, though.

She didn't reply or turn to look at him, but she could see out of the corner of her eye that his hand was coming up to reach for her and she sprinted forward at a speed she didn't know she was capable of and she made good distance from him. She ran off the path and into the thick of the forest, dodging the trees, zigzagging between them, and she could feel the tears slipping down her cheeks, and she could hear him gaining on her, now that he'd had time to make up for the unexpectedness of her flight. Then, out of nowhere, she heard another voice calling her name. Tino. She stopped and turned and he was standing there, surprise in his face and anger too. She called his name and he walked towards her and took a hold of her wrist. He looked round and listened.

'Who's there?' he asked, and she said nothing.

She could feel Tino's anger growing as he led her out of the forest and back across the river. He pushed her through the door of the *pagliaro* and went back out again and she sank down to the floor in the space between her sisters and she slept.

Signora Clara moved away from the pen and glanced over at the house. Concetta could see that she had finished now and would be coming back in. Francesco sighed and took his hand away and Concetta felt its absence.

Signora Clara opened the door wide and put her head in warily. She pulled off her boots, put her house shoes on and looked at Concetta and her son in turn.

'I brought you some beans,' said Concetta. 'Felice picked them. I would have picked them myself, but I'm not able to go back to work yet.'

Signora Clara glanced over at the beans and nodded her thanks.

Concetta moved towards the door. 'I'll be going now. I have another errand to run before I go home.'

Francesco walked her out to the path. 'Take care of yourself,' he said, and touched her shoulder again with his hand.

She nodded and then started away. She walked on until she reached the cemetery, then she went past the open gates and the carved gravestones at the front and past the mausoleum until she reached the masses of wooden crosses. She searched out the one Francesco and his mother had erected for Peppe, his name scratched onto the smooth side of a piece of dry bark, a single nail pinning it to a piece of wood planted in the ground. She stood by it for a while and thought how sad it was to be standing at a grave without a body.

After some moments, she moved off towards the back of the cemetery where there was a piece of wasteland with no markings on it of any description. This was unconsecrated ground for those that had never been baptized, and here again Concetta stopped and stood for a while.

19

O nce the *feste* of sant'Antonio and san Giovanni Battista had come and gone, when the days were at their longest, the people prepared for *la metetura,* the harvesting of the wheat. All year they had been nurturing the grain: the sowing of the seed at the beginning of winter, the turning of the soil and the frequent removing of the weeds so as to keep the young plants from being strangled. Now that the wheat had grown to head height, its ears rippling back and forth in the evening breeze, the time had come to cut it and thresh it and store it away, and then mill it into flour for bread.

Concetta felt strong enough to join Felice and the others for the cutting of the wheat. Felice hadn't wanted her to, he said she wasn't well enough yet to be out in the fields all day under a hot sun, and Franchina had agreed and told her to help out at the house instead where Giovanni would be preparing the grain to be milled. Concetta felt, though, that the time had come to return to her husband's side and she promised him that she wouldn't push herself too hard. She wouldn't try to make up for lost time.

The day was hot, but there was a breeze stiff enough to

push the ears of wheat this way and that. Perfect weather, they said, as *la metetura* needed the heat to keep the cut wheat dry and, later, the wind to separate the wheat from the chaff. Once Concetta and Felice got to the fields, they were greeted by his brothers and Nunzia came over to kiss Concetta on the cheek and to bring her over to that part of the field where she and Paolo were working. Concetta took hold of the sickle that Nunzia handed her and together they began scything at the wheat, sweeping at it from the waist and binding handfuls of it together with straw.

After some time, Concetta stopped, took a handkerchief from her waistband and wiped her brow. She shielded her eyes from the sun and looked over at Nunzia. 'Nothing like it was last year, thank God.'

Nunzia took a moment to understand. 'Ah, the heat,' she said, nodding and looking thoughtful. 'We said it was earthquake weather and so it was.'

'Everything feels different this year,' said Concetta. 'As it should be.'

Just then, as though Nunzia had called his name, Paolo lifted his head and smiled and Nunzia smiled back. She bent down to bring a handful of wheat towards her and then stood back up as though she'd just thought of something. 'You remember?'

Concetta nodded. 'The sun that came too close. How old Paolo's dog died in the midday sun. How someone hid sant'Emidio and then we had the earthquake.'

'We knew the earthquake would come one day,' said Nunzia gently, 'and we know it will again.'

'Yes, but not for a long time yet. Once in a lifetime, maybe twice.'

Nunzia eyes rested on Concetta's belly. She opened her mouth as if to ask something and then, thinking better of it, she turned away.

Concetta put a hand to her belly. It felt hollow.

It took them a week to cut down the wheat. They tied it up in loose bundles and wove these together to form a more solid whole. The constructions they made grew as tall and intricate as houses. They left the rest of the wheat stalk uncut; these would be cropped later and burned. In the meantime, they prayed as they did every year that there would be no rain in this period and they gave sloping roofs to their towers of wheat so that any rain would run off the sides and not penetrate within.

Once the wheat was dry enough, they pulled it down and took it to the threshing floor by the flour mill, a wide, smooth area that had been cleared of stones and grasses. Giovanni Totila hitched two oxen up to a rounded stone as wide and heavy as a tree, which needed six men to carry from the barn to the threshing floor. It was a hard brown sandstone, durable enough to serve this generation and the next, and it had been quarried on the banks of a river several days' walk away. Giovanni and his sons took turns to walk the oxen round and over the wheat to batten it down and separate it out from the chaff. The others, including Concetta, came in later and, with pitchforks, they threw the mix up into the air and left the chaff to blow away in the wind, as it was lighter than the wheat and of no use for anything.

The tramping of the wheat and the winnowing, the separation of the wheat from the chaff, was a long job even with a dry, strong wind behind them. The grain was plentiful, enough to give them bread for a year. Once Giovanni had prepared his own grain, his floor and mill were used by others in the village. Everyone pitched in to help and so the harvesting of the wheat stretched out for many days and sometimes weeks.

They ground some of the grain into flour and the rest they kept in cloth sacks to mill during the year when it was needed. Half of the grain, though, would have to be taken to *lu conte*, the count, in lieu of payment as the land they worked belonged to him. The men travelled in a group to Villamagna, the count's residence, half a day's walk away, with some of the sacks loaded onto donkeys and the rest carried on their backs.

Each family was to hand over *lu mezzetto*, half of what they made. Concetta's father, with only a small family to support and a few strips of land to work, set aside four capons at Christmas, thirty eggs at Easter, half of the grain and pressed olive oil and most of his wine. There was more owed besides: basketfuls of chestnuts and spinach and winter salad, the rump of the pig, a sackful of potatoes, another of sweetcorn, bowls of broad beans and spring onions and tomatoes, and as many armfuls of fruit as could be carried. *Lu conte* had taken pity on them the year before because of the earthquake and the heat. *Lu mezzetto* had been waived for half a year, but would have to be made up over the years to come and, as her father said, they would forever be in debt to *lu conte*.

On the day the men were due to set out for Villamagna, very early in the morning, when people were still in bed, the earth shifted itself. Concetta had woken and for a moment she was unsure whether the movement was real or dreamed and then, as if from a great distance, she heard a deep boom rumble briefly to silence. In its wake, she heard the flapping of wings in nearby trees and, much further away, the ululating howls and hootings of distressed animals. She glanced down and saw that Felice had his eyes open. He reached up to her elbow and squeezed it and they waited in the darkness to see if there would be more to come. She knew that they should get up and run outside to be safe, away from the house with its walls and heavy masonry, and far away from the trees, which could uproot and topple over.

'All right?' asked Felice. His fingers were still at her elbow. 'You're not afraid?'

She shook her head. She felt no fear any more.

'There's still a few hours before dawn.' Felice opened his arm out for her and she turned to put her hand to his cheek first and then sank down close to him. They lay there in silence for what seemed like a long time and outside the animals in the forest grew silent again and there was just the single plaintive call of a bird near by. She knew that Felice was waiting for her to make a sign that she was ready. Her hand went to her belly. It didn't feel empty any more. It was like there was something hard and sharp inside, and she turned her face away from her husband and closed her eyes.

Later that morning, after Felice had set off to join his father and brothers for the trip to Villamagna, Concetta stayed on at the house to clean out the animal pen and to tidy up the room. She used the leftover water from the pail that she and Felice had washed themselves with and got down onto her hands and knees and scrubbed the floor. The brush was an old one of Franchina's; its bristles had become soft with use and there was too much give in them, and she had to pick at some of the more ingrained dirt with her nails.

It was another hot day although the wind, which had turned earlier, had since grown still. She could sniff the *mufita* in the air and she knew it would hang there until the wind changed again and no amount of scrubbing would rid her of it.

It was while she was sitting back onto her heels to dip the brush into the water again that she heard a noise outside, a twig snapping underfoot. She stilled to listen closer and cocked her ear. She had her back to the door, which was ajar, so that anyone outside might see her before she would be able to turn round to see them. When there was no further sound, she got to her feet and dropped the brush into the water where it made a quiet plop.

There was no further movement or sound, but she felt herself gathering her strength. She was alone and there was no one in earshot to shout for help but she felt calm. It was as if she had been waiting for this moment ever since the birth, since the remembering, and perhaps long before that.

She wiped her hands down on her apron and turned to face the door. Everything remained silent outside and, for a moment, she wavered and wondered if she had imagined the presence, but she knew he was there, waiting for her. He had bided his time, but so had she.

She walked over to the wall and unhooked Felice's rifle and powder bag from where they hung. She glanced up at the door, imagining a shadow falling across it, but the light remained steady and she cast her eyes back down to the rifle. She remembered how Peppe had taught her to fill the muzzle and where to place the bullet and she did this now, even though this was a different gun to Peppe's, a newer one with a plain wooden handle. It felt light in her hands and she would have preferred the sheer antique bulk of the other, but she steered the muzzle towards the door and took a step forward.

It was so quiet both inside and out that she feared again that there was no one there and that the presence was all in her mind. She wondered if the force of her will to have this moment had led her to imagine things, but then she heard it again. A snap. This time, though, it was a small stone dislodging, scraping against the metal hobnail of a boot. She expelled a deep breath and moved out of the cottage. Outside, she looked right and left and then she caught a movement just up ahead out of the corner of her eye and she raised the barrel of the gun towards it.

'Come out,' she called.

From just beyond the animal pen, Pasquale stepped out, holding a cockerel in his hands. It strained to open its wings and, unable to, gave off a low gurgling sound from its throat. 'It's a good one,' said Pasquale, laughing. 'He's got some fight in him.' But then he held it still, close to his body, and looked back up at Concetta. He nodded at the rifle. 'There's no need for that, is there?'

'Let the bird go,' she said. Her voice was toneless, not her own, and she could see that it had affected Pasquale, too. He looked down at the bird, shrugged and let it drop and the cockerel cawed loudly and deeply and stalked away in a flurry of feathers.

'There,' he said softly. 'See. You got your bird back.'

Concetta moved forward a few steps, keeping the barrel held high against her arm. Even though it was light she could feel the pull of it and how already her muscles were tense and aching from carrying it. She looked Pasquale up and down and noted his tattered clothing and his whiskery beard grown more through slovenliness than intention. She could see, even from here, the dirt deep in his fingernails and she remembered the smell of him, a pungent smell of an animal bedded down in its lair. She felt sick. She had willed this moment to come and she was overwhelmed now by this feeling of sickness that came from the hard, sharp thing inside her. She wanted more than anything to rid herself of it.

Pasquale looked away from the barrel of the gun, out towards the forest. He sniffed the air as though catching a scent of something and Concetta thought to herself that he really was like a feral beast, a fox or a wolf, that finding itself at bay would never look you straight in the eyes.

After a long time, he turned to face her. 'You remember now.' He nodded slowly. 'That's good.'

She lifted the muzzle and looked into his eyes. 'You deserve to die. You were like my own brother.'

He shook his head and gave a sad smile. 'No,' he said. 'Never a brother. I was never that.' He took a step forward. 'We had a promise. You keep quiet and so will I. Remember that I saw you and that boy together.'

'Peppe's dead.'

'Yes,' he said, with meaning. 'I know.' He looked down the barrel of the gun pointing at him and then back up to her.

Concetta felt her grip slacken. 'What do you know? He died in the earthquake.'

He shook his head. 'It was before.' He looked briefly away again towards the forest. 'Before the earthquake. He came for me that morning, just after dawn.'

Concetta put a hand to her head and let the muzzle of the gun droop. 'He went to find you.' She hadn't thought of that. She hadn't imagined that Peppe would seek revenge. He had been distant with her when she'd finally told him, angry with her it seemed, and she had never thought he would act on it.

Pasquale looked back towards the forest. 'He was like a crazy man. I couldn't stop him. He jumped me and had his hands on my neck. I fought back. What else could I do? It happened in a moment. No time at all. He went out fast, like a candle.' He kept his eyes on a dark dome of trees in the distance.

'Where is he?' Concetta's voice was hard.

'I buried him there and then, close to where we were. I was afraid someone would find him.' He hesitated. 'It's just behind my hut. I marked the place with a cross.' He cleared his throat. 'I didn't mean to do it. I had no quarrel with him.'

Concetta sank down to the ground and rested the rifle beside her. She felt slack as though she'd been emptied out. 'What do you want of me?'

Pasquale shook his head. 'I don't know.' He put his hands to his face and rubbed his eyes. He took a few paces forward and stopped. 'I want you to come and take him away.'

She covered her eyes against the sun and looked back up at him. 'What's to stop me telling Francesco, his mother, everyone?'

Pasquale glanced down at the rifle. Its butt end was lying close to him. He only needed to lean forward to pick it up. 'We're family. Blood ties. Shame on me will be shame on you and your family, and your children.'

Concetta felt the hard knot in her stomach again. She thought of the children to come, the ones she hoped she and Felice would have, but she wanted more than anything what was owed to her. She wouldn't speak of this, just as he'd known she wouldn't talk about that night in the forest. She lunged forward, picked up the rifle and drew herself up tall. She searched out his eyes and, understanding her intention, he dropped his hands to his sides. She looked at him down the barrel. 'Tied by blood,' she repeated, and inched her finger forward until she found the trigger. Pasquale seemed to be hesitating, not sure whether to run at her or stand his ground and then, before she knew it, she was pressing down, just like Peppe had shown her, and she felt the gun stutter in her hand and recoil. A short crack of noise followed and then a fainter echo in the hills.

Pasquale stared at her stupidly, as though he couldn't quite believe she'd done it. After a few moments, he glanced down to check himself and, in doing so, staggered and fell to the ground. He rubbed his arms and legs to check he hadn't been hit and, realizing that he hadn't, he looked back up at her and frowned, not understanding.

'Go away from here,' she said. 'Far enough away that nobody knows you.' She turned round and walked back into the house. She closed the door and stood with her back to it for a few moments until her breathing became steady. Then she went to the window, keeping just clear of it so he couldn't see her from where he was, and she kept her eyes trained on him until he moved away. He walked back towards the forest, from where he had come.

20

After Concetta had been pushed into the *pagliaro* by Tino, she slept a heavy sleep. The next morning, her sisters had to shake her hard to wake her and even then she had not wanted to get up and stayed where she was for a while without moving. Nunzia blamed the weather again and Concetta nodded in a tired way at her sister's plea to the skies for rain. Water, she thought, might wash the night away.

Over the next few weeks, with no break in the weather, their father had the girls work on the fruit trees on the edge of their strip of land. Concetta could see along the lines of trees that the fruit was withered and dry and that those that were gathered would be bitter to the taste and only good for the pigs. Immacolata and Nunzia pressed on into the orchard, though, and began to pull at the fruit from low and overhanging branches and so Concetta trailed after them and did the same.

One morning, several weeks after that night in the forest, they returned to the orchard earlier than usual. Dawn had not long broken, although the day was already hot and there was a stifling quality to the air as mistiness, distant rainfall, spread across the skyline. Nunzia glanced up overhead through the branches, but even she was weary now of asking for rain. The girls worked mutely and were glad at least of the shade from the trees, as the rising sun was already fierce.

Before midday, to allow the time it took for them to walk back to the village, their father gave a piercing whistle from the field. The girls stopped working and gathered what fruit they had into their aprons and walked it back to the field to tip into baskets. Their mother went to get the donkey, which stood panting in the shade under a nearby oak tree, and they loaded the baskets up onto its back and, in a single line, they trudged along the path that edged the field and through the lanes that brought them back up to the village.

Nunzia and Immacolata started up again about the heat and the oppressive force of it, but talking soon sucked the energy out of them and they fell silent. Concetta was tired, her legs were heavy and the boots felt like lead weights on her feet. She stopped a moment to get her breath back and hitched her skirts up a little to let the air in. She saw the dried blood of a graze down one of her calves and dropped the skirt again so no one would see. The others, though, were further ahead. They were walking slowly, but Concetta dropped further back and even her mother didn't have the heart to turn to call for her. She stumbled along and was glad of the time alone.

By the time she got to the part of the road where the fallen tree lay, the rest of her family were far ahead. Nunzia had stopped and called a few times, but her voice had sounded feeble in the distance and Concetta had waved her to go on. As she passed the tree stump, she noticed a flutter of colour. She stopped and walked towards the tree and found a small blue handkerchief tied to one of the branches. She untied it. A circle with a cross inside had been scrawled on it in charcoal and she immediately thought of the target carved on the tree and knew that Peppe had left it for her. She pushed the handkerchief down the front of her dress and walked on more quickly, now thinking that she might catch the others.

She knew it was a sign from Peppe that he would be waiting for her that night outside the house and she felt a small leap of gladness. She put a hand to her breast where the cloth lay. Being away from him, being forced to stay away, had stifled something vital inside her. But now things had changed; a terrible thing had happened. It was something that must never be spoken about, something that she must forget.

Despite the heat, she broke into a run and the damp trickling down her face and under her arms and between her legs made her run all the faster.

That night, Concetta and her sisters slept at the house. Concetta had known they would be able to sleep in the village as they had been out at the *pagliaro* the night before and the girls complained about being there two nights in a row.

As soon as her sisters had climbed into bed, dog-tired, she heard their steady breathing and she lay still on her back for a few moments before gathering herself and carefully moving across Nunzia to get off the bed. She heard a spring decompress and she stilled. Immacolata muttered in her sleep and turned into the empty space that had been left. Concetta picked up her clothes and padded into the other room so as not to wake them while she dressed. She walked out into the yard and stood by the tree where Peppe had emerged the time before, and she waited.

She glanced up at the moon; it was just a sliver and it gave off a wan light, as there was humidity in the air and, now and then, wisps of clouds trailed across it. She heard a horse from a neighbouring stall whinny and she crouched down low against the tree so as to be sure of being in shadow. She heard a light step, a boot tapping its approach, and she took the blue handkerchief from her breast and waved it at Peppe so he could see her.

He was surprised to see her waiting and, when he opened his mouth to speak, she laid a finger to his lips and he nodded. She indicated with her head that they should walk on and she took his hand and led the way.

She hadn't really known where to go or what she wanted to say to Peppe. She knew only that she had wanted to see him, that she wouldn't be denied that, and that even this simple thing would make her feel better. It was as though her whole life had turned on its axis and that the only thing she could cling to, the only thing worth holding on to, was Peppe and this time they had together.

They walked silently down several side streets, but there were windows open to let the night air in and they could hear the soft moans of people as they slept. Concetta had walked without really having a clear idea of direction. She wouldn't go as far as the forest, she knew she couldn't do that again, but it was dangerous to stay in the village. She stopped a moment and tried to think where to go.

Peppe frowned. He had been expecting to go to the forest again.

'No,' said Concetta. 'It's too far.'

She thought of the deconsecrated church of Santo Stefano, which was just to the right of them in a small *piazza*, but then she thought it would be worse if they were caught together in a church. Then she remembered the underground passage that Francesco had shown her. They traced their steps back towards Concetta's house and Peppe pulled the grate up from the ground.

'How do you know about this place?' he asked.

'Francesco. That time he brought me back.'

Peppe raised his eyebrows. 'He must trust you.'

They dropped down through the hole and walked some way in darkness down the narrow passageway until they came to the part where the space widened into a small room. Peppe scraped a match against the wall and it flared briefly, bringing some of the strange etchings on the wall into sharp relief. He lit a taper he had brought and used some of the dripping wax to set it on the floor and Concetta found the bench carved out of the wall and they sat back onto it together.

They stayed in silence for a long time and Concetta thought to herself that she would be happy if she never had to speak again because there were so many things that were best left unsaid and to say them would make them real again and this was something she did not want. They were far below street level here, deep enough for the quiet and the coolness to wash over her, and she thought to herself that peace was mostly something you noticed when it was absent.

It was Peppe who spoke first. 'He's gone.'

Concetta turned, not understanding.

'Francesco. He left a week ago. Some men in San Michele said they'd take him with them to find work. But it's far away, many days on the sea to get there.'

She thought of the distance to San Michele, a place that seemed far to her, and the hills and mountains beyond that. But this was a place further away, much further. Some men never came home and some were never heard of again, no message through those returning, no money or gifts. People spoke of a lifetime's money to be made in just a few years of labouring, and what was hard work to men such as them who had worked all their lives? 'How long will he be gone?'

'A year. Less maybe. Time to earn us enough to get some land of our own and build a bigger house.' He glanced shyly round at Concetta. 'We will need the space for our families and room for poor *Mamma*, too, of course.'

Concetta looked down at her hands. 'I didn't think you'd come out again like this. After last time.'

'We were reckless.'

'And now?'

She could hear the smile in his voice even without turning towards him. 'Even more reckless.' Then she could sense the smile fading. 'Francesco was right, though. I don't think before I act. I should know that these things would hurt you far more than me.' Concetta felt him reach for her hand. 'We can't meet like this any more. It's too dangerous.'

Concetta nodded. 'Yes,' she said. 'I know.'

'This must be our last time together.'

She nodded and felt a tear slip down her cheek. She put a hand out to stop it in its tracks and turned to stare down the dark passageway so that he wouldn't see her crying.

'In a year or two, once your sisters are married . . .' His voice trailed off.

'Yes,' said Concetta. She thought how much had happened in a few weeks and how much more could happen in a year or two.

They lapsed into silence again and when the candle went out Peppe didn't light another immediately. Concetta wiped her tears away with the back of her hand and sniffed. 'We'd better go back now.'

Peppe turned to her. 'It's hard on me, too. I want to be with you but' – he hesitated – 'it's not fair on you.'

'No.'

'Once your reputation is gone, you can't get it back.'

Concetta swallowed. 'I would be ruined.'

'Yes.' Peppe nodded and felt for her hand again. 'I don't want you to suffer.'

'You'd give me up, though.'

'I'd do it for you. Not me. I don't care about me. I don't care what people think.'

'What if I don't care?'

'I wouldn't believe you. Anyway, it's not the same for you. You'd suffer afterwards and you would care. Your family would care.'

Concetta turned to look at him. His hair was getting long. She put a hand out to push a lock of it back, to stop it falling into his eyes. His ear, when she brushed against it, felt oddly warm and smooth in the cool air. She remembered the spirit then that had reached out to touch his father's ear, and she felt a quiver of fear run through her as it had when Peppe had told her the story in the forest.

'I'd wait for you.' He spoke hesitantly, as if not sure of himself. 'I'd wait as long as it took.'

Concetta's hand fell away.

Peppe shook his head 'You don't believe me?'

Concetta shrugged. 'You mean it now, but who knows in a year from now or longer. So much can happen.' She sighed. 'So much already has.'

'I mean it.'

Concetta watched him for a few moments and she thought that there was no one in the world now whom she trusted more, not her sisters, or Tino or her mother. She reached for his hand and drew her skirts up to her knees and brushed his fingers along the damaged skin on her calf.

'You're hurt?'

'Yes.'

Peppe rubbed it with his hand and smiled up at her. 'Is that better?'

'It's my ruin.'

She could see Peppe frowning to understand and he took his hand away and reached inside his pocket for a match and relit the candle. The flame leaped against the wall and then steadied.

'It's just a scratch.' Peppe blinked at her uncomprehendingly.

'A few weeks ago I slept out in the *pagliaro*. I was with my sisters.' She swallowed, wondering whether she should go on. 'And I fell. It is just a scratch. Nothing.'

She reached to pull her skirts down, but Peppe put his hand over hers. 'Tell me.'

Concetta turned to face him. 'If I do, I'm ruined.'

His hand gripped hers and he pulled her upright.

She looked down at the candle on the floor. It flickered only a little now and had grown mostly calm.

'I couldn't sleep. I left the *pagliaro* and went into the forest. I tried to keep to the river, but I lost my way.' She stopped, still unsure whether she should make it real again by saying the words. 'I turned into the forest, but I was lost by then. I was frightened. I imagined so many things, spirits and bandits and wild animals, and I couldn't think properly.'

'What happened?' Peppe's voice was quieter now. It was as though he had already guessed what she would say.

'I heard someone and I hid but when I saw who it was I went to him.' She turned to face Peppe. 'It was my cousin. It was Pasquale.'

Peppe looked away towards the gloom of the passageway.

She couldn't say the words of what had been done. It seemed as though to speak of it would be to create a monstrous thing in her mind, something real and, if it were not for the graze, she might have persuaded herself that it wasn't real. 'So I'm no good now, for anyone.'

Peppe didn't say anything and it seemed as though the darkness of the tunnel was growing. She wanted to say something to make him understand that she had done what she could to stop her cousin, but then she thought to herself that she hadn't done much at all. She had hardly fought and all she had to show for it was a small graze. She looked away and thought that there was nothing more to say now and that she should go back. She remembered something then. 'He saw us that time in the forest.'

Peppe turned, not understanding.

Concetta looked down again. 'When we kissed by the tree.'

Peppe nodded.

More time passed and after a while he said, 'I was probably close by, with Francesco, at the river. I was probably there.'

She remembered then Peppe's voice, that she'd heard him and Francesco, and that she'd been alarmed at the thought that they would see her again out alone at night and think ill of her and so she had strayed from the river and into the woods. She put her hands to her face and groaned and tears slipped down her face.

Peppe didn't turn to her or say anything and even when she had finished crying and the candle had gone out in a soft puff of smoke, he continued to stay as he was. It was only when she rose to indicate that they should leave that he got up. They walked back through the tunnel and up into the street again, and it was lighter up there because the day was about to break.

When Concetta left Peppe, she didn't go to bed but stayed in the yard. Her sisters, she knew, would be rising soon as it was nearly dawn. Already it was hot and the day, she felt, would be the hottest they'd had so far.

When her sisters emerged from the house, they headed to the fields to join their mother and father and Tino. It was the last day of *la mancanza*, the waning moon, and there could be no planting now for two weeks until the moon grew full again. They raked for potatoes while there was still some chill in the air, but the earth was as dust in their hands and the pieces they found were small and shrivelled.

At midday, they returned to the house. Concetta removed her boots and let her bare feet rest awhile on the stone floor before getting into bed. Her sisters were already asleep by the time she found her place in the middle and she didn't remember the falling asleep, only the waking up again. Her mouth was dry and her limbs stiff, as though she had been still in one place for a very long time.

She had woken for no reason that she could fathom. She slipped out of bed and found the old grey work dress that she had discarded and pulled it over her head. Immacolata had left a pair of old sandals by the bed and she put these on and went to the window and pushed the blinds up to see outside. It was quieter than usual, the hum of the cicadas hardly a murmur, and the birds were very still in the trees. She let the slats of the blind fall and tiptoed through into the other room; she didn't look at her mother or father or brother, but pushed on out of the house.

The heat outside seemed to roll up from the ground in waves. The very force of it was like a roar in her ears and all at once she felt disoriented and she stumbled. She regained her balance and walked on out into the street and she stopped to listen to the noise again and it was as if something were straining with all its might and ready to give. The branches of the trees in the distance were waving as though a great wind was moving through them and she stopped to open her hands, expecting to feel the brush of hot air.

The push, when it came, nearly brought her to her knees. It was not the wind that shivered down the street towards her, but the very ground itself that rose and fell. A terrible creaking started up, of metal scraping against metal, of hinges snapping, of bricks scratching loose and tiles pulling free. Concetta felt the force of the motion pass through her and she wondered that she didn't fall, but nothing was as it should be.

She glanced towards the doorway of a nearby house and knew that there, under the heavy stone arch, she should seek her cover but already there was dust settling all around her, a fine dust that sparkled in the light and that was soft against her hair and face. She looked up to see the glass from an upstairs window bursting out of its frame, the pieces flashing sharp against the sun, and then a door opened and a woman in black, a neighbour of theirs, stumbled out.

'Earthquake,' she said to Concetta, as though a time of waiting were finally over. 'It's the earthquake.'

About the Author

© Rich Tatham

Maria Allen is half Italian, half English and has lived in different parts of Italy and the USA. She has worked as a journalist, in TV research, publishing and most recently in teaching. She lives in Loughborough.

Acknowledgements

Many thanks to my agent Lucy Luck for all her support and Alan, Emma and the team at Tindal Street Press for their valued input.

On the writing side: very special thanks to Nicola Valentine for all her help but especially for believing in this project throughout. Thanks also to Richard B, Paylor, Richard P, Jonathan and James. I'd also like to thank all the Nottingham Trent tutors for their support.

On the research side: many thanks to my mother Rosaria Scotti and my grandmother Fiorentina Brida for inspiring me. A big thank you also to Giuseppe Di Marino, Carinda Brida and Antonio Scotti for their invaluable information and advice on how it used to be. A mention also to Maria Giovanna Agresta, Leontina Brida (RIP), Salvatore Brida, Sister Anna Patricia, Valerio Carelli and Richard Allen.

Finally, I would like to thank il comune di Villamaina, its past and present residents and all those that trace their origins back to there and places like it.

Some of the Italian terms in this novel are conveyed in a dialect of the Campania region, and not in standard Italian.